I'm Just a Girl

Susan Ravagni

First published by Dog Ear Publishing
4010 W. 86th Street, Ste H
Indianapolis, IN 46268
www.dogearpublishing.net

ISBN: 978-160844-159-4

Printed in the United States of America

Prologue:

I'm Just A Girl, Livin' in Captivity

(Just A Girl, No Doubt)

I am not an adventurous person. I got A's and B's in high school. I never cut class. I was never sent to the principal's office. I went to a state university. Got an average job and have an average life. In the words of Gwen Stefani, I'm just a girl.

Up until a few weeks ago that would have been very, very true. The first thirty eight years of my life were average, middle-of-the-road, run-of-the-mill. Un. Note. Worthy.

Probably the most unusual, quirky thing about me, up until lately, was that I hear music. Well, that doesn't sound quite right; after all most of us <u>hear</u> music. I guess what I am trying to say is that I hear music in my head and it is associated with whatever events are occurring in my life.

When I was a little girl I would pretend, in my ego-centric little mind, that I was the main character in a movie featuring my life. Like all kids' movies, songs would play for each particular scene: pillow fights (*Girls Just Wanna Have Fun*), running bases when the ball is hit (*We Are the Champions*), or pedaling your bike like a maniac while bullies chase you (*Wicked Witch of the West* music from the Wizard of Oz). Then I grew up and realized no one would watch a movie about me (booooring!). But the songs continue in my head unbidden. For example, every time I get ready to go out – which isn't often, trust me – I hear Blondie singing "Call Me" as I choose my outfit – laying out selections in Richard Gere fashion. Then, feeling fully '80's, I attempt to resist the urge to tease my hair to monstrous proportions and apply globs of mascara to my puny lashes – move over Tammy Faye Baker. Like I said, I don't go out much so don't worry about the flashback. It doesn't happen often.

Anyway I was pretty average up until a few weeks ago: hockey mom, working stiff, didn't do anything wilder than make my sons hike a mountain with me or take Bikram yoga; both pretty darn crazy by my standards. So I had no idea the life changes this regular gal, this Average Jane, this Milquetoast Millie was going to encounter.

Well, it all started with an incident seemingly unrelated to me. What I thought was a simple tragedy ended up being a wild and scary adventure into a dark, dangerous world; one that changed me completely and irrevocably.

Ok, so now you think I am this exaggerating, dramatic person who speaks in grand terms and deludes herself. Well, judge for yourself...

Chapter 1:

Be My Baby

(Be My Baby, The Ronettes)

Okay, so the Ronettes are little before my time. But when great music speaks, hey, one must listen, right?

My name is Amanda Buscemi, nee Brown. On our first date, Bobby Buscemi took me to see Dirty Dancing. While Johnny taught Baby to dance on a rainy afternoon, I felt Bobby slip his arm around my shoulder and pull me close. A kind of psychosis overwhelmed me. This was the kind of mental derangement that caused a young lady (um, me) to have a lapse in judgment provided by the extreme emotion of the moment ("no one puts Baby in a corner") and thereby conceived her first child on and around the gear shift of Bobby Buscemi's truck. Be My Baby was playing on the oldies station at the time. Prophetic, huh?

Any time I hear the song I can't help but smile wistfully at the memory.

Now you are thinking I wind up living in a trailer on welfare, right? No, but thanks for the vote of confidence. Ok, so it was north Boston suburbia. And we had to scratch along with baby, bills, and dreams. Sometimes people make it....and sometimes they don't. I'd like to be philosophical about this but then - *you haven't been married to Bobby Buscemi.*

Bobby is a true-blue, American flag-waving, get-your-deer-hunting-license-early, gut-scratching (or crotch, depending on the day) good ol' boy. He should have been born in the South. His stork must have got lost in the hurricane that blew in the day he was born. The hurricane is true, by the way. It is one of the myriad fond stories with which Mama Buscemi loves to regale us.

Instead of Bobby being born to his rightful parents, probably some folks named Verleen and Billy Bob who live in the hills of Arkansas, Bobby was born to Elizabeth and Charles Buscemi (pronounced boo-skemm-ee) of Somerville, Massachusetts. E and C are first generation Italians. They are Catholic to the core with sound working-class ethics. All that took a backseat to spoiling their one and only son: Robert Anthony. As I learned, boys are the princes of the family; they can do no wrong. The girls, on the other hand, are the slaves; doomed to eternal drudgery, no dating, at mother's beck and call. At least, this is what his sisters told me one day hunched over their coffee mugs, compulsively wiping the kitchen counters and picking miniscule specks of dirt off the floor.

According to Maria, Anna, and Lisa, Bobby was the prince who didn't have to help with chores, didn't get in trouble for bad grades, and could stay out as late as he wanted. They, on the other hand, had to do all the chores...late into the night....with no thought to having a potential social life. Meanwhile Bobby was busy playing high school hockey, sneaking beers into the state park, and later impregnating me. Pretty auspicious beginnings, eh?

Actually the sisters were quite nice to me. Remember, Milquetoast Millie? What was there to hate about me anyway? Who they *should* hate is their bratty sonofabitch brother. But, again, that would go against everything they were raised to believe. Instead they think he's right up there with sliced bread. When Bobby walks in the room they all light up like he's Brad Pitt or something. Sheesh.

According to local legend Bobby was a real pistol growing up. When he ever-so-quietly cut the pigtails off of Angela Piscatelli in class, would he own up to it? No, they "fell" off. Momma Buscemi didn't force him to apologize ("boys will be boys"). Neither did a punishment ensue when he spray painted his name on the house ("he's expressing himself"). Not to mention when he took the neighbor's new John Deere mower on a joy ride destroying the newly laid sod, flattening the saplings, and emulsifying flowerbeds. His NASCAR career ended when the mower got stuck in three feet of muck in the swamp out back. The punishment for this youthful abandonment? He was grounded for a week. This was reduced to two days because there was a Red Sox game he was supposed to go to with a friend and it "wouldn't be fair to the friend" if he couldn't go.

Oh yeah, these people were real tough nuts. It isn't hard to understand why Bobby never learned to worry about the consequences of his actions.

As Prince Bobby grew, the antics increased. Mailboxes were introduced to his baseball bat. He took his father's electric razor and gave the neighbor's cat a buzz cut. He claimed he saw it on a Saturday morning cartoon and wanted to see if Fluffy would look like the cat on TV. Fourth of July always had the Somerville Police visiting the Buscemi house for complaints of unauthorized fireworks. Bobby's mother would cover for him, "Oh no, he's been in his room the whole time, officers". Meanwhile he and his delinquent friends would be wheeling the Old Ironsides-sized canon used to launch the incendiaries back behind the garage, out of official sight.

I met Bobby in an over 18 club my first year out of high school, a freshman in college. He was yummy, yummy, yummy. Curly, dark brown hair, striking blue eyes, and ready smile, he made my knees weak the very first time I laid eyes on him. My three date rule lasted for four hours on our first date and we walked down the aisle five months later, my belly quietly expanding. The wedding gown was too tight to zip so I had to be sewn into it. Literally. This was certainly not the fairy tale wedding of which every girl dreams. My poor, quiet, Protestant, French-Canadian parents came down from the pristine mountains of New Hampshire for the nuptials. They desperately clutched each other throughout the ceremony and then into the reception where the boisterous Italian segment took over in a delirious eat-your-guts-outs, drink-your-liver-fatty celebration. Ever see that annual hot dog eating contest where the Japanese kid always wins? I'd like to see him pitted against the Buscemi clan. That would be a show for ESPN!

Anyway, little Philip arrived and we lived with Mama Buscemi until we could "get on our feet". Nine years later I had had enough. Flat broke from Bobby's incessant gambling and bitter from his continued cheating, I packed my stuff and left the Buscemi fold. Mama begged me for another chance but Bobby didn't. I guess that's what finally made me close the overstuffed trunk on my car with resolution and drive off to bunk with my friend, also newly single mom, Linda. We have been our own little family for the last ten years.

Linda and I joke that now that it's legal we should get married. It would be funnier if it wasn't so close to the truth. Rumors roared for a while about the lesbians in the neighborhood. Old ladies would wag their fingers and the men would wink. Ugh. Nothing is further from the truth but try changing people's minds? Not easy. It doesn't do much to dispel the notion when so few men are seen visiting. We both got divorced in the same month and had a moratorium on men for the first year of our new-found singleness. After that it just seemed like a good idea to not let a lot of men into our home and lives.

Don't get me wrong – I have dated. I have even become serious a couple times. But in the end nothing panned out. Bobby jokes that he has ruined me for other men. Asshole.

Ok. So now you have the basics of my life. My sex life is somewhere between languishing and non-existent most of the time. I try not to think about it. Too much. But I do have a hand-held shower massager. Sometimes I call him Hal.

Chapter 2:

It's the glamorous, glamorous life

(*Glamorous Life*, Fergie)

The alarm startles me awake. And, unlike Fergie in her video, I'm not getting up to jet away to some fabulous locale. I'm going to work. I turn my head and groan as thousands of muscles, large and small, remind me that I have done the Bikram yoga class with Linda last night. Every time I go, I can barely move the next day. Linda says if I went more often that I wouldn't be so sore. I say if I don't go at all I won't be sore at all. Put that in your pipe and smoke it. Logic is a two-way street, baby.

I roll to my side and push up, knowing from past experience that I do NOT want to use my abdomen for this endeavor. The aroma of coffee drifts my way as I walk, okay stagger frankensteinishly, down the hallway.

"Well, good morning, sunshine," Linda comments, regarding me over the tops of her reading glasses. She is in her usual spot at the kitchen table, blue fleece robe stretched across her midsection, her mop of curly, ash blond hair already looking perky and ready for the day. A small smile plays across her lips.

"Erg," I groan. I have made it over to the counter and slop cream into my mug. I attempt to pour the coffee but my arm is protesting at the weight of the coffee carafe. I have to lift it with both hands to actually get it high enough to fill my mug.

"Lemme, guess, you're sore," her smile broadens.

"Ding, ding, ding," I say as I point to my nose. Oh man, even that hurts. What the freak have I done to myself?

Linda folds the newspaper back up and moves it aside to clear a spot at the kitchen table for me.

"Ow, ow, ow, ow," I whine as I carry the mug over to the table. I ease myself into one of the chairs as if I am a hundred. I try to glare at Linda but she is having none of my mood.

"You'll feel better after a shower and you move around some more. You're just stiff right now," she assures me.

"Yes, yes, I know you're right," I tentatively flex my foot. Sweet Mother of God, even my toes hurt!

Linda changes the subject, "What time is Philip's game tonight?"

Philip, as you already know, is my oldest son. He has his father's looks and athletic ability. I'd like to think he gets his charm and sweet nature from me. In reality, he is his own person and I am incredibly proud of him. He got recruited by Boston College to play hockey for them and has almost a full scholarship. This is his first game and none of us would miss it for the world.

"Seven thirty. We're meeting him at the doors at six thirty before he goes in to wish him luck. Then we'll get a drink. Can you be there by then?"

Linda scrunches her lips, looks up at the ceiling as though it holds her calendar, and then nods. "Yeah, I think I can get there by then. Bobby coming?"

"Wild horses couldn't stop him," I say.

We hear a thunk from down the hall and then feet pounding toward us.

"The native awakens," I say and sip my coffee (ow, ow, ow as I raise the mug; eee, eee, eegh as I lower it).

Brendan, my younger son who is eleven apparently has two speeds: nothing and warp. When he wants to get somewhere he runs. He can drink a glass of milk in four seconds flat and belch for twenty seconds straight after that. Banisters are the preferred mode of transportation, either hurdling over or sliding down them. Descending one step at a time does not seem to be an option. Wish I could bottle that energy and joie de vivre.

"Well, that's my signal," Linda pushes away from the table, stretches seemingly unaffected (bitch), and walks out of the kitchen.

At the doorway Brendan and she almost collide. "Hey, Scooter, watch where ya going," she playfully pinches his bottom. He yelps but gives her a hug. Then he bounds over to me.

"Whoa," I hold up my hand forestalling what could be an extremely painful hug, "Mom is beyond sore this morning, how 'bout a kiss instead?"

"Let me guess, yoga?" he smiles and leans in for the kiss.

"Yes, yoga," I push back the hair out of his eyes and kiss him on his forehead and then his nose, which is dotted with a smattering of small freckles that become more prominent in the summertime sun. "Your Aunt Linda insists I torture myself every so often." We grin at each other.

"So," I smack the table for emphasis, "name your breakfast, buddy, we have to get a move on."

"Pancakes!" Brendan straightens, throws his hands up like he's signaling a touchdown and dances around the kitchen, hip hop style. Like I said, wish I could bottle it.

I arrive at the lab and Deke, straddling a lab stool, is at the chemical-stained, black workbench with a row of flasks containing clear liquid in front of him, swirling away on a rotator as he dumps some dry chemicals from a plastic measuring boat into one of them.

"Heya, Deke, how's it hanging?"

"Dude," he replies in his best Keanu Reeves as Ted in Bill and Ted's Excellent Adventure. Dude is his name for me. But I think it is like aloha or shalom; it means a

7

number of different things. In this case 'dude' probably means "good morning my bodacious lab mate and my balls are hanging just fine". I'm not kidding; I'm getting really good at reading the nuances of his speech.

Deke is from Ventura, California and for some crazy reason gave up all that nasty sunshine for the splendor of bleak New England winters. He doesn't even have to open his mouth and you can guess he's from So Cal. The longish, blonde hair and OP surfer shirts are a dead give away. I was sure he was going to bale after the first bad winter. But it is three years later and still he is here. Good thing I'm not a betting woman. I would have lost that one for sure. But sooner or later Deke will move on. He is about three quarters of the way through to his doctorate.

"Paul in yet?"

"Come and gone, my friend. He has that early class today." Wow, two full sentences. This day is really shaping up into something truly special.

"Hey Deke," I pause thinking, why the hell not, "my oldest boy is playing his first game for BC tonight. I have an extra ticket. Would you like to come?"

Deke looks up at me and smiles, "Righteous," he exclaims. I think that means he'd be honored to join me.

I gingerly pull on my lab coat (Linda was right, the shower helped – I am only partially disabled now) and get busy with what I know I need to do for the day.

I work for Dr. Paul Herzog in his biochemistry lab at the university. That's my day job. But it doesn't quite pay all the bills so I moonlight over in the lab at City Hospital a couple off-shifts every week. See? It's the glamorous, glamorous life.

Chapter 3:

We will, we will rock you!

(We Will Rock You, Queen)

It's pretty quiet outside the arena when we get there a little before the appointed time. Brendan is nearly apoplectic with excitement. His teacher called earlier to tell me how he insisted that tomorrow had to be Show and Tell in his class so he could tell everyone about his big brother's first college game. I guess we have inherited some of the Buscemi humility: we all think Philip is right up there with sliced bread.

Brendan hops from foot to foot dissipating some of the excess energy he can't contain. He's singing to some song on his iPod.

Around the corner come Bobby and Pete. After we separated Bobby moved in with Pete, his best friend. Pete lives in Cambridge and is a fireman. Bobby decided that he wanted to be a fireman too. So he took the paramedic courses and such and now they both work for the Cambridge Fire Department. In my humble opinion this is just another aspect of the gambling syndrome. Bobby gets a rush from taking risks: whether it's putting money on the roll of the dice, having sex in a public place, or running into a burning building to save lives. He is an adrenaline junkie, plain and simple. I hate that he risks his life so often. The boys would be devastated to lose him. But I stay out of it. It's his life. The dumbass.

Speaking of dumbasses, there's not one but two of them. My lucky day. Enough testosterone even before the game begins to wipe out my measly estrogen in one fell swoop. Where is Linda when I need her?

Brendan sees his father, let's out a whoop of pleasure, and makes a mad dash. Bobby scoops him up and swings him around. Squeals of laughter bounce back to me. My heart breaks a little more as I see this. Wishing for what could have been. I shake my head to clear the thought. No sense getting upset when this is such an exciting evening.

"Hey 'Manda," Bobby leans in and kisses my cheek, "been waiting long?"

"No, we just got here. Hiya Pete." I nod his way.

"Amanda, you look good as always," Pete looks me up and down. Not sure what there is to check out. I am wearing my cold weather gear as I am a total wimp. From November to March you can only find me outside for brief moments in time as I scuttle like a crab from building to building. I am not the poster child for hearty New Englanders. So even though it is early October, I anticipate a cool evening and the arena will probably be cold. I have learned over the years to dress warmly.

"Dad," Brendan interrupts, "where do we go to meet Phil?"

"I think the team uses the side entrance over there. Are we waiting on Linda?"

"Yes, I spoke to her a few minutes ago. She should be here in less than five."

"Cool, we'll wait." Bobby says.

So for the next few minutes we chat while Brendan flits around and finally Linda comes huffing up the hill.

"You guys didn't have to wait for me," she says as she comes within speaking distance of us. "Hi Pete, hi Bobby. Scoot's are you ready for an awesome game?"

"You bet!" Brendan bounds up to her and they do this body slam cum handshake cum boogey dance that they made up in honor of Philip's new status.

We all clap as they end it. It's pretty cool. My friend is cool. She's the greatest.

We walk over to the entrance Bobby said the team goes through and slowly young men start showing up to go get ready for the game.

Brendan hops up and down and is the first to spot Philip making his way. He runs up and they high five and low five.

We all greet him in our own way and then I say, "Ok, not to be weird or anything but I want to get some pictures."

We pose in various groupings with increasing amounts of silliness and then it's time for Philip to go in. Just as he picks up his bag and turns to go I call, "Philip!"

He turns back. I run up to him and I say in a low voice so only he can hear, "Look, I am so proud I could burst. You are the best son a mother could ever wish for."

"Mom...." He glances down, maybe a little embarrassed.

I don't care, I am going to have my say. "I want you to try your hardest tonight but, *please*, be careful too. You're playing with the big boys now."

He looks like he is about to say something but hesitates. I lay my hand on his arm, "Just play smart, okay?" My voice cracks a little as I say this. I hate when I get emotional and take a deep breath to control myself.

He glances down and then nods. Every time he goes out on the ice I think of the Boston University player that ended up paralyzed from a hit he took in his very first college game. It sends fear up my spine.

"Hey, I love you," I whisper. I lean in and hug him real quick so as to not embarrass him further.

"Love you too," he whispers back. My heart swells. I pat him on the arm and he turns and walks into the entrance. My baby is a man. I sigh.

"Ok, gang," I turn to everyone else, "Let's go get that drink."

We raucously make our way down the street to what we assume will be our favorite haunt for the next four years.

The pub, Dobsky's, is dimly lit with dark wood ceiling beams and brick walls. It is made cheery by several crisply burning fireplaces and whaling lamps on each table. An energetic girl with a name tag that reads "Cheri" greets us and asks what we'd like to drink.

"Stella Artois if you have it" Bobby says.

"Yes, we do"

"Make it two," I chime in.

Pete asks "How about that new energy drink, Ripped?" she nods, "I'll take that with vodka."

Brendan orders root beer.

"What's that all about, Ripped with vodka?" I ask Pete.

"It's what all the college kids drink now, vodka mixed with energy drinks and Ripped is the best," he explains.

"Let me guess, your latest conquest is in college," I smirk.

Typical. This guy carves notches on his bed post, I swear. Someone should carve a notch on his penis. I smile at the thought. I mean sure the guy is good looking and buff. But scratch the surface and underneath you find just pure, unadulterated bullshit. Probably horse, monkey and goat shit too. Let's not limit this to one species.

I've seen puddles with more depth than Pete.

He takes advantage of every opportunity to chase skirt. I actually saw him hand out business cards to young women at a fire once. I bet the fools called him too. It isn't like he trolls for girls at the Mensa club.

Okay, so I am not a fan of Pete. He aided and abetted Bobby in some of his more ill-advised exploits. A true friend should encourage fidelity and fiscal responsibility. So in my book he is worse than useless.

"Hey, I'm young at heart," Pete holds his hands up as if to say 'what can I do?'

"Nice tee shirt," I snort as I read the material stretched across his well-toned chest:

Cambridge Fire Department –
Find 'em hot,
Leave 'em wet.

Oh my God. Unbelievable. What self-respecting girl would date someone who wears a shirt like that? That's even worse than the mud flaps he has on his truck showing the silhouette of a voluptuous girl.

"Thanks," he grins and does some stupid pec flexing thing that is supposed to impress the opposite sex and wiggles his eyebrows at me. Ugh.

I look over at Linda who rolls her eyes. Exactly, girlfriend.

We finish our drinks and head over to the arena. It is time for the game. I wipe my hands surreptitiously on my jeans. I'm a little nervous for my boy. This is the big time. All those years of carting him around at all hours of the day and night, freezing my ass off in some of the most God-forsaken arenas, shelling out what little money I had for equipment, hockey camps and trainers. This is the payoff and it is sweet: a hockey scholarship and the possibility of the NHL. It has been worth it.

At the entrance Deke is waiting for us and after introducing him around (Brendan immediately gets tagged "Little Dude" by Deke) we go in and find our seats.

Soon the players come out on the ice to warm up. BC is playing St. Francis Xavier and, according to Bobby, they should beat them.

As the game starts we bide our time until Philip's line is out on the ice. I bounce excitedly in my seat as he blasts out onto the ice. Philip plays defense. He has lightening fast reflexes, skates like the wind and is like a brick wall when opponents try to check him...if I do say so myself. While his line is on the ice he doesn't let anyone skate in close to the goal. So far it hasn't been a very physical game, thank God. Those bone-crunching slams into the boards scare the crap out of me.

Philip's line is out for their second shift near the end of the first period. BC has the puck down in St. Francis' zone. BC's two wings have been trying to get the puck in to no avail. One of them shoots it up to Phil and in a flash he slaps it at the goalie. Whoever number 12 is tips it in for the first goal of the season. We all stand and cheer. Actually we scream, jump up and down and hug each other. I think I even have to wipe tears off my cheeks. This is the best! The first goal of the season and Philip has an assist.

I look over and see even laid back Deke is celebrating. He is sitting to the left of Brendan and does a whole series of high fives with him and pronounces it a "truly nasty goal." Nasty, if I understand the current lingo, is the new awesome.

The game continues on with a catch up goal by St Francis. In the second period Philip shoots the puck up the boards. His teammate scrambles down the ice and reaches it just ahead of the St F guy. He gets slammed really hard into the boards and goes down. Ouch! I wince at the impact and then crane my neck to see what is happening. It looks like the player is lying prone on the ice.

The ref blows the whistle and the game halts. Both refs go over to the fallen kid. He still hasn't moved. My stomach clenches as I whisper a little prayer, "Be okay."

They motion for the coach who comes out on the ice. They are all kneeling around the fallen player and we can't see anything. One of the refs skates rapidly over to the BC bench and confers with the other coach, maybe the assistant. This guy then quickly turns and runs out.

What the heck is going on? A murmur starts to run through the stadium. I lean forward, straining to see what is occurring down on the ice. One of the men moves and now I see that the coach is doing chest compressions on the fallen player. Oh my God, my heart does a flip flop, this cannot be good.

The arena turns deathly quiet as we begin to realize something very serious is happening. The assistant coach rushes back in with a case that he hands to the ref who has remained by the bench.

I quietly gasp as I recognize the symbol on the outside of the case. It's a defibrillator. Linda and I clutch each others arm and my other one slides around Brendan.

"Mom, what's going on?"

"I'm not sure sweetheart but it looks like the player got hurt really bad," I try with limited success to keep my voice from cracking. I hold my breath and feel tears forming in my eyes.

We watch in horror as they rapidly cut through the hockey shirt, tear his pads off, apply the paddles and shock the young man. A collective intake can be heard as his body jerks at the electrical jolt.

Apparently it didn't do the trick because they shock him one more time and then resume performing CPR. I notice a few more people have come out on the ice now. One man takes over the compressions after checking the prone figure's pulse at the neck. Maybe he's a doctor?

Paramedics arrive. They continue the chest compressions and place an oxygen mask over his face. Eventually they have him on a stretcher with all kinds of medical paraphernalia attached to and coming off him and wheel him urgently off the ice.

Now that the ice is cleared of this dreadful spectacle I turn to look at Bobby. His mouth is compressed into a fine line and I see the tension in his jaw. Our eyes meet and we silently acknowledge the horror and, dare I say, the relief that it was not our son at the center of this horror. He gives a little nod to let me know we are on the same wavelength.

Minutes later an announcer tells us that the game will not continue and will be rescheduled for a different time.

The whole place is very subdued and eventually people begin leaving.

Brendan seems freaked, "Mom, is that guy going to be alright?"

"I'm not sure Bren. We'll call Philip a little later to find out. We should go home."

We all agree that's the best plan and join the growing lines as people filter toward the exits.

As we get to the front entrance I turn to Bobby. "Look, I think I should get Brendan home. Are you going to wait for Philip?"

"Yeah, Pete and I'll wait for him and get him some dinner or whatever he needs."

"Okay, have him call me on my cell tonight."

I turn to Deke, "Deke thanks for coming. Sorry the evening ended in such a sad way."

Deke pushes his hair back and nods, "Dude, that was a major bummer. But it was nice to meet you all."

And with that Deke leaves and Brendan, Linda and I go home.

Deke was right, it was a major bummer. It was a mystery what caused the player to collapse. And the mystery would deepen even further the next day.

Chapter 4:

It's a bittersweet symphony, this life

(*Bittersweet Symphony,* The Verve)

I awake before my alarm sounds, pulling myself out of a sleep which ends with a vaguely disturbing but rapidly fading dream. Philip had called me about an hour after we got home that night. He was shaken up about his teammate and didn't have any news about his condition or what was wrong. I had wished him a good night and crawled into bed for a troubled, restless sleep.

My morning starts the same way it usually does. Linda is up before me and when I come into the kitchen she holds up the paper and says, "Looks like that boy didn't make it."

"What?!" I grab the paper and scan the piece. His name was Mike Donowski. He had been taken to City Hospital where he was pronounced dead on arrival. Cause of death is unknown pending autopsy.

"Oh my God, how terrible," I look up at Linda, "He was out on the ice with Philip." My unspoken fear is that it could have been my son and not this boy that got clobbered and now laying on a slab.

Linda's kind gray eyes reflect her understanding. She reaches out and squeezes my arm. "I know, Hon. But we don't know if the hit into the boards is what killed him."

I nod. Linda is right. But still I feel like we had an uncomfortably close brush with death.

I stand up to get my coffee and try to shake the bad feeling percolating inside me.

Stirring my coffee I give myself a mental headshake and purposely turn my thoughts to the day ahead,

"Tonight is when I work the evening shift at City," I remind her.

"Yup, I'll pick up Brendan and do the Mommy stuff for you."

"Thank you," I call over my shoulder as I take my coffee back down the hall and go get ready for work.

Showered, dressed and properly made up, I head out to catch "The T". The T is the train/subway system for Boston and surrounding towns. Sometimes it can be a pain but it saves a lot of money and headaches since parking in Boston and surrounding areas is expensive and at a premium. So I choose to use it for city travel.

The T has been around for a really, really long time. I read in a Boston Globe article once that it was conceived in 1895. The Park Street station was intended to be the central point from which the different "lines" would meet, interconnecting everything together. Work began digging out the Park Street station soon after that. Within a few years workers discovered a common grave with nine hundred bodies in it. For awhile negative stories circulated regarding this revelation.

The original vision for the T had four lines: the red line extending from Cambridge in the north, across the Charles River, through downtown and then into South Boston; the yellow line mimicked the red line but in an east-west direction curving from Charlestown in the northeast to Roxbury, west of Boston; the blue line was to be an outward thrust from downtown to East Boston; and the green line was to make a small semi-circle in Boston for those who just needed to get around town. To a large degree if you superimpose the original concept over the current version it is almost identical except that the lines have lengthened over time with a few branches added to accommodate the growing population's needs. It's amazing that something more than a hundred years old still serves the needs of the people so well. At least it serves me.

As I step outside our house I see Mr. Ziegler, the neighborhood busybody. He is out smoking his cigar and leaning against the gate to his front walkway.

"Morning Amanda," he rasps out in his thick Boston accent. "Morning" sounds more like "mawnin'"

"Morning Mr. Z," I respond back, "what kind of a day is it going to be?"

"Sunny, up to sixty sweetheart (pronouncing it shweet-haht)," he growls.

"Excellent. Have a great day and stay out of trouble!"

"You too darling (dah-lin)."

Our relationship has not always been this cordial. When I first moved in he would merely grunt when I greeted him. But I wore him down over time; I'd always make sure to say hello, compliment him in his garden, or ask about the weather. Finally one day I was helping him carry groceries in to his house and he told me I wasn't so bad after all "for a lesbian." I tried to set the record straight but he wouldn't believe me.

As I explained earlier, everyone in the neighborhood believes we are lesbians. We've never given them reason to think that. It seems they just want to believe we are. I guess it makes for more interesting gossip.

The neighborhood is rife with characters if one believes all the rumors. There's a big dilapidated house in which resides a loosely-knit family of Russians, all adults. The rumor-mill says they are in the Russian mafia. No real reason for this general belief, apparently, it just makes for good speculation.

And then there is the witch across the street and down one house on the left. Yeah, I said witch….like, Wicca witch. Neighborhood lore is that once some telephone workers were blocking the driveway to her house and they had a heated exchange when she came home and thought they should move the repair truck. They refused saying she could get by them just fine. Five minutes later the guy in the bucket working on the lines gets zapped. Spooky, huh?

The day is uneventful in Dr. Herzog's lab. Deke is focused on his experiment and keeps pretty much to himself.

I hustle over to City to start my evening shift. I work in the "Core Lab" which is the designation for the section of the lab that does most of the basic Chemistry and Hematology testing. I go over to the bench I am assigned and begin setting up for my shift.

I see my friend Milagros several benches over and wave. She is this hot South American chic, 15 years my junior. One might think we are an odd pair, but we get along really well and always go on break together. Every once in a blue moon she talks me into stopping for a nightcap at the dive two blocks down from the hospital.

"Chica, I got to talk to you," whispers Milagros who has sidled up beside me.

"Jeez, Milagros, you almost made me jump out of my skin," I reply. The ambient background noise provided by the larger instruments running in the lab has blocked me from hearing her approach. I am still on edge from the bad news earlier this morning and have not been able to shake my funk all day.

"I am serious! Don't say anything more just let's go for a walk at break." And then she hurries away before I can question her.

Sometimes she has a flair for the dramatic.

Milagros was born in Paraguay to affluent parents who sent her up to Boston to get an American education. She stayed in the area after graduating.

When dinner break finally comes we go outside for our walk. Night has descended and the air is frosty. I turn up my collar and then bury my hands deep into my coat pockets as we begin walking up the well-lighted, still-busy street.

"So what's the big secret," I ask.

Milagros glances over her shoulder, "Something weird happened last night in the lab."

"What all the guys didn't drool when you took off your lab coat?" I joke.

"I'm not kidding," she grabs my arm for emphasis, "listen to this. You know that BC hockey player that died last night?"

"Do I? We were all there at the game. It totally freaked us out. Philip was out on the ice with him when it happened," I exclaim.

Milagros glances around again and then lowers her voice, "Well, they brought him to City and we got the lab work on him. One of the tests they ordered was a BNP test."

BNP is a blood test that you usually run on old people to check for heart failure. This doesn't make any sense. Why would they order that test? "Really?" I say, puzzled. "That doesn't seem right."

"I thought so too, chica. I put the test on and was running some other labs when they called from the ER to change the order from BNP to BMP. Someone must have misunderstood or keyed in the wrong test."

Now that makes more sense. A BMP, or basic metabolic panel, checks the basic chemistries for kidney function, electrolytes and glucose.

"Ok, so it was a mistake. What's the problem?" I ask. I can feel the tip of my nose turning cold and bury it a little deeper into my coat collar.

"I forgot to cancel the test. Later, when things calmed down, I noticed the BNP result was almost 1,000."

"Wow," I say. A normal result should be under 100, especially for a young, healthy person. Actually, I would expect it to be much, much lower than 100. "Could you have mistakenly put on the wrong patient?"

Ravagni

"I looked at the tube and it was labeled correctly," her brows are knitted.

"Well, that is strange," I admit, "So what did you do?"

"I called down to the ER to tell them about it. They took the message and that was that." Milagros pauses and then pulls me closer so my head is almost touching hers, "But it troubled me, you know? Like did they mix up some other patient's blood tubes? So I came in early today. I decided that I would grab the other purple top from Hematology and run a BNP on that." [Note: blood is collected into different color-topped tubes, each color represents a different anticoagulant. BNP test is run on a purple top as are some Hematology tests such as a complete blood count] "And guess what?" She hisses, "The tube wasn't there."

"Milagros," I sigh, "maybe it was just misplaced."

"That's what I thought but I looked through all the racks and there were no tubes anywhere on this patient."

"What? Are you sure?"

"Of course, mommy."

Hmm. I ponder this for a few moments. "Maybe they were all pulled for some particular study." I am the voice of reason to Milagros' melodrama.

"Again, I thought the same thing. So I asked Melanie if she knew where the specimens went." Melanie is one of the chemistry supervisors, "She had no idea and asked around."

"And she didn't come up with anything?" I ask.

We have come to a stop at a busy intersection. Her face is orange from the sodium vapor lights. Milagros looks me straight in the eye, "Nada. So today, just before you came in I went to pathology to see if they had pulled them. They hadn't."

"Look," I turn her around for our return trip to the hospital, "it does sound odd but there's probably a reasonable explanation for the missing tubes."

"Maybe," she concedes, "but I don't like it. I want to know why I got that high result and now I have no way of double-checking."

"I hear you but it looks like you reached a dead end," I tell her.

Just then a panhandler approaches us for money. Politely we turn him down. I feel that slight tug of guilt you get when someone asks for your help and you don't give it. But every time I *do* give money I feel like a chump that just got taken. It's a lose-lose situation.

As we move along Milagros continues, "Well, I got a friend in pathology. I am going to ask him about the autopsy results."

"Just be careful," I warn her, "we aren't supposed to go looking into patient charts and invading privacy." That's a good way to get in deep trouble. We both know that.

"I'll be careful, querida. I'll be like, real discreet."

And with that we leave the cold autumnal night and go back into the warm embrace of the hospital. So far Milagros has all but called in the National Guard over the missing specimens. Discretion is not a word often used to describe my friend. But stubborn sure is.

Little did I know where this was going to lead us in the following days.

Chapter 5:

She blinded me with science, and hit me with technology

(She Blinded Me with Science, Thomas Dolby)

The next day was once again spent in Dr H's lab. I resolved to help Milagros put the funky lab result to rest. So during my down time I traipsed through the internet reading up on BNP.

BNP, which stands for B-Type Natriuretic Peptide, is a fairly new test. It is a hormone released from the heart when it no longer pumps efficiently. As the heart overfills with blood, the chambers stretch and this causes BNP to be released into the bloodstream. BNP's purpose is to help the body compensate for the pumping imbalance: it increases urine excretion which in turn reduces the overall blood volume. It also increases the strength of each heart contraction so that more blood is pushed out of each chamber to reduce the over-filling.

Fascinating stuff but at the end of my reading I still don't see anything that would explain why a normal, healthy young adult would have an increased level of BNP.

My eyes are burning from staring at the computer screen for so long. Rubbing them I phone Milagros to tell her about my research. "Hey," I say when she picks up her cell phone, "I've been reading up on BNP. It's pretty interesting actually."

"Oh, so now you agree with me?" She wants to know.

"Let's just say that I think we should understand if there is any possible way this kid *could* have had an elevated BNP."

"Well, that's at least something," Milagros concedes.

"So you want to meet for lunch so I can tell you about my findings?" I want to know.

"I was going to go see a friend of mine, Benny, who works down in pathology at lunchtime. You want to meet me at City and we can go see him together?"

"Sure, let me check with Deke to see if he can do something for me."

I walk over a couple benches to where Deke is carefully applying some chemicals to a gel sheet. I ask him if he can put my tubes in the centrifuge in forty-five minutes to finish the extraction I am doing.

"No, prob', dude" he says without looking up.

"Ok, it's a go," I tell Milagros, "Meet you in the lobby in thirty?"

"Sure chica, let's do it."

I am the first to arrive in City's lobby but Milagros breezes in right after me. She looks amazing as usual. With her long curls and tight jeans it's no wonder that men stop to stare at her. Actually it wouldn't surprise me if they bayed at the moon and slobbered on themselves. She is gorgeous; she looks like a young Catherine Zeta-Jones.

We go down into the basement where pathology does all their "posts", as in post mortems. It is definitely different from the hustle and bustle of the hospital lobby. We pass a few people in lab coats or scrubs. Otherwise we have the corridor to ourselves so I tell her about the BNP research as we walk down the tiled hallway.

She listens and then says, "So anatomically you would see an enlarged heart because it is stretching out?"

"That's my understanding, but that happens as the disease progresses. It might not be enlarged for several years. I'm only taking a guess."

We push through the double doors into pathology and the smell hits us. It isn't overwhelming but if you have ever smelled a dead body, well, you know where you are even blindfolded.

Sitting at a table in what looks like the lunch room we come upon a young, good-looking, muscular African American man.

"Hey, Benny," Milagros flashes her knockout smile, "how's it goin'?"

"Hey Milagros, good to see you," he blushes. Obviously he has a thing for Milagros, as does most of the male population. I have this urge to check under the table for a woody.

"Benny, this is my friend, Amanda."

"Hi, how ya doin'?" He stands to shake my hand. He is well over 6 feet tall. I can't help but glance down. No telltale bulge. Obviously Benny is a man of immense self-control.

"Doing okay, thanks," I answer. My hand disappears in his.

"So did you get the info I tol' you about?" Milagros gets right to the point.

"Uh, yeah, lemme grab somethin' and I'll be right back," and Benny strides out of the room.

I look around the room while waiting. Over on a bulletin board there are different pieces of paper: announcements, reminders, an apartment for rent sign, jokes: "Friends help friends move... REAL friends help friends move bodies." And another, "Good health is merely the slowest way to die". Morgue humor.

Benny comes back in with a folder clutched in his massive paw. "Let's go out this way."

He leads us out of the pathology department, pushes through an exit door and we are out in a small parking area. A black hearse is pulled up to the doors. Incongruously a bird is singing and the sun shines brilliantly. We continue up the driveway toward the street and over to a low brick wall separating the sidewalk from the hospital's back property. We sit down: first Benny, then Milagros and finally me - like a wart on the end of an otherwise beautiful nose.

"Y'see, I don't know how much I am going to be able to help you," Benny looks at both of us, "What exactly are you looking for?"

"Anything unusual, poppie. Like why this kid croaked." Milagros says.

"Uh, well, look I shouldn't do this because of confidentiality."

"Come on Benny," Milagros starts a little pout, "we work at City too. I'm just following up on a lab result that makes no sense."

"Jus' so you understand that this is on the down low and it isn't gonna come back to haunt me," Benny looks intently at Milagros.

"Amanda and my lips are sealed. Honest," she crosses her heart which probably works in her favor because he looks a little distracted as his eyes are drawn downward. He looks up and sighs.

"Alright, I can't tell you the cause of death yet but he *did* have diabetes."

"Could that be what did him in?" Milagros interjects, "he had messed up blood sugar?" Our hopes soar. Here might be the answer.

"I doubt it," Benny shakes his head, "his glucose level was in normal range."

Bummer. So much for an easy answer.

He pauses and then says, "Nothing was noted regarding the sort of sequela resulting from long-term diabetes." Sequela is a term for events that follow from a pre-existing disease or injury. For example stroke or kidney damage can be sequela of high blood pressure. Or nausea and hair loss sequela of chemotherapy

"You mean, like for diabetes there might be eye or kidney damage?" I say.

"Yeah, but his diabetes was well under control. His BUN and creatinine were normal. Besides," he adds, "it certainly wouldn't have made his heart just stop beating."

BUN and creatinine are blood tests for kidney health. To have those in the normal range and for the pathologist to note normal healthy kidneys upon gross examination probably means that, like Benny just said, the diabetes was well-controlled and not doing the sort of organ damage you see in older adults with diabetes.

"Interesting. Anything else?" Milagros prompts.

"Well, the thing is that I just read through the report and some of it isn't like I remember the autopsy."

"Explain," Milagros and I lean forward.

"Well, when we opened the guy up his heart looked pretty big. And it weighed more than it should have. I recall it being almost five hundred grams."

"What's normal?" I ask.

"Around four and a quarter is the upper limit of normal," Benny states, "So I remembered because the pathologist whistled when he put it on the scale."

"So what was different in the report?" Milagros wants to know.

"The report states the weight as four hundred thirty."

"Could you have been mistaken originally?" I ask.

"I 'spose, I mean it might have just been slightly over normal limit but then why would Burns whistle like he did?" Benny shrugs, looking a little confused.

"Can you check with him? Maybe he remembers," Milagros says.

"He's not in today. So I went to pull the voice recording made at the time we posted the body. It's used to transcribe the report. I figured I'd sort it out for myself."

"Good idea, and....?"

"Gone." Benny holds up his hands as if to say, what can I say?

"Holy freakin' shit." Milagros mutters.

❖ ❖ ❖ ❖ ❖ ❖ ❖ ❖ ❖ ❖ ❖ ❖ ❖ ❖

We are walking slowly up the street to where we can catch the T. After thanking Benny for his help Milagros and I are in stunned silence; both lost in our own thoughts.

The day has turned gloomy and the birds are silent. The only background sounds are street noises: cars accelerating as a traffic light turns green, vibrating rap music leaking through the windows of a car as it passes us, a distant honk followed by a police whistle.

"I have to get back to work," I finally tell Milagros.

"What are we gonna do?" She says as though I haven't spoken, "I think something is being covered up, Amanda." Now she is serious. Rarely does she use my given name.

"I hate to sound like a conspiracy nut, but this *is* looking kind of suspicious," I agree.

Milagros grabs my arm, "I mean *all* the lab specimens disappear, and *then* the autopsy report gets changed."

"We *think* it got changed," I correct her, "but I do agree that something doesn't smell right."

We continue walking when a thought hits me, "Hey, I have a friend who's an ED doc. Maybe we can talk with him and he can help us understand all this better."

"Perfect, chica. I got an idea too. You see if we can go see your friend after work today and I'll check out my idea a little. Call me." She blows a kiss and takes off.

The T pulls in as Milagros click-clacks down the street in the opposite direction. Well, I think as I climb aboard, maybe Dr. Ronald Lee, emergency room physician extraordinaire, will have some insights for us.

Chapter 6:

Doctor, doctor gimme the news...

(Bad Case of Lovin' You, Robert Palmer)

Ron, my friend who is a doctor, is working that night at Beth Israel Hospital. When I speak with him in the afternoon he tells me I should just come into the Emergency Department and have the secretary page him.

At home I read with Brendan, tuck him in to bed allowing him a half hour of TV before it is lights out and book out letting Linda know that I am leaving for a couple hours. Philip is planning on coming home this evening and sleeping over. But I am figuring that he won't be in until much later.

As I turn down the sidewalk I notice the glow from Mr. Ziegler's cigar from up on his front stoop.

"Hey Mr. Z," I call out to him as I pass by, "everyone in the neighborhood behaving themselves?"

"Just you and those Russian mobsters are out and about, sweetie" he replies.

"What are they smuggling this time?"

"Don't know, but I'll keep an eye on it and let ya know."

"Okay, see you later," I make it down the block, chuckling to myself. Anyone else coming and going from their home, it would be considered normal activity. But when the Russians stir it could only mean some sort of nefarious activity according to Mr. Ziegler.

I meet Milagros in front of Beth Israel Hospital and we walk into the ER waiting area. It is filled with an assortment of people in varying levels of distress and boredom. A college-age girl wrapped in a blanket is hunched over a small plastic trash can perched on her lap.

A man in dark blue coveralls holds a bloody white hand towel around his hand. Lost in their personal misery, most ignore us. Sponge Bob's maniacal laugh erupts from a television set entertaining a few children gathered around it as we approach the reception desk. Ron very thoughtfully has told the receptionist that we would be coming in and to let us through into the urgent care side where he's working that night.

Once through the ER doors we sidle up to the nursing station in the urgent care area and a splendid African American woman with gorgeous skin, long braids and even longer fingernails is tapping away on the computer keyboard. Milagros and I lean in to see how the hell she is managing the keystrokes. She doesn't pause for a moment as she says, "May I help you?"

"Yes, please, um Shaneeta," I say, observing her name tag, "I'm a friend of Dr. Lee's and he told me to come see you to have him paged," I explain.

Rat-a-tat-tat, she finishes whatever she's doing and then looks up and says, "Sure thing sugar," but it comes out more like shore thang shugah. "You wait right here." (you wait raight hee-yah).

She taps into the computer again, pausing while the computer catches up with her commands and then taps some more. This must be the paging system they use.

"Damn, mommy, how you keep those nails clean?" Milagros blurts out with a little awe in her voice.

Embarrassed I elbow her. But Shaneeta seems unfazed by the question and holds up her hands proudly.

"Jes' like you would hon' I wash 'em ev'ry once in awhile," and with a flick of her hair she goes back to her computer.

We turn as the sliding doors from the ambulance bay open up and in rolls a gurney with a startled-looking young guy on it. His skin is red as a beet. I spy Ellen, Ron's longtime girlfriend who is also an ER nurse. She's coming around a corner as though she expects this delivery.

"Over in three," she directs the EMT's, never breaking stride. She passes the nursing station by which we are standing while she consults a chart and briskly enters a room a few doors down, ponytail bobbing authoritatively behind her.

I tell Milagros who she is as they wheel Beet Boy into room three. Milagros and I follow their progress like this is a tennis match. I am wondering if they serve popcorn here, it's getting interesting.

Ellen pops out of the room she had been in and goes into room three pulling the privacy curtain closed around the bed.

Milagros and I both lean forward to try to catch the conversation but can't hear anything.

"Hey Amanda," I turn at the sound of Ron's gentle voice. Ron is somewhat shy and retiring. Intelligent eyes regard us behind frameless glasses and his conservative haircut adds to the whole geek-doctor persona. He and I went through undergrad together. We suffered through Organic Chemistry, Biochemistry and Genetics together. He went on to med school, I went on to raise a family. We've stayed in touch through the years.

"Ron, it looks busy. Can you break away for a few minutes to talk?" I ask.

"Sure. It's like this every night," he assures me. "Let's just go over here," he points to an empty room maybe fifteen feet from the secretary.

After introducing Milagros I get right down to business describing the death of the hockey player and the unusual lab result. I leave out the autopsy for the moment as I don't want to admit that we entered the tricky ground of patient privacy.

"Hmmmm," he says, taking it all in, "so how can I help you?"

"Well, I'm not sure. But we wanted a better understanding of what might occur in the ED when a patient arrives with this type of situation. What you would do, and what might explain the high result," I say. Ron's a genius. If anyone can sort this out, he can.

"Ok. If he came in DOA, there isn't much I would do since I am in the business of trying to save lives." He says this with no rancor, just stating the truth. Ron is a pragmatist to the bone.

"Sure," I say, "but if you were uncertain about the status of the patient..." I prompt.

He shrugs and sighs, "I guess it would depend on the presentation. You said it was this hockey player so I am assuming certain things here...."

"Yes," I prompt.

"Well, I heard it was sudden cardiac arrest. So they were probably doing CPR as they brought him in. I would order ABG's and hook him up to get an EKG."

I look at Milagros who nods, affirming that they did get ABG's (arterial blood gases: it checks on the oxygenation of the blood) on him.

"Okay, anything else?" I pursue.

"That would be my first line of action," Ron says. "I guess if I thought there was some hope of resuscitating the patient I would want to know his electrolytes."

Again, this makes sense. The basic electrolytes in our body, sodium, potassium, and chloride, can get messed up as the body is in distress. Once too much of an imbalance occurs, such as too much potassium, the heart will go into an arrhythmia – an irregular heart beat – that is difficult, if not impossible, to pull out of.

"So you'd order a BMP?" I ask.

"Here, I'd order a seven." He corrects. A seven is a really, really old term for the basic chemistry panel. It's similar to a BMP as far as I know.

"Okay, you just want to make sure his 'lytes aren't so messed up that you could do something for him?" I lead him along the thought trail I am following.

"Yes, that's the idea. If there's any hope in saving the patient, you have to understand his electrolyte balance, especially his potassium."

I turn to Milagros, "So the order which they claim was for BMP is probably correct," I point out to her.

"Alright, so nothing suspicious about ordering the BMP which is mistaken as a BNP," she concedes, "but the BNP did get run and it was really high. How do we reconcile the result with the cause of death?" We both look at Ron.

"That *is* interesting," Ron pushes his glasses up his nose, "I certainly would not expect to see a BNP level like what you recovered. Perhaps he had a heterophile antibody that interfered with the BNP result."

"Ah," I say, "*that* would explain a high result." Antibodies are what the body's immune system forms to fight foreign objects such as viruses. Heterophile antibodies are a group of antibodies used to describe more of a non-specific reaction. The most common time you see them rise to a detectable level is during and after a case of Infectious Mono, the kissing disease. The incidence of Mono is highest in high school and college kids. When you run a certain type of lab test, called an immunoassay, these heterophiles can do funny things to the test and you can see a falsely lowered result or a falsely elevated one. BNP is an immunoassay test.

"I suppose but if that is the explanation I would expect him to have been quite ill. I can't recall ever seeing such a massive interference to drive a result up that far even with full blown Mono," he says hands in his lab coat pockets. "I suppose it's possible, though."

"Let's play devil's advocate," I say, "and this is not a false elevation. What, as a doctor, would you expect to see in a patient like this if he's still alive?"

Ron looks down at the floor for a couple beats and then looks up and says, "That value indicates an approximate Class Three or Four heart failure. This would be a person who struggles with normal exercise. He would be extremely short of breath in a rapid amount of time. Blood is going to pool anywhere below the heart so swelling of the lower extremities is expected as well."

"What if he just went into heart failure?" Milagros asks.

"I think it would depend on the individual. The heart failures I see are usually dramatic – the patient is struggling to breathe. But heart failure is caused *by* something. It typically starts out with very few symptoms and worsens over time. There would have to be a precipitating incident. I would look for a history of heart attack, long term high blood pressure, malformation of the heart, or endocarditis or cardiomyopathy from a viral infection."

"None of those sound realistic for a college hockey player," I observe.

"Probably not," Ron agrees. "Although I wouldn't rule it out based solely on his age."

"He had diabetes," Milagros mentions.

"That too can lead to heart failure," he says as his beeper goes off. He glances down at it and starts to usher us back over to the nurse's station. "Diabetes might be the best avenue to pursue but I'd also check his blood for heterophiles. I just find it difficult to believe that an athlete could sustain the kind of performance required at the college-level if he is a Class Three heart failure. The more plausible answer is that the test was inaccurate."

"Makes sense," I say as we end up back at the desk where we met him.

Just then Ellen pulls back the curtain in room three and we see that Beet Boy is now completely covered in a thick layer of white cream from his waist on up.

"Hey Amanda, I didn't know you were here," she comes up to the counter.

"We came in to get Ron's help on something," I explain. I introduce Milagros to Ellen and then ask her what happened to the patient in room three.

"Oh, this is a good one," she smirks. "He wanted his car engine all sparkly and clean for some car show," Ellen says and lowers her voice. "The dumbshit cleans the engine by soaking some of the parts in gasoline, puts it back together, wants to make sure that it still works. Tells his friend to start the engine while he's standing over it. Boom! He get's blown ten feet back from the fireball. Shoes were still right in front of the car where he was standing when the paramedics arrived," she snorts.

Milagros and I turn our eyes back to this prime example of male stupidity. I now see that his eyebrows are gone as well as the front section of his hair. He is wearing this surprised expression on his face, like he still can't believe what happened to him.

"Is he going to be okay?" I ask.

"Yeah, he can't hear all that well right now but that should come back in awhile. Ear drums don't like explosions. Hon'," she turns to Ron who had been speaking with the secretary, "room eight is ready to sign out."

"Okay, thanks," Ron acknowledges her. He turns to leave, pauses, turns back to me once more and says, "One more thing I thought of that can produce heart failure," he says, "sometimes a drug, chemical or toxin can injure the heart and lead to failure."

"We appreciate your time, Ron," I say. "Have a good evening."

"You too. Milagros, nice meeting you." We make our goodbyes to Ellen as well and then leave.

Outside the BI I say, "Did you think this was helpful?"

"Yes and no," Milagros tucks a piece of her long curly hair behind her ear. "I mean, it would be easy to say the result was due heterophile interference. But I can't test for that *since all the blood is gone.* And Benny remembering a much larger heart than what was put in the report goes along with a high BNP result."

"Is he going to check with that pathologist to see if he remembered correctly?" I ask.

"He tol' me he would so I'll call him on Monday."

"So we can wait until Monday and think about it over the weekend," I am trying to wind her down.

"Not me, chica. I found out that since the next few games for BC are going to be rescheduled, the hockey team has some free time and is getting together tonight at a bar near the college."

"So what does that have to do with you?" I want to know.

"Remember I said I had something to do this afternoon? Well, I did a little digging and found out who Mike Donowski's best friends and closest teammates are. I am going to go over to that bar to see what I can find out about his health and activities the last couple of days before his death."

"What?" I yelp, "You shouldn't do that. These people are grieving. The last thing they need is someone coming around and asking all kinds of questions," I argue with Milagros.

"Querida, I am not an insensitive fool. I will just hang around, listen, and ask a few questions here and there when it seems appropriate."

"So, you are going to go into a bar. All by yourself. At night. Just on the off-chance of hearing something or talking with someone," I enumerate the problems with her hare-brained scheme.

"You can come with me," Milagros says in a little sing song voice and gives me that look – it is the look that says well if you are going to go all Mommy on me, then you should come to protect me. This is emotional blackmail. I have lectured her on being safe any number of times. And going to bars all alone is one of my recurring themes.

"Or we can just both go home," I say back in the same sing song voice she used.

"But that don't get us no answers," she sings back.

"You are nuts," I sing back once more.

"Look, loco or not I am going to do it. I can't just sit on this the whole weekend. It will drive me crazy. I promise I won't make a nuisance of myself or act suspicious." Milagros has folded her arms over her chest, "Now, you coming or not?"

Ravagni

I sigh heavily to show her my disapproval and take out my cell phone to call home. Linda assures me everything is fine and not to worry. Sure, easy for her to say.

Chapter 7:

Bubbletoes

(*Bubbletoes*, Jack Johnson)

We enter the Keg and Kettle Alehouse right around 9:30pm. I have the mellow tunes of Jack Johnson playing in my head as I ooze into the crowded bar behind Milagros. I'm taking Jack's advise, 'just go with the flow'.

I didn't have time to vamp myself up, for which I am sure society at large is grateful. But I did manage to comb my hair and put on some lipstick. Back when Philip was a little guy he would follow me around as I got ready in the morning. I used to joke with him. He would sit in the bathroom and watch me do my hair and face and ask me why I was putting on the makeup. I'd say so I wouldn't scare people. Ha, ha. Thought I was being funny, not realizing that children take everything literally. One morning I overheard him tell one of his teachers at pre-school that his mother has to wear makeup so she doesn't scare people. That teacher never could look me in the eye again after that.

Anyway Milagros is navigating the poorly-lit bar and I am following behind, weaving around people and trying to keep up as best I can.

"Over here, querida," Milagros pulls me to a small bar table pushed against the wall. The chairs are missing but the table looks reasonably clean so we put our coats and purses on its surface.

"So what do we do now?" I want to know.

"Let's just have a drink and blend. I'll keep an eye out for opportunities."

I have no idea what, in this loud and crowded place, she thinks she is going to see or hear but at least she isn't doing this alone. All I would be doing right now is sitting at home and worrying about her safety.

"Those are some of the guys on the hockey team," Milagros points out.

I see a group of young men and a few girls with pitchers of beer in front of them. They are sitting around a couple tables pulled together. They are talking but don't appear nearly as animated as the other patrons. I don't recognize any of them but I haven't met too many of Philip's teammates yet. How, I wonder, does Milagros know that these are guys on the hockey team?

I scan the crowd. There're mostly college kids from what I can tell. I feel old as dirt and a little out of place here.

All of sudden I hear some people call, "Booze! Booze!"

Now normally one might think that they are asking for refills in a slightly unorthodox manner, like at one of those medieval dinners where you are holding a turkey leg in one hand, beer stein in the other, and telling the serving wench to bring you more spirits. This however is not the case. Instead I see that Philip has come in and I know that they are calling him over to their table. Booze has been his nickname ever since junior varsity hockey when he'd score a goal and the announcer would say, "Goal! By Booooooooz-kemee". It doesn't thrill me but it is kind of understandable.

Drat. I should have realized he might show up. I wonder if he is going to think I am spying on him. We've already ordered our drinks and I decide that I will stay for one drink, keeping a low profile, and then leave; Milagros or not. I watch Philip walk up to the table and do the guy hug thing with his friends. Someone has pulled another chair over and he joins the group. A waitress that was bringing another pitcher of beer hands him a glass as well after he shows her his fake ID. Neato. A chip off the old block.

I feel a tap on my shoulder and turn to look right into the broad chest of Pete, Bobby's friend. "What are you doing here?" I blurt out before I can stop myself. Jeez has everyone in the universe gathered at this one particular bar?

"Well hello and nice to see you too, Amanda," Pete grins.

"Uh, sorry, you just surprised me," I can feel my face color. I'm not his biggest fan but I should use the manners my mama taught me. "So how are you?"

"Fine, and you?"

"Okay, I just stopped in for a drink with my friend. You remember Milagros?" I touch her arm since she is still focused on the hockey group.

She turns and says, "Oh, hi Pete. Nice to see you again."

Our drinks arrive and before I can stop him, Pete pays for our drinks. Oh great, now he thinks he can hang around.

Almost as though Milagros has read my mind but in the reverse she says, "You know, I think I might see someone I know over there. Since you are here Pete, I won't feel bad about going to say hi."

"Sure, sure, you go right ahead, *Milagros*," I say as sarcastically as possible. This appears to be completely lost on her since she starts making her journey to the other side of the room.

"So, are you meeting someone here?" I ask. Not because I really care but rather I feel the need to fill in the conversational void. I sip my wine.

"Not really. I knew Philip might be hanging out and I just wanted to make sure he's okay. Bobby's on tonight." Meaning he's got a shift at the firehouse.

"That's really sweet!" I exclaim. I am genuinely touched that he cares so much about Philip. In spite of his chauvinistic attitude towards women, he might have a redeeming quality. He just went up a couple notches in my book.

"It's nothing. He's a great kid," he sips his drink. So I take another swig of my wine. It's a little warm in here so I remove my cardigan sweater, exposing my pink Red Sox chick tee-shirt.

"You know Amanda, you look really good. Have you lost some weight?" Pete leans in a little closer.

"Uh, maybe a pound or two," I admit moving away slightly.

"Well, you look really, really good, honestly," he says admiringly.

I take another slurp of wine. Pete has flirted with me off and on for a number of years now. I consider it harmless but still feel disarmed by it.

"Thanks. I don't get to work out like I should though," I babble about being busy and working.

"There's a Gold's Gym near you. I'm a member. I could meet you there a couple times a week and we could work out together," he suggests.

Great, just what I need: Pete and Me Time. I look around for Milagros who is over talking with a girl by the ladies' room.

"Um, that's okay, Pete, I'm not sure how often I could get over there. It's probably too much of a commitment," I say lamely.

"Well, then how about dinner sometime, like tomorrow night?" he asks.

"Huh?" I drag my eyes away from Milagros and back to Pete, "like all of us?"

"No, Amanda," he smiles, "just you and me, like a real date."

What the heck is this all about? I flounder in my thoughts. I'm not sure what to say so I reply, "Aren't I a little long in the tooth for your tastes?" I try for some levity but it comes out sounding catty.

"Look, I know I've dated a few women younger than myself but that's because I don't think age is a big deal, either way," he says levelly.

"Oh, so you'd date someone, say ten years older than you?" I ask.

"Actually I would if I really like her but you are getting away from answering my question: will you go out with me?" he persists.

I drain the last of my wine to buy some time. Just then the waitress brings another glass to me. How did that happen? Gratefully I take it and have another sip right away to stall giving him an answer. Looking around the room I see Milagros disappear with that girl into the restroom. I swivel my eye's back to find Pete is looking at me pointedly, eyebrow cocked like some stupid swashbuckling pirate.

"Um, you *are* Bobby's friend," I remind him.

"Yeah?" he looks amused.

"Well, don't you guys, like, have a code or something?"

"A code?" he asks.

"Yeah, like a brotherhood code. You know: thou shalt not date your buddy's ex-girl." I splutter and suck down more wine. Boy, it is getting *really* hot in here. Can't anyone else feel it? People are sitting around in sweatshirts, jackets and sweaters. Here I am sweating like a pig in a Louisiana heat wave. I flap my napkin in front of my face. The draft this action creates wouldn't cool a flea.

"Babe, how long have you and Bobby been divorced?" he drills me with his eyes.

Babe??!! "Uh, nine years," I answer increasing the napkin flapping.

"Exactly. Even codes have expiration dates," he says.

"Really, I thought it was forever, you know, like Twinkies," I say weakly.

"Not in my book," Pete answers.

"Well, you might want to check in Bobby's book for that one," I say lifting my hair off the back of my neck and sopping up the perspiration that's beaded there; anything to cool myself down.

Pete turns me around and blows on the back of my neck, "Does that help?"

"Kind of," I say. Actually it feels terrific, it's working way better than the napkin-thingy I'm doing. And then I feel Pete's lips touch the back of my neck.

Panicked, I try to turn around quickly and stagger a little.

"Are you ok?" Pete has a hold of my shoulders to steady me – I think – and looks with concern at me.

"I'm jes-a-lil-tot," I slur.

"What?" Pete asks.

"Fa-gil-il hot-ot," I say with no control over my tongue.

"Oh for God's sake, are you drunk on two glasses of wine?" he demands.

"Noooooo!" I deny, "jes a man-eeee eesa plee-ple," I attempt to explain, waving my napkin in the general direction of the crowds.

"Here, come with me," he says taking the wine glass out of my hand and grabbing my arm.

We wind through the throngs of people as I start to giggle. I am moving like a jellyfish, rhythm is not. Whatever those words are...flow a-go-go hot, hot, hot. Giggle.

Pete pushes through the front door and now we are out in the cool crisp air. That's the last thing I remember.

Chapter 8:

Say "nighty night" and kiss me

(*Dream a Little Dream of Me,* as sung by James Dean)

Filtered light seeps into my consciousness as does this really annoying sound. I swim through layers of mental fog toward the sound and realize it's my alarm clock making the noise. It continues to squawk at me until I sluggishly reach over and fumble to switch it off.

I crack open a crusty eye and take in my surroundings blearily. I look at the digital date readout and realize that it's Saturday and I don't have to get up. Cursing my stupidity at forgetting to turn the alarm off before going to bed, I groan. Now my mind starts clicking into place regarding the events of last night. Like a slide show I see the crowded bar, drinks, and Pete kissing the back of my neck!

"Aaagh!" I sit up straight in bed the last remnants of lassitude wiped away with an adrenaline rush. Rifling through my memory I determine that my last conscious thought was Pete with his arm around me outside that bar. I throw my covers off and wildly check to see if I'm naked. All my clothes are still on except for my shoes which are down on the floor by the foot of my bed. I think to myself, Thank God I didn't sleep with Pete; aka When Hell Freezes Over.

I dash out of my room and down the hall. I look in Brendan and Philip's room. Brendan is not in his bed but there is a big hump under the covers in Philip's. A foot and a portion of a hairy leg is all that sticks out. Steadying myself on the wall I quickly move down the hallway. As I approach the kitchen I can see Brendan watching TV in the living room and eating cereal.

Linda is at the sink but turns when she hears me as I enter with a huff and a snort.

"Hey, kiddo, how do you feel?" she says with an arched eyebrow.

Holding onto the door jam for balance I say, "Oh my God, Linda, I have no idea what happened last night. The last thing I remember is Pete dragging me outside when it got hot in this bar," I flop down on a kitchen chair.

"Oh yeah, Prince Charming brought you home. You were out like a stone-cold fish," she says.

"Jeez," I exclaim, bending over and clutching my head in my hands. "What in the world happened?" Fear has replaced fuzziness in my brain.

"Well, according to Pete, you got drunk and he had to bring you home."

"I only had maybe a glass and a half of wine," I protest. "How could I have gotten drunk on that?"

"I don't know, but he said you were talking gibberish about jellyfish, called him Jack, and giggled a lot."

"Did the boys see me in that condition?"

"No. Brendan was down for the count and Philip came home a couple hours after Pete and I tucked you in bed," she says.

"Thank God for small favors," I exclaim. I am so embarrassed. I can't remember the last time I got drunk; or at least so drunk that I couldn't remember getting myself to bed. I guess I am now officially a light weight.

I have a sudden thought, "My car must still be over there, then."

"No, Pete drove you home in your car and then took a taxi back over to the bar to get his," she dangles my keys in front of me.

Squinting at them I try to digest what she just told me.

Finally I say, "Wow, he's more human than I thought." This act of chivalry astounds me. He gets me home, tucks me in bed, doesn't molest me (I'm pretty certain), and then leaves my car for me.

"Yeah, he's the one that brought Phil home and then came in to make sure you were okay," she smiles.

I shake my head in wonderment.

"Milagros!" I yell out as it suddenly dawns on me that I abandoned her at the bar. "Oh my God, she was still there and I left her." I grab up my phone and start clicking through the numbers to find hers.

"Hey, I'm sure she's alright," Linda tries to assure me. "I bet she goes out all the time by herself."

"Yeah, but not on my watch!" I say as I land on her number and spastically press the Send button.

"You do realize it's only a little after seven in the morning?" Linda reminds me.

"Uh, yeah, but screw it, I have to know she's alright," I announce in full-blown mama-hen voice. I know I am being a paranoid twit but I can't help myself.

Her cell phone rings once and then goes directly to voice mail.

"Argh!" I huff as I press the End button, "the phone's turned off!"

"She's probably asleep and doesn't want to be disturbed," Linda reasonably explains to me.

"Well, that's not acceptable! What if I need to reach her?"

"Amanda, honey, Milagros is a big girl. I'm sure she's had many evenings out by herself," Linda says attempting to reach the rational part of my mind which cowers in some dim corner while the lunatic rages.

"I know, I know but I got a bad feeling about this," I say as I am thinking about her zeal to get to the bottom of our little mystery.

"All of a sudden *you're* relying on intuition," she cocks an eyebrow at me.

Okay, the history behind Linda's comment about intuition is that I think that "sixth sense", intuition, gut feelings etc, etc, are, at best, explainable, at worst, superstitious malarkey that harkens back to the Dark Ages;

where you had to study the entrails of some animal or interpret tea leaves or some such nonsense to decide whether it was okay to make a trip, marry a certain girl or plant your harvest. Linda and I have had many conversations about this. I am the antagonist, the debunker for all things mystical. Let's just say that I lost my sense of wonder and ability to believe in the intangible a long time ago.

"Look, I don't have time to explain, but I've got to go check on her. You gonna be around?" I ask as I grab the keys from her.

"For awhile, but Phil is here. Before I go out I'll wake him up to watch Brendan."

"Sounds good," I say high-tailing it out of the kitchen, "I'll have my cell phone if there's any problem."

I show up at Milagros' condo building fifteen minutes later. I punch her intercom button and stand there waiting, hoping, that she'll answer.

"Come on. Come on!" I mutter, fidgeting, unable to keep still as my trepidation rises. I press the button again and again. No answer. I back up and look up at the set of windows I know are hers. All of a sudden the lock release buzzes. I jump toward the door and yank it open. Bounding up the stairs I see her door cracked open.

I push open the door and Milagros, who was standing behind it, quickly closes it. She's wearing a gray sweat suit, her face is pale and she has dark smudges under her eyes. Relief floods over me.

"You didn't answer your cell phone. Are you okay?" I ask.

"What happened to you last night?" she asks instead of answering my question. Wrapping her arms around her middle she sits down on her couch.

"Pete brought me home. I guess I got drunk although it doesn't seem possible. I mean I did drink my first glass quickly," I blabber. I throw up my hands. "I didn't even finish my second glass of wine," I finish weakly feeling foolish and irresponsible.

Milagros is silent through my monologue. Finally she draws in a breath and says, "We were set up, chica."

"What do you mean, 'set up'?" I ask.

"After I noticed you were gone I decided I had better leave too. I was parked a couple blocks down and so was walking to my car when these two guys approached me."

"What?" I shriek.

"Yeah, and they knew my name. I asked if I knew them from somewhere and they said, no, but that *they* knew *me*," if possible her face is even paler as she recounts this to me.

I feel my throat constrict and say with a catch in my voice, "So then what?"

"I took off running like the devil was chasing me," she says.

"Did they run after you?"

"They might have but they didn't catch up to me and when I got to my car, I got in and locked it right away and the street was empty."

"I *knew* I screwed up," I exclaim, "Oh, Milagros, I am so sorry! You're just lucky you thought fast and took off like you did."

"I don't think they actually meant to hurt me, chica," Milagros states.

"How do you know that? They even knew your name!" I say.

"Because as I was running away one of them called out to me and tol' me to be a good girl and to stop poking around in business that wasn't mine," her eyes are like saucers.

"Huh?" I say.

"Amanda, I think they purposely tried to make sure I was out on the street alone so they could scare me."

"So what, like someone slipped me a micky or something to get me out of commission?" I ask.

"Exactly," she states. "Tell me what happened to you."

"I was talking with Pete and drinking my wine. I started to slur my words and I was getting clumsy. Pete thought I was drunk and brought me outside. Linda tells me that he brought me home and they got me to bed but I don't remember any of that."

"That's why I said we got set up," she says. "I think that whoever is behind this hockey player death is trying to cover something up and we are getting in the way. So if someone scares one of us we might stop."

"If that's the case then they did a good job," I say. My stomach is churning at the thought of Milagros being in danger.

"So this has to be related to all the investigating we are doing," she says.

"Maybe," I say. Even with this latest scare, I still have misgivings about jumping to conclusions. As I said before, Milagros can have a little flair for the dramatic. It is possible she is reading more into this than is there? "Listen, I didn't eat dinner last night so maybe I *did* get drunk. Someone drugging me in a crowded bar is really reaching."

"Oh really?" She stands up, goes into the kitchen. I hear her rummaging around and then she comes back with a small plastic bowl and cover. "Pee in here," she commands.

"Are kidding me?" I say, "What are you going to do, test me for drugs?"

"If that will convince you that I am right, then yes," she thrusts the bowl at me.

"Milagros, you know all kinds of people. Are you sure that you heard right about what those guys said to you?"

"Yes, mommy, I am. Now go make water," she places the bowl and cover in my hand and then gently pushes me toward her bathroom.

"I cannot believe this," I mutter as I go in the bathroom. "Promise me you will drop this conspiracy thing if the test is negative," I yell through the door.

"No problem," she yells back, "'cause I know I am right!"

We go into the lab at City Hospital. Since we both work there we just go over to the bench where the urine drug screens are performed and start the testing on my urine. We barely even get a glance as everyone is intent on their tasks. Saturday mornings are typically very busy.

While the clock is ticking away for the ten minute reaction time, Milagros goes over to one of the computers and does a search engine for Rohypnol which is the date rape drug of choice.

The site she pulls up describes the drug as "tasteless and odorless, so most victims are not aware that it has been slipped into their drink."

"See," she points out, "you wouldn't have noticed if someone put it in your wine."

We read on, "Within ten to fifteen minutes the drug can take affect. Some of the effects are dizziness, drowsiness and confusion; worst of all, victims have reported not being able to remember what has happened or where they have been."

"I *was* dizzy and confused," I admit. "And I certainly don't remember Pete getting me home."

"We will know soon enough if someone monkeyed with your drink," Milagros grimly states. We both look at the timer; two minutes to go.

Rohypnol disappears fairly rapidly in the body but it's been less than twelve hours so we have a good chance of detecting it. If it is there, it will show up in the benzo-diazepine drug class on the test card.

The timer dings and Milagros transfers the reaction onto the testing lane, waits about ten seconds and then adds several drops of the wash solution. As the liquid soaks through the membrane we both lean over and stare at the test card lying on the counter. A strong pink line comes up next to the label that says "BZO" on it.

Stunned we straighten back up and look each other in the eye.

"Holy crap," I whisper.

Chapter 9:

I'm not ready to make nice,
I'm not ready to back down

(*Not Ready to Make Nice*, Dixie Chicks)

We're outside the hospital now, walking back to my car.

"Okay, no more arguments on my part. I am a true believer," I say. Up until now I was playing my usual role of devil's advocate. Not anymore. I am really shaken up over the fact that someone drugged me and that they did it so easily. What if Pete hadn't been there?

"That's good chica. I have to admit, what happened last night really scared me," Milagros says. "Proving that you actually got drugged only confirms that we are dealing with some bad people who mean business," she states, "but I am not going to give up on this."

"What?" I exclaim, "Oh yes you are! Immediately we are going to stop. No more! That kid is dead and gone and there's nothing we can do about it."

"But I haven't told you what I found out last night," she says.

"Talking to that girl? Why, what's the big discovery?" I ask. We arrive at my car. I click open the locks and we climb inside.

"That girl was Mike Donowski's girlfriend. She's real broke up over his death."

"I'm sure she is. So we have to take on evil villains just for her?" I ask.

"No querida, listen to the whole story and stop being so crazy."

"Oh, I'm sorry! I'm a little sensitive right now what with getting drugged into oblivion and you being threatened and chased down the street by hoodlums," I reply sarcastically.

"Well just listen. So Caitlin, that's her name, tol' me that Mike hadn't been feeling very well lately. That he was feeling run down and didn't have energy at hockey practice," she pauses.

"Mhmmmm...." I say to get her to continue the story. I am tempted to make the rolling hand gesture but she might just smack me up side the head. I do have to agree that his symptoms are fitting the picture of heart failure, new onset. It could also be about a million other things as well, like Mono as Ron suggested.

"So I asked her if there was anything unusual that he had been exposed to lately. I was looking for something that could have brought on the heart failure."

"You didn't tell her about what we found out, did you?" I ask alarmed.

"No, I am not stupid," Milagros looks slightly indignant. "I had told her my boyfriend played hockey and I felt really bad for her. I was real careful not to make her suspicious. Anyway, she said she didn't think he had been exposed to anything. Then I asked her if he had had any illnesses 'cuz I knew you would want to know about the possibility of him having heterophile antibodies from like, Mono, or something."

"Good, good," I say.

"She said that he just complained about an overall not feeling well but no definite symptoms that would make her think had an illness. He mentioned about going to some clinic about his diabetes. He thought maybe the new treatment he was doing was the cause."

"The diabetes was under control, though, according to the pathology report," I say mulling over what Milagros just told me.

"A pathology report that got *altered*," Milagros reminds me.

"I give you that it *might* have been altered concerning the heart size but what would be the value in changing the glucose level? I think we are barking up the wrong tree with the diabetes," I say.

"So I have an idea," she says.

"Oh, no! No, no, no!" I protest, "No more ideas. No more going around asking questions. No more," and here I hold up two fingers on each hand and curl them several times, " 'investigations'."

"This won't be much of anything, really," she says.

"That's right. It won't be much of anything. It'll be nothing!"

"But all I need you to do is go visit your son in his dorm," she wheedles.

"Why am I thinking there's more to it than that?" I ask.

"I found out Philip is on the same dorm floor as Mike Donowski was," she says.

"And???" I say. I have visions of breaking into Mike Donowski's dorm room and bumbling around like Inspector Clouseau looking for clues.

"Maybe you could have Phil introduce you to the roommate, whose name by the way is John McSweeny, just so you can ask him a few questions, you know?"

"What," I say, "what could he possibly know that would help us figure any of this out?"

"First, see if his story is the same as Caitlin's. You know, with the heart failure symptoms. And see if there is additional information that could point us where to go next."

I fold my arms across my chest and put my head back against the car's headrest. "You are certifiable, you know that? When are you going to be satisfied? When those thugs make good on their threat?" I rant.

"Just do that for me. If this kid was in heart failure there has to be a reason for it. And that reason maybe the *something* that someone doesn't want us to know," she says.

"I'll see what I can do. It can't be this weekend since Philip is home already. Monday would be weird. But I can make brownies maybe and bring them over on Tuesday. I suppose I could stop in to give my condolences to the roommate," I say grudgingly.

"Perfect, chica," Milagros squeezes my arm and beams at me.

"I'm glad you're satisfied," I grumble, "now I gotta get home. My teeth are growing fur," I run my tongue over the fronts of my teeth. Yuck!

I drop Milagros off at her place and then gratefully speed off toward home to spend the weekend with my family. A few days of R and R with the boys will be my best medicine. Little did I know that the upcoming week was going to open a can of worms that no lid would contain.

Chapter 10:

Stacy's Mom has got it goin' on

(*Stacy's Mom*, Fountains of Wayne)

Tuesday afternoon finds me moving down the dormitory hallway toward Philip's room. In one hand I am balancing a huge plastic container with two batches of brownies (with pecans and chocolate chips baked in just the way he likes them) and in the other hand I have my purse, a grocery bag, and a dripping umbrella that knocks against my left leg getting my jeans all wet.

"Knock, knock," I announce myself and then push my foot against the partially ajar door to his room.

"Hey, Mom," Philip jumps up from his bed, grabs the precariously balanced container and leans in to give my cheek a kiss.

"Hi Mrs. B," Ryan, his roommate calls out from his bed as he reaches over to his stereo and turns the volume down to a respectable level.

"Looks like you boys have been busy cleaning." My eyes dance around their room. It appears suspiciously clean. I had called Philip while driving over and my guess is they both raced around tucking dirty underwear under their pillows and tossing chip bags, soda cans and other trash into their closet. When I was in college I knew some guys that took great pride in not washing their sheets or cleaning their room for an entire semester. I always figured the college's cleaning crew had to go in with Hazmat suits to decontaminate those rooms. I've been kind of expecting Phil to end up living like a slovenly troll and am pleasantly surprised to see he is being very responsible.

"Just a little cosmetic surgery," he smiles and tears off the container's lid. "Mmmmm, brownies."

He snags one and then hands the container to Ryan who takes one as well.

Ryan takes a bite and says, "Oh my God, these are better than sex!" His face heats up as he realizes his social gaff, "Uh, oops. Sorry Mrs. B. I just meant they are really, really good." He mumbles around a mouthful of brownie.

I smile and assure him I am not offended. We chat for a while as they consume the first layer of brownies. I pour the milk I brought into cups for them amazed as always by the stomach capacity of young men.

"So the game is on for tomorrow?" I finally ask trying to segue into the request to go meet Donowski's roommate.

"Yup. You and Dad coming?"

"Yes, but Brendan is staying home with Linda. I don't want him out too late on a school night."

Philip nods his understanding as he wipes his mouth and stretches. His shirt rides up and his incredible six-pack is displayed. How did I every spawn such a phenomenal creature, I wonder to myself.

"You think your team is mentally ready to play?" I ask.

"I guess so. I mean, what can we do, right? We got a season to play," Philip replies.

"Yes, I know," I wait a beat, "Hey since I'm here I thought I would give my condolences to his roommate. Is he around here?" I ask as nonchalantly as I can. No way was that subtle, I think. I might as well be waving a banner, blaring a horn, and shouting, 'I'm playin' ya, dude'.

Instead Philip responds, "Yeah, he's right down the hall."

"Well," I say grabbing up my purse and umbrella, "can you introduce me on my way out?"

"Sure," he stands up. This was too easy. Philip doesn't suspect anything.

"Ryan, good to see you," I say on my way to the door.

"Same here Mrs. B. Thanks for the brownies." He's pulled up a fleece blanket and looks like a bear about to hibernate; brownie coma.

"You're welcome," I say as I follow Phil into the hallway.

"This way," Philip turns the opposite way I had come in.

As we start down the hall we hear a yell followed by some laughter. There is a crash and then two boys come running out of a dorm room almost colliding with us. They go dashing down the hall, roaring with laughter and then slamming out the exit. Another boy then comes out of the same room screaming, "Very funny! Come back here you assholes!"

I look at his face and see that they have shaved off one of his eyebrows. He looks hilariously comical. It's hard not to laugh.

"Booze, which way did they go?" He asks Philip. Grinning Philip hikes a thumb over his shoulder and the boy takes off running in that direction. "Prepare to die, suckahs!" He yells as he throws open the same exit door.

Ah college days, filled with pranks. With no parents to put on the brakes, I am sure it can get out of hand sometimes. I reminisce about the punishment I received at the hands of some college boys during my freshman year. My dorm mates and I got caught putting peanut butter on the underside of all the door handles to the boys' dorm rooms one floor above us. We would have made it out undetected but Bill Wilson, that little weasel, was just walking on to the floor when we were leaving and spied us. I put my finger to my lips and did this begging motion quietly beseeching him to not alarm the other boys. But he let out a war cry and we weren't able to outrun them. My friend Carolyn got thrown in the showers but I got a swirly; they stuck my head in the toilet and then flushed. I still feel kind of sick when I think about seeing the black scum on the underside of the toilet bowl and the smell!

Ugh, I washed my hair five times and still had the skeeves for a week.

Anyway, Philip and I arrive at a room maybe six doors down from his. He knocks and we wait for a few seconds until we hear a voice call, "C'mon in."

Philip pushes the door open and we see a disheveled young man sitting at a desk with a couple notebooks open along with his laptop.

"Hey, John, my mom wanted to meet you. Mom, this is John McSweeny."

"Hi John," I say holding out my hand to shake his. "How are you doing?"

"Ok, thanks. Nice to meet you," he replies politely, shaking my hand.

"Same here," I say. "I know that all the guys are very upset about Mike's death and I just wanted to tell you how sorry I am that you lost your roommate in this way."

"Thanks. Mike was a good guy. I miss him a lot. It was so wrong."

"Have you heard anything else about what caused it?" I ask.

"No, we were just told sudden cardiac arrest. That's really weird, huh?"

"Yes, it is," I agree. "I wonder did you see anything unusual or different about Mike in the weeks leading up to his death?" I am so not smooth, I say to myself.

"Yeah, he seemed a lot more tired. One day he couldn't drag himself out of bed and skipped some morning classes."

"And this wasn't typical for him?"

"No, he usually got up before his alarm. He'd go running or over to the gym. He hadn't done that in the last week or so before he died, at least, not that I saw."

"Did you ask him what was wrong?"

"Yeah, I came back from morning classes and he was still in bed, he woke up when I came in the room and asked me what time it was. I told him just a little after ten and asked if he had gotten up yet. He said no, that he just couldn't seem to get out of bed. I asked him if he was sick. He said he wasn't sure. He didn't have a fever or anything."

"Did he go see his doctor or maybe the campus health clinic?"

"Not that he told me. He said he had the weekly follow up for the study he was enrolled in for his diabetes. He was going to tell them about his symptoms."

"Do you know what exactly the study was for?"

Milagros had said that Caitlin mentioned a new diabetes treatment. Maybe he was enrolled in a clinical trial for a new drug. Although I didn't see how this could be associated with sudden cardiac arrest I guess I shouldn't dismiss it out of hand.

"It was some new diabetes treatment that uses an inhaler along with the regular insulin shots. He was excited about it because as the medicine from the inhaler starts to work the need for insulin decreases. I didn't really understand what it was all about but he mentioned one time that he had been able to decrease the amount of insulin he was giving himself. I guess his sugar levels were becoming more stable or whatever you call it." Mike shrugged.

"Do you recall the name of the study or who was conducting it?" I ask.

He shakes his head, "No idea. If you'd really like to know ask Tyler Brooks. I don't know him but I heard Mike mention him a number of times because they were both enrolled in the study together and went to BC."

"Well, I just wanted to tell you how sorry I am for your loss. I heard he was a good guy."

"Mike was the best. It all seems so random," he sucks in a jagged breath.

Jeez, there are no easy words for something like this. So I tell John again that I am sorry for his loss and wish him a good semester. I say goodbye to Philip, reminding him that I'll see him outside the arena tomorrow night.

Mulling over what John McSweeny has told me, I try to fit what I just learned with what I know about heart failure. If the heart is getting progressively ineffective at pumping, there would be a decrease in the amount of oxygenated blood being delivered to the body. This would definitely make a person feel weak and run down.

My cell phone rings and it is Milagros.

"Hey, girl," I answer the phone.

"Hey, what's going on? Are you free to talk?"

"Yes, I just left the dorms and am heading back to my car," I tell her.

"So, did you talk with the roommate?"

"Yes, you would have been proud of me. I got Philip to bring me down to see him." I tell her about the diabetes study in which Mike was supposedly enrolled and his fatigue.

"So we have at least two independent sources saying that he had heart failure symptoms. That makes it heart failure in my book," she says with confidence.

"You sound like a detective, 'two independent sources'," I say.

"No, I dated a reporter," she says as I roll my eyes, "and he tol' me that when researching something you had to have two or more independent sources telling you the same thing before you could use it in a story. So I figured the same thing applies to this."

"Makes sense," I allow.

"I called Benny to see if he spoke with the pathologist."

"And?"

"He said that the pathologist recalled it just like he did, with the heart being enlarged and weighing close to five hundred grams."

"Huh," I say, "so what about the report?"

"When the pathologist learned the tape was missing he went and asked the transcriber about it. She claims that she always transcribes exactly what's on the tape and then stores the tapes in order. They couldn't find the tape, though. He finally told Benny to forget it. That it wasn't worth driving themselves crazy over it. He did however put a notation in the report saying the original transcription tape was missing."

"That doesn't really help all that much does it?"

"Well, it helps confirm Benny's story. But if you're talking evidence that holds up in a court of law, I'd say we don't have much."

We are silent for a few moments. Then I say, "If he had heart failure, we still we don't know what caused it."

"I know," Milagros states, "His kidneys were fine and you'd think that if the diabetes was wrecking his body so much that his heart was affected, then the kidneys would be too. So if it isn't the diabetes, what caused it?"

"I have no clue," I say getting into my car. It stopped raining while I was visiting the boys and now it is cold and damp. I start the car and turn the wipers on to get rid of the beads of water on my windshield and turn on the heater to dissipate the chill that's settled into my bones.

"Maybe he got exposed to something, like the drinking water in his town."

"Okay, knock it off," I say, exasperated. "I know you'd like to solve this but we don't have the resources to do anything more."

"Hmmm," Milagros says.

"Milagros," I say in my warning voice, "Remember - scary guys drugging your friend and chasing you down the street?"

"Yeah, that's why I am so stuck on this. Like, what is it that's so important that someone needed to try to scare me?"

"I don't know and frankly it isn't worth taking any chances."

"Obviously this is important to them," she points out.

"You have a point there," I agree. "It is a dumbass move. I mean all they had to do was sit back and let us run into a dead end. We would have dropped it."

"Right. But instead, because they made such a big deal, we just got convinced that something really *is* going on." She pauses and I don't say anything. "Well, let me think about this a little bit. I'll call you to plan our next move."

"Milagros," I say completely aggravated, "this is it! Whatever is going on, I think it is too dangerous to get involved in anymore."

"No problem, mommy. You don't have to get involved anymore."

"You are making me nuts! Please reconsider," I beg her.

"Querida, we will talk later. Love you," and she hangs up before I can say anything more to her.

Oy. How can I convince her to back off? I chew my lip as I throw my car in gear and drive home.

Bobby is already at the arena entrance when I arrive the following evening. He is backlit by the entrance lights so all I see at first are his broad shoulders and narrow hips. In his late 30's he is still a fine specimen. When we were together and even for a period afterward all I could picture were those broad shoulders over me and then superimposed over some other woman enjoying them. I shake the thought.

"Hey, Bobby," I greet him.

"Manda," he acknowledges me.

I wonder if Pete has told Bobby about what happened in the bar. I examine him closely to see if he is showing any signs of mirth, or worse, contempt. I am hoping Pete kept this incident to himself but don't see why he would.

We make some small talk waiting for Philip. The night darkens further and a distinct chill sets in. We finally see Philip trudging up the hill towards us.

"Hey Mom, Dad," he says coming up on us.

We greet him, give him the parental good lucks and send him on his way.

Over at Dobsky's we settle in with our beers and catch up on kid news. Brendan has started drum lessons at school and got one hundred percent on his math test. We decide he is going to sleep at Bobby's on Friday night.

While Bobby tells me about the latest firehouse politics I sip my beer. My stomach unknots and my limbs start to loosen. I didn't realize I was tense but as it slowly dissipates, I realize that I was all clenched up. I think about the snooping Milagros and I have done, ending with our last conversation after I had visited Phil. I know Bobby wouldn't approve so I keep all these thoughts to myself.

In a conversation lull I say, "I stopped at Philip's dorm yesterday. Brought the boys brownies."

"Yeah? I like his roommate. He seems like a good kid," Bobby rejoins.

"I agree." I keep to myself that I visited Mike Sweeney, though. I don't need him getting a whiff of what we are up to. Suddenly I remember that I wanted to ask Bobby something that I overheard.

"Hey, Bobby?"

"Hmmm?" he says as he goes to take a sip of beer.

"What's a milf?"

Bobby coughs and splutters foamy beer out across the table and, it looks like, through his nose. He starts hacking uncontrollably and I run around behind him and whack him on the back. Finally he gets the coughing under control but his face is all red and his eyes are watery.

"Are you ok?" I ask alarmed.

"Where the hell did you hear that word?" he finally chokes out.

"Uh, when I was leaving Philip's dorm floor," I say as I return to my seat.

"Uh-huh, and what *exactly* was said?" Now his eyes are no longer watering but his face is still pretty red. I am starting to think maybe I shouldn't have asked him about this.

"Um, well, I overheard these two boys talking and I, uh, thought one said, 'did you get a load of Booze's mom?' and the other one said, "yeah, she's a real milf'. That's all." I cross my arms defensively.

Now he's face is even redder than before. I see storm clouds forming in his eyes. Then all of a sudden he roars with laughter.

"What?" I say.

He holds up a finger to indicate that he needs a minute while he tries to get the laughing under control enough to speak. Now I am annoyed. Obviously I am the butt of some joke.

"Hoo-hoo, you seriously don't know?" He finally says. Once again he is wiping his eyes.

"If I did, would I be asking you??" I lean forward and start jiggling my leg up and down in annoyance. I should have let him choke, I decide.

"Okay, okay, calm down. Oh, this is rich." He blows his nose on the bar napkin, looks at me with a huge grin and says, "Ok, milf stands for Mom I'd Like to F-"

"Holy crap!" I yell out.

Bobby's grin widens as he watches my face go from a normal color to probably more like clam chowder pale as I digest this piece of information.

"That is so sick!" I finally groan.

"Why? It's a compliment."

"Oh sure," I respond sarcastically. "Horny boys want to screw me. I am so hot!"

"Manda," Bobby reaches out and touches the back of my hand, "you *are* hot."

I look into his eyes but do not see any teasing. He actually looks like he means it. Oh, great; here's my ex-husband who didn't think I was worthy of fidelity but is still attracted to me. A swirl of emotions roils through me and my heart does a flutter. This is not good and I decide to brush it all off.

"That's sweet of you, Bobby, but you don't have to build my ego. Hey, how 'bout them Red Sox?"

"I *am* serious and not trying to patronize you. You are a beautiful woman."

"Right," I snort, "so beautiful and hot that I have men chasing me constantly. Why, I have to carry Mace just to keep them at bay."

"Listen," he catches my hand in his, "there are some things I have never said to you. Basically because it took a long time for me to grow up and realize what an asshole I was."

"Bobby..."

"No, Manda. Seeing your reaction right now makes me feel like a huge heel. I never meant to make you feel so bad about yourself."

"Well, I'd be lying if I said my self-esteem didn't take a hit." This is an understatement. By saying my esteem took a hit is like saying a nuclear bomb is a little explosion; World War Two was a minor skirmish; a tsunami is a small wave. By the time I left Bobby, I had gone through so many years of heartbreak and blaming myself, that I felt completely unattractive, unlovable and nonsexual.

Bobby leans forward a little more and says, "See, I was so selfish I couldn't see what I was doing to you. Manda, I was too young to get married and too inexperienced to recognize it. I resented being tied down at a time when my friends were still running around."

"You still managed to get out there," I remind him as I try to swallow the lump that's formed in my throat.

"Some," he allows, "but every time I had to say no to my friends, I blamed you for cramping my style. And every time I did go out I felt like a jerk. Again I blamed you for that. I was irresponsible and selfish. So what I am trying to say, after all these years, is that I'm sorry. You didn't deserve to be treated that way."

"Jeez, Bobby, I never thought I'd hear you say something like that." I feel tears burning my eyes.

"I should have told you this a long time ago but it wasn't until just now that I realized the impact my actions made on you."

I clear my throat and cautiously say, "Okay, well, thanks for telling me that. I guess we were both young and handled things in a less than mature way." I don't know what else to say. He had crushed my spirit and made me feel ugly. I look away so he can't see the tears swimming in my eyes.

Bobby grips my hand even tighter, looks at me intensely and says, "Amanda, you have to stop this!"

"Stop what?"

"Minimizing what a jerk I was. 'We were both young,'" he quotes me. "You still blame yourself. Just stop doing that and accept my apology."

I look at him in amazement. When did Bobby Buscemi grow up and become a nice guy? Introspection has never been his forte. It feels a little surreal.

I sigh and give him a small smile. "Okay, apology accepted. I never thought you had misgivings or even thought about what went wrong between us."

"Well I do," he gives my hand a final squeeze and then lets go. "What do you say we go watch that game?"

"Sounds good to me," I reply with some relief.

We pay the bill and go watch Philip play with a new found peace between us. Who'd have thought? Not me. But that wasn't the end of Bobby's surprises for me this week.

Chapter 11:

I feel like walking the world,
Like walking the world
(*Suddenly I See*, KT Tunstall)

"Mommy, what are you doing tomorrow?" Milagros'
strident voice chirps from my cell phone.

"I don't know. Nothing, I guess. Bobby has Brendan
for the weekend."

"Excellent. I'll pick up you at 9am. Be ready."

"Whoa, what are we doing?"

"It's a surprise. And don't ask me anything else, 'cuz
I'm not gonna to tell you," and with that she hangs up.

Harrumph, I think, this better not have anything to
do with the dead hockey player. She has been alarmingly
quiet on that front for a few days now. I am hoping she
has dropped it. But in my heart of hearts I don't think so.
It's been like waiting for the other shoe to drop.

I turn back to carefully weighing out the dry chemicals I need for an experiment. I hear the door open but
don't take my eyes off the scales as I add one more grain
to the weigh boat. A gentle throat clearing causes me to
raise my eyes to this stunning woman who looks a few
years older than me but light years away on the social
strata. Her upswept hair and designer dress with matching coat – in Jackie Kennedy style – are eclipsed only by
the honking-big diamond dangling from her neck with
matching sparklers on her ears. Holy crap, this is serious
money.

"Can I help you?" I ask.

"I was wondering if you could help me locate
Decatur."

"Illinois?" I ask in confusion.

"No, my son," she states with just a slight lift to one of her salon-tweezed eyebrows.

"I'm sorry," I say, bending back down to carefully remove the weigh boat from the scale and carry it over to my bench, "there's no Decatur here."

"But of course he is here. He works here," she follows me.

"Look, I'd like to help but I don't know any Decatur. Maybe you can call his phone and ask him where he is."

"This is where he told me he works."

Just as I start to reply Deke walks in. "Mother?" He says.

"Decatur, there you are!"

"Decatur?" I ask, "Your real name is Decatur?" A slow smile starts to spread across my face.

Deke's face turns red and he looks uncomfortable, "Dude, this is not something I advertise."

No shit, I think. This is blowing his whole surfer-guy image right out the door.

"Why not?" His mother exclaims, "It is a wonderful family name: Decatur Ainsley Falworth Albright."

"Decatur Ainsley Falworth Albright," I repeat slowly, savoring each syllable. This is awesome. I am already thinking of ways I can torment him. I can feel my eyes sparkle with delight.

Deke looks as though he'd like to sink into the floor. He turns to his mother, "What are you doing here?"

"Your father and I came in for a charity event. I thought I'd surprise you and take you out for lunch."

"Uh, I'm in the middle of an extraction, mother, I can't just drop everything. You should have called ahead of time."

"Oh dear!" she creases her suspiciously unwrinkled forehead. "I didn't think this would be a problem."

"Don't worry about it," I step into the conversation, "I'll finish what you're doing. You go have a nice lunch with your mom."

"How sweet of you. I'm Patricia Albright, by the way."

"Very pleased to meet you. Amanda Buscemi," I shake her soft, well-manicured hand with my chapped, nails bitten-to-the-quick hand. We could be a different species.

"Well, then is it all settled?" She turns to Deke.

"Sure, thanks Amanda."

I can't remember the last time he has called me by my first name; another sign that he is thrown off-balance by the parental visit.

"No problem......Decatur," I say with an evil smile.

After they leave and I have done what I need to do for both his experiment and mine I take out my decadence for the week: a peanut butter and potato chip sandwich. Munching slowly I Google Deke's name and learn some interesting things. Deke's father, Douglas Albright, is the CEO of Mead Albright Mutaki, a pharmaceutical company based in Modesto, California. He is also one of the founding members of said company. Douglas Albright and Alston Mead were scientists that started their own company with the help of Japanese American businessman, Oshu Mutaki.

So the apple doesn't fall far from the tree. I ponder why he has never told me about his family and I realize that he has never said too much about anything personal. The picture I had was that Deke grew up on the beach as the love-child of people named Gidget and Moondoggie.

But I couldn't have been further from the truth.

Hmmm.

Milagros picks me up, as promised, at nine on Saturday morning.

"Ok, so where are we going?"

"You'll see soon enough," she answers enigmatically.

I decide to sit back and not worry about it. She has this satisfied little smile that continues to play across her lips. Obviously she is enjoying keeping me in suspense.

We drive into the city and park at the Copley Square Plaza garage. We enter the mall and Milagros steers me past pricey store, after pricey store until finally halting in front of a salon called Cher Tresses.

"Here we are querida."

"What, a hair salon?"

"Si, we are going to get you a fabulous new hair style."

"Ha ha! Good one, cupcake. Now seriously, what are we doing?"

"I am serious!" She digs in her purse and pulls out a credit card. "You are getting a full makeover compliments of Bobby."

"Bobby. As in Bobby Buscemi?" I try to process what she is telling me but it makes no sense.

"Yes, of course Bobby Buscemi, you silly girl. Here, he wanted me to give you this too," she hands me an envelope.

I rip it open and there's a note from Bobby:

Amanda:

After we talked the other night, and I realized what a jerk I have been, I wanted to do something nice for you.

I know that this doesn't make up for all the hurt I have caused but I'd like to do something for you.

There's $1,000 on this card. I asked Milagros to help you get a makeover so that you will realize how really beautiful you are.

Have fun and spend every dime. I mean it.

Bobby

I refold the paper and look at Milagros, "So you conspired with Bobby to give me an overhaul?"

"No, this is all his doing. He called me, chica, and said he wanted me to go with you for this. That you never spend any money on yourself and that you deserve it. You ask me, it is about time he did right by you."

Conflicting emotions collide in me. First, embarrassment: how dare he think I need a makeover; am I really that atrocious? Second, disbelief: where did he get the money for something like this? And third, giddy delight. I decide to go with the last emotion and just enjoy the moment.

"Hell, Milagros, let's do it. Get me in there and let's see what happens!"

A look of relief washes over her face. She must have seen my internal struggle. She links her arm through mine and says, "I was hoping you would say that."

Inside the salon she tells the receptionist that I have a ten o'clock appointment. We sit down to wait and soon my stylist comes out to get me. He has short, spiky black hair but the tips are dyed silver. He's dressed all in black except for a skinny fuchsia tie. His eyebrow is pierced by a little hoop and he is wearing a sparkly lip gloss. He introduces himself as Javier – pronouncing it Ha-vee-air. He holds out his hand for me to take and grandly escorts me to his chair.

"My darling Amanda, I am going to transform you into a goddess today. You have the most amazing cheekbones and eyes. We must cut and color to flatter these striking features." He gestures flamboyantly as he talks. Milagros has followed us back and she and Javier discuss highlight colors. Overwhelmed I sit in stunned silence as the experts take over. I can't even remember the last time I had a haircut. I either pull my hair back or just wear it down and long.

Satisfied, Milagros leaves me to the labors of Javier.

Two hours and forty minutes later Javier is pronouncing me done and turning the chair around so I can look at myself in the mirror.

"Wow," I squeak out as I examine my new locks. Flashes of gold shimmer as I turn my head this way and that. The highlights seem to match my eyes perfectly. The blunt cut with wisps around my face makes me look ten years younger and twenty pounds lighter.

"How you like?" Javier beams at me as he puts a hand on his jutting hip.

"Javier, you are a magician. I had no idea my hair could look this good."

"It is no lie, I am the best. You come see me again. And," he wags a finger at me, "do not let any Neanderthals near your hair!"

"You got it!"

He kisses me on one cheek and then the other, pats my hair one more time, sighs dramatically, then turns and sashays off.

"You look amazing, mommy," Milagros has arrived back at my side. She grasps my shoulders, turns me toward the door and says, "I got more for you to do."

Next come makeup, lunch, and then some clothes shopping. Two day and one evening outfits later we have spent all of Bobby's money. I am exhausted as we head back to Milagros' car. KT Tunstall's song, *Suddenly I See*, is playing in my head as I pull down the visor one more time to admire my new look. I never thought I could look this good. I give myself a full smile and see that it reaches up into my eyes. I feel like a million bucks.

We break open a bottle of wine and kick our shoes off at my house. As we pour out our second glass Linda comes trooping through the door.

"Hello ladies, holy mother of God!" She exclaims as she gets a good look at me.

I grin and hold up my glass to toast her reaction, "My new look compliments of Bobby."

"Bobby. Bobby Buscemi?" She says, almost an exact imitation of what I said seven hours earlier.

I nod and Milagros and I look at each other and start to laugh. Then Linda starts laughing too. Now we laugh harder and harder until we are clutching our sides. We laugh and laugh until we can't breathe and we finally have to stop. Wiping our cheeks from the tears that have leaked out and gulping air trying to get back some oxygen, I tell Linda about Bobby's epiphany the other night and how it lead to our wild day at the mall.

Linda shakes her head in amazement. None of us saw it coming.

❖ ❖ ❖ ❖ ❖ ❖ ❖ ❖ ❖ ❖ ❖ ❖ ❖ ❖

A few hours later Milagros and I are out to dinner to continue the celebration. Linda had plans to go over to her daughter's so she couldn't join us.

I have this heady moment when we walk in the restaurant and many of the male heads turn to look at us. That is not unusual when traveling as part of Milagros' posse. What's different this time is that some of them are looking at me. I surreptitiously run my fingers through my hair and a little smile twitches at the corner of my mouth as one man actually stops mid-bite to stare at me. *Me!*

And now a warm glow suffuses us as we are finishing our shared dessert and coffees but then Milagros gets a funny look on her face.

"Chica, I got a favor to ask," Milagros says.

"Shoot."

"There's this man at the bar. He's been watching us and there's somethin' about him that makes me nervous."

"What do you mean, nervous?"

"Well, I'm not certain but he might have been one of the guys from the other night that chased me."

"Are you kidding me?" I say in a strangled kind of whisper, resisting the urge to turn around and look, "How certain are you?"

"Not real, but my gut tells me something is wrong about him. He isn't interacting with anyone else at the bar and he's ordered a beer but has only taken maybe a coupla sips and it's been sitting there a real long time."

I feel my stomach turn over.

"Act like I just said something funny and we have no concerns," she says plastering a big grin on her face and gesturing as if telling a funny story.

I throw back my head and bray out what I hope is a realistic laugh. I wipe my eyes as though I am overcome by the hilarity of her story when in fact I feel like tossing back up the dinner I just consumed.

"Milagros, what have you been up to?"

"Just following up on a few leads," she says smiling broadly and stretching as though very relaxed, just having a good time with her friend.

I try to match her expression but my face muscles feel all numb and twitchy, "You are absolutely impossible. I told you to drop this whole thing."

"I know, mommy, but I just couldn't and once I tell you about it, you'll understand why."

"Oh swell."

"Look, I am going to go into the bathroom to try to figure out what we should do. Can you pay the bill so we'll be ready to leave quickly?"

Before I can answer she rises, grabs her purse and saunters back to the bathroom. I bend to get my purse from beside my feet and surreptitiously turn to look back at the bar. All I see are a bunch of people mingling, talking and laughing. Then I see him. He has on a baseball cap pulled low and is wearing a black leather jacket. He appears to be looking into his beer glass but I see his head turn slightly to watch Milagros' progress.

Damn it! What I am supposed to do? I draw my wallet out of my purse and with numb fingers take out a couple twenties to cover our bill. I decide putting on lip gloss will give me something to do and kill some time while I wait for Milagros to come back to the table. I check out the bar again in my little makeup mirror. Black jacket is still at the bar but I see him start to swivel his head toward me and I quickly clamp closed the mirror. Breathing shallowly and trying to ignore the hammering of my heart in my ears I look for Milagros. No sign of her yet. I glance at the other patrons. Everyone is involved in their own conversations, unaware of the little drama playing out around them.

"Excuse me," someone touches my shoulder.

"Ahg!" I jump; startled as I am sure Mr. Black Jacket has snuck up on me and is now holding a gun to my head.

I look up to see the guy from earlier in the evening who had interrupted his meal to stare at me as I walked past.

"I'm sorry, I didn't mean to startle you," he smiles.

"Oh no, it's okay. I was just surprised," I say trying to recover and swallow my heart back down my throat.

"I saw you getting ready to leave and, well, I don't do this very often, and please tell me if I am out of line, but I couldn't let you just leave without introducing myself."

I am temporarily shocked into forgetting the present dilemma as I look into these really dreamy, beautiful eyes and think, this doesn't happen to me, this happens to Milagros. I wonder if I am wrong about his interest in me and he is going to ask me for an introduction to her. Bracing myself for disappointment I smile and say, "Oh, well, my friend went to the ladies' room if you want to sit down for a moment."

"Thanks," he pulls out the chair and sits down. "Tris McEvoy," he says, holding out his hand. I take it and tell him my name.

"Tris, that's not a name you hear every day," I say.

"It's short for Tristan, as in the legend of Tristan and Isolde."

"Your parent's must have been romantics."

"My mother is an English professor, not sure about the romantic part."

"No one wants to think of their parents in that way. I'm sure my sons don't." Great I give myself a mental head slap. In case he's interested, that'll drive him off.

"Oh, I'm sure my daughter feels the same about me," again the stunning smile. Tris McEvoy is a good-looking guy. Why in the world is he sitting across from me?

"Daughter, does that mean you're married?" I ask.

"No, divorced. You?"

"Divorced." We smile at each other.

"Look," he says after a moment, "I don't want to interrupt your evening with your friend but when you walked in I thought you were so stunning and confident. I thought, now this is the kind of woman I would love to get to know better."

I don't say a word, basically because men do not say things like this to me and I am at a complete loss. My heart beat has once again quickened and I get a warm tingly sensation that starts in my stomach and moves all the way to my toes.

"Anyway, I was hoping you'd consider going out with me," he finishes with a little self-deprecating shrug.

Finally, finding my voice I say, "Sure, that would be nice."

He smiles again and says, "That's great. Here's my card. Will you promise to call me?"

"Um, okay," I say taking his card.

"I'd ask for your number but I don't want to make you uncomfortable. So I'll let you make the next move. But I really hope you call."

Once again I promise to call him as I slip his card into my purse. We wish each other a good evening and he leaves to rejoin his friends.

Just then I look up to see Milagros coming back to the table. She sits down across from me with a little smile. Thoughts of Tris McEvoy vanish as I remember our present dilemma.

"Ok, so what's the big escape plan, Houdini?" I ask.

Just then a shrill alarm sounds. Everyone starts looking around for the source of the noise. Smoke has started pouring out from the back of the restaurant. There are exclamations of surprise as people begin to notice the smoke and start standing up at their tables. Within moments the front door to the restaurant bursts open and firemen in full gear come crashing in.

The firemen are shouting for people to exit the restaurant and to get out of their way. People are yelling, the overhead sprinkler system starts spurting out water all over the place. Someone screams, chairs crash, glass breaks, and pandemonium ensues.

Panicked I look at Milagros who grabs her coat and crouches down under the table. She grabs my arm and pulls me down too.

"What are we doing?" I shout to her over the general chaos.

"We are making our escape."

"Did you do this?" I cough as the smoke begins to irritate my throat. "Nice one!" I reply sarcastically.

"We needed a diversion!"

"Well, we got one. Now what?"

"Follow me!" Hunched down she starts to duck walk between the tables toward the back of the restaurant.

I follow closely behind her. When she gets to the hallway that goes down to the bathrooms as well as the kitchen, she pauses and we both look around the chair legs and table tops to see if Black Jacket is still in the restaurant looking for us. I think I see him near the front door.

"We got to sneak out the back way," Milagros yells to me over the alarm.

"The firemen are going to see us."

"We got to take the chance."

All of a sudden the alarm shuts off. Milagros nods at me as if to say, now or never. She makes a dash down the hallway and I'm hot on her heels. At the end of the hall is the exit door. We push through the door and into the alleyway. Milagros grabs my arm and pulls me behind the dumpster. We slam our backs against the wall and catch our breath.

"Sweet Jesus, Milagros. You just committed a felony. What were you thinking?"

"I was thinking we needed to get out of there. All I did was light a cigarette and start a fire in the trash can. There shouldn't be any damage."

"Let's hope not. The fire department showed up really quick."

"I know. That's why I called it in before I lit the fire."

"Then that explains why they were there within minutes of the alarm sounding."

Just then the back door opens and light spills out onto the pavement. We instantly stop talking and crouch down a little so we won't be visible. We hear some voices but it doesn't sound like anyone comes out.

"Let's move away," Milagros hisses into my ear. I nod my understanding and begin inching away from the open doorway and down the alley toward the street.

We move slowly around a second dumpster and then a stack of smelly discarded boxes. Steeping over loose trash I carefully place my feet so as not to ruin my boots. Senses on hyper-alert I notice a very slight movement at the end of the alley. I abruptly stop my forward progression and Milagros bumps into me from behind.

"What's wrong? Why did you stop?"

"Shhh!" I whisper. Fear has made my mouth dry and the hairs on the back of my neck are standing on end. My eyes are open so wide I think they might pop out of their sockets. There's another movement that's barely discernible. "Go back, go back!" I command in a harsh whisper.

We start to shuffle the opposite way down the alley. It is a much longer route to the street at the other end. I keep glancing over my shoulder, unnerved by the sensation that we are being followed. At the edge of a dumpster two back from where we are I see the bill of a baseball cap peek out.

"Oh shit! Go faster, Milagros, faster! I think he's behind us."

Milagros let's out a tiny squeak of fear and starts to run like a commando in a war movie; all crouched down and darting around the alley debris. I'm right behind her but continue glancing back. Again, I think I see movement a ways back. Yards from the end of the alley, we do an all out sprint to safety.

"This way," I say careening around a corner, trying to put as much distance and zigzags between us and the alley. I round another corner and plunge head first into someone and fall on my behind.

Scrambling to my feet I go to take off but hands are clutching my arms.

"Let me go! Ah, Milagros," I yell, kicking and thrashing with all my might.

I hear Milagros calling my name over and over again. I look up to see Pete holding on to me.

"Amanda! What the hell! Calm down," he's yelling at me.

I stop struggling and he let's go of me. I bend over putting my hands on my knees. I think I'm going to be sick. Panting I look at Milagros who is leaning against the building trying to catch her breath.

"What is going on? Why were two running like the devil was chasing you?" Pete demands.

Before I can say anything Milagros tells him that we were at this restaurant and there was a fire. We got disoriented and went out the back to get away from the smoke. Thinking someone was in the alley we got scared and were running to get out of there. Mostly the truth but I wonder why she is being slightly evasive with her answer. Maybe it is time to come clean.

Pete goes around the corner to check out the alleyway and I look at Milagros as if to say, what the heck. She puts her finger to her lips and shakes her head. Maybe she's worried that he would report her if she confessed to setting the fire.

Pete comes back shaking his head, "No one's there that I can see. Are you guys okay?"

"Yes, we just got spooked," Milagros again speaks for both of us.

"What are *you* doing here?" I ask my breathing now under control. This guy keeps turning up like a bad penny.

"I was in the neighborhood to meet some friends and came to see what all the commotion was about."

"From what we could tell there was a fire in the kitchen and everyone was evacuated," Milagros again speaks.

"Can I give you a ride home or anything?"

"No, no, we're alright. Thanks for asking," Milagros answers.

We finally convince Pete that we can manage on our own, say goodbye and on shaky legs walk down the street to find Milagros' car.

Our evening isn't over, though. Milagros has some explaining to do.

Once we've locked ourselves in Milagros' car and peal out I turn to her, "Okay, of all the hare-brained things you could have done! What if someone identifies you as being back in the bathroom right before the fire?"

"I know, Amanda, but I didn't have a lot of options. I didn't see you coming up with any ideas!"

"That is so unfair," I fume. "*I* am not the one who got us into this predicament. I *told* you to stop snooping and you continued to do it anyway!"

"Well let me tell you about what I found. Okay? I went to see Tyler Brooks, the other boy that John McSweeney told you was in the diabetes study."

"Oh jeez," I mutter.

"Some of the people in the study formed an impromptu blog group. Tyler's been chatting with people from all over the country. He posted that Mike Donowski died. That's when he found out there was another sudden death in Florida."

"What kind of death?"

"This person was stabbed and died of his injuries."

"That's not exactly heart failure, Milagros."

"I know chica, but what if that person was going into heart failure and he was killed so it wouldn't be discovered."

"That is a huge reach. It's one thing to cover up a scandal; it's another to murder people!"

"Oh really? You think after everything we've gone through that this is not a possibility?"

"You might have a point. But it could be two unrelated incidents. But maybe Mike's heart failure was caused by something unrelated to the drug study. Remember Ron said it could be caused by a drug or chemical that is cardio toxic? Maybe he had some exposure like that company in Woburn they made a movie about. They were dumping chemicals that got into the drinking water and people were getting cancer."

"Yes, mommy, I am one step ahead of you. I got a sample of the drinking water and had it analyzed."

"And how did you do that?"

"I went to Mike Donowski's parents' home. I said I was from the Water Department and we needed to test the end user water for purity. I got a sample and sent it out for analysis."

"They didn't question you?"

"No, I think they were too upset to really think about what I was up to. They didn't even ask for my credentials."

Her audacity is astounding. I sit in stunned silence.
Finally I say, "Did you get the results?"

"Preliminary, yes. And no chemicals or toxins were
found."

"Well I applaud your tenacity but all you managed to
do was eliminate one potential cause for the heart failure.
And you haven't linked the other person's death with
Mike's. *And* this is a little outside of our ability to investigate."

"Not for me, I am going to Miami."

"What?! Stop! Right now, stop! I can *not* believe I
am hearing this with my ears. Milagros, you have to stop
this right now."

"You think it is okay for people to be dying?"

"Of course not, but I don't want you to be one of
them!"

"I can handle myself, don't worry."

"Look maybe we should just go to the police."

"Oh please," she actually snorts, "you think they are
going to believe us? All we have are suspicions. We need
to get some more facts."

"And what kind of facts are you going to get? Can't
you read the news to get the 'facts'?"

"I already read everything there is. No one saw the
assault, police have no leads."

"Great. And what do you think you are going to
accomplish by going there? Solve the murder for the
police?"

"No, I'm going to find out if he was in heart failure."

"Can't you do that without going down there?"

"People are not going to be as willing to talk to me
over the phone. I got to go. I have a flight tomorrow
morning, coming back in the evening. No one will even
know that I'm gone."

"Aghh!" I yell in frustration, "How can I stop you
from doing this? It's crazy!"

We are sitting at a light, waiting for it to change.
She sighs, puts her head back on the headrest and turns

to me. "I know you think I shouldn't continue investigating, but I won't be able to look myself in the mirror if I don't do this." She puts her hand on mine and squeezes, "I can't explain any better than that."

The traffic light turns from red to green and casts her face in a death pall shade of green. I shiver at this foreboding vision and make up my mind.

"I'm coming with you then," I decide. "Not sure how I am going to pay for a round trip ticket but I can't let you go alone."

A little smile curves her lips and she says softly, "I figured you would say that, mommy. I already bought you a ticket too."

I close my eyes and pinch the bridge of my nose to keep my brains from exploding out the front of my skull.

"You played me like a concert piano. I don't know whether to laugh or scream."

"Instead how about we go get some sleep so we can be ready for our flight and not worry about how you feel?"

Suddenly exhausted I say, "That's probably the best plan you've had all day."

Chapter 12:

You know I'm no good

(*You Know I'm No Good,* Amy Winehouse)

Extremely early the next morning we are on our way to the airport. Amy Winehouse's Back to Black album is playing on Milagros' car stereo. As she croons about being trouble and no good I look over at Milagros and think, yup, that's you: trouble with a capital "t". I'm still not sure I am ready to forgive her for continuing this mission and emotionally high-jacking me on the latest excursion.

I had to ask Bobby to keep Brendan for the entire weekend. It wasn't a problem but he was less than thrilled when I evaded his questions about what I was doing. I'm not quite ready to confess to what we've been up to. He probably thinks I'm dating someone and that I wanted a weekend alone with my new man. Any other time this would have filled me with an evil kind of glee but since he was so nice to me I feel slightly guilty that that is his suspicion.

I am such a schmuck.

I didn't go home since Milagros lives closer to the airport. We picked up a toothbrush at the drugstore and now this morning I am in one of her black tank tops with my jacket zipped up to cover the super-tight fit. Milagros' boobs are about two sizes smaller than mine and what looks like a cute little top on her looks like hooker getup on me.

We go from the crisp, cold New England morning to the mid-morning sunshine of southern Florida. As we walk out of the air-conditioned airport the humid air hits us with the promise of a steamy, sultry day. My skin turns instantly clammy from the cloying atmosphere.

On the way down I had read every inch of a magazine someone had left in my seatback pocket. It had a run down on the history of the Miami area. I learned that for thousands of year various American Indian tribes had populated the area. Next came the Spanish colonization and then the French pushed in from the west. Americans finally sunk our teeth into Florida in the early eighteenth century making things very miserable for the Spanish until they gave up and we finally added Florida to our growing country's acquisitions. Along with the Indians and people of European decent, there was an influx of people from Haiti and other Caribbean islands – some of which were former or fleeing slaves. So Miami was probably one of the earliest melting-pot American cities.

I learned that Miami used to be called "The Magic City" back in the first part of twentieth century. This was when the population tripled, then quadrupled and then astoundingly quadrupled again in less than twenty years. For a while it seemed as though it was going to be bigger than NYC but then the Great Miami Hurricane in 1926 pushed the region into an early start to the Great Depression. The forward momentum slowed even more significantly on into the World War II. Once Fidel Castro came into power on the nearby island of Cuba, disenfranchised Cubans came seeking refuge and freedom. I'd like to think America welcomed these poor people with open arms but nothing goes quite that well, now does it? To make matters worse Castro diabolically opened his prisons and dumped the dregs of his society onto ours. What a guy. So the Little Havana section of Miami that had the highest concentration of decent, hard-working Cuban families began to see increases in crime and violence. Welcome to America!

The rest of the magazine had articles on deep sea fishing (best time for marlin is April through July if you really want to know), an article on a group called Mamborama that plays a blend of modern Cuban rhythms, and filled me in on the best South Beach casino stops. They had a picture of a bar where beds and couches were placed all over the outdoor area surrounding a walk-in pool with fountains and a waterfall. It looked so decadent, like something out of a Caligula movie – well, without the orgy part of it maybe. I gave up on the crossword puzzle (don't know enough Spanish words and Milagros was sleeping) but I did do the Sudoku puzzle and took the Are You A Genius quiz (I am, by the way, if you disregard the fact that I looked up half the answers in the back and then agreed with them that they were right and I knew the answer all along – I was just confirming).

We get an economy rental car from some budget place. Walking up to it we stop, taking in the vehicle.

"What the heck is it?" I ask. It is a brilliant green color that does not exist in nature except, maybe, on a parrot and looks like one of those improbably small clown cars you see at the circus.

Milagros stands with her hands on her hips inspecting. "Daewoo?" she says reading the name off the key set they gave us.

"Huhn. I think that's Korean," I say, walking up to the vehicle in question and kicking the tires. I am suspicious. I've seen children's bicycles with bigger tires.

I'm starting to sweat in my jacket so I take it off and we fold ourselves into the clown car. Milagros starts it up. I am reminded of a moped engine and wonder if we're going to get stuck on inclines. Maybe we'll have to put our feet down on the pavement and make it go Fred Flintstone-style. She puts it in gear and I say, "Yaba daba doo!" as we slowly putter out of the rental parking lot.

Julio Rodriguez was a twenty-four year old Hispanic male. He was found near his car in a mall parking lot.

His wallet was missing so it appears that he was a victim of a robbery gone wrong. The first stop we make is to talk with his cousin, Daniel.

Daniel is a small, wiry guy with five visible tattoos. Daniel and Julio shared an apartment so Milagros figures he will be the best person with which to start.

I don't even ask her how she got this information. I am counting on it being something illegal. This is my strategy for when the fuzz finally catch up with us: I was an unwitting participant and had no idea what she was up to. I hope to minimize the number of counts on my indictment. I figure I'll get five to ten and have a cell mate named Helga who wants to take showers with me. That's if I'm lucky and the bad guys don't get me first.

Daniel has no problem letting us in. Not sure if it's Milagros' drop dead good looks or my boobs straining to burst free from the tank top. Either way he probably decides we can't possibly harm him and if we *are* potential assassins it will be the male version of death by chocolate.

Milagros tells him we are researchers from the diabetes study. We figure he'll have no way of knowing otherwise and it makes asking medical/symptom-related questions appropriate. This is my idea; my one flash of brilliance. Don't smirk, I have my moments!

After we give our condolences we get down to our questions. The first is: has he noticed anything unusual in Julio's energy level.

"No, not that he mentioned," Daniel responds.

"No complaining of being tired at all?"

"Not that he told me."

Milagros writes in her notebook that we bought at Staples on our way over. We figure it would look more official.

Next Milagros asks him if Julio complained of any shortness of breath.

"No."

"Chest pain?" I ask

"No."

Persistent coughing?

"No."

Weight gain? Frequent urination?

"No," and "no."

Ugh. Swelling of his extremities?

"No."

We pause, looking at each other. Appetite?

"I think it was fine."

Confusion or dizziness?

"No."

Now we are out of questions. We need to figure out our next move but I'm beginning to think Milagros has sent us on a wild goose chase. If he had no symptoms of heart failure why would he be a target?

Milagros asks him if there are other family members or friends we might interview. He says that Julio was close with his older sister, Cecilia. He looks up her phone number and address for us. We get ready to leave. Milagros gives him her cell phone number in case he thinks of anything else that might help.

Climbing back into the clown car I say, "It doesn't look promising. Maybe his death has nothing to do with the diabetes study."

"Maybe," she allows, "but I got a feeling about this."

"Yeah, you and your feelings," I grouse. "Have you ever heard of Occam's Razor?"

"No, what it that?"

"It's a scientific rule"

"Really, and what is this rule, chica?" She raises a questioning eyebrow at me as we putter along. For a second I think I see an insect that's bigger than our car passing us on the left.

"Occam's Razor:" I say, "when you hear hoof beats, think horses not zebras."

"What are you talking about?"

"It's a rule that's applied to explain something; the simplest solution is the most likely explanation. Such as when you hear hoof beats it is more likely to be horses making the noise, not zebras. Another example might be crop circles. They are more likely to be a result of a human prank instead of the result of alien space crafts landing in wheat fields."

"Huh. So what's the simple explanation for this?"

"That Julio is a victim of a random act of violence instead of being eliminated because of some huge conspiracy."

"So then how do you explain you getting drugged, me being threatened, and us being stalked?"

"I'm not saying something isn't going on. But we can't connect Julio's death with Mike's. Mike had heart failure, we think. Julio did not."

"We don't know that yet. Let's go see the sister," she says. We have stopped at a light. When it turns green Milagros presses on the accelerator. The engine gives a little cough and we take off on all two of its cylinders.

We finally find Cecilia's house. It is in this well-maintained neighborhood of small homes all with tropical trees and cactus-type plants landscaping the front yards. Few have lawns and those that do, the grass looks really different; the blades are thicker and look sharp, like it would cut your feet if you walked barefoot on it. Large awnings cover the windows as well, giving the homes a more closed in look.

We are sitting in front of the home plotting our strategy while peppy Cuban music drifts toward us from someone's backyard. People are laughing and I hear a big splash and then some squeals of delight. I envision some barrel-chested uncle jumping into a pool with the kids while the ladies are all sitting around drinking margaritas and gossiping. I am suddenly thirsty and wish I could join their party instead on sweating bullets on the vinyl seats of the clown car.

Finally we decide that since the researcher shtick worked with the cousin that we'll try it on the sister. We peal ourselves off the seats and start up the walkway to her door. I realize my pants are soaking wet and clinging to my butt. I daintily pull the material away and wish I could do the same for my underwear.

Cecilia has two children that we can hear even before she comes to the screen door. One child is in her arms and has the most adorable mop of curls. The other one clings to her leg and looks younger; his wobbly Pillsbury dough-boy legs exposed under a Winnie the Pooh tee-shirt and diaper.

We tell our lie again about being part of the research team and she buys it hook, line and sinker. After giving our condolences and apologizing for dropping in on her unannounced we go through our battery of questions relating to heart failure symptoms. She hasn't invited us in and so we stand there baking on her front stoop as we quiz her.

Once again we come up with zilch.

"Thank you for your time," I say trying to wrap it up, "I hope they find who did this to your brother although we heard it was a random crime with no witnesses."

"I'm no' so sure 'bout that it ees random crime," she says, wiping a stray tear from the corner of her eye.

"Really," Milagros says, sliding her eyes towards me surreptitiously.

"Yeah, jus' that morning, when Julio an' I were talking on thee phone he say that he thought he was being followed thee day before."

"Did he get a look at who it was?" Milagros asks.

"No, eet was more like a feeling he have," she sniffs back her tears.

"So he never really saw anyone?" I clarify.

"No, but he was *not* thee kind o' person who goes around all crazy paranoyho, you know?"

"Gotchya, well, again, we are sorry for your loss," I say grabbing Milagros' arm and propelling her back to the car before she starts asking all kinds of questions and blowing our cover.

Back on the road I say, "I think we've reached a dead end here. He didn't have signs of heart failure and even if he was killed for some reason to do with the study we have no proof, no connection."

"But he said he was being followed," she argues.

"So what?" I say exasperated. "Even if he *was* being followed, even if his death *was* related to the study, which is a preposterous leap of reason, we have nowhere to go with it. Let's go home. Maybe we can get an earlier flight."

"Uh oh, chica," Milagros is looking in the rear view mirror, "we have company."

"Are you kidding?"

"No, I am *not* kidding."

I lean toward her a little to get a view from the driver's side mirror. Directly behind us is a sports car, a black Camaro I think, with darkened windows that are rolled up so you can't see who is inside, giving it a very sinister look.

"How long has that car been behind us?"

"I think since we pulled out onto Dixie Highway."

"If they're following us they aren't doing a good job of being sneaky. They're right on our ass!"

"Maybe 'cuz they want to scare us."

"Or worse," I say. Horrified I see the car ease into the lane to the left of us and slowly start to gain.

"Oh crap, Milagros, it's coming up next to us. Go faster!"

"I'm trying! I'm trying!" She yells, "I've got the pedal pushed all the way down!"

The clown car does a little groan and emits this whining protest as it strains to accelerate. The speedometer creeps from fifty to fifty one to fifty two at an impossibly slow pace.

We look in terror as the Camaro continues to gain on us. I grab Milagros' arm and compulsively push my feet into the floorboards as though I can help the stupid car go faster. Slowly the Camaro pulls up even with us and the passenger window begins to slide down. Expecting to see the muzzle of a semi-automatic we hold our breath. But instead there is the smiling face of a young Hispanic male.

"Hey baby, wanna take a ride in a real car?" He yells over to us.

Relief floods my body but it quickly turns to anger as the adrenaline flooding my bloodstream in a fight or flight response tries to find an outlet. Evidently Milagros has the same reaction because she yells back, "Sure, show me a *real* car."

His smile waivers a little.

"This is as real as it gets," he rejoins; master of the witty comeback.

"Oh sorry, I guess I'm getting confused. It's a real car but no real man!"

Now he looks a little angry as he says, "Hey! Come here and I'll show you how real I am."

"No thanks pequeno muchacho. Go bother simple girls who will be impressed with your silly car."

He gives us the finger as he rolls his window back up. Revving the engine he peals out leaving a cloud of exhaust that we roll through.

"Pequeno muchacho?" I ask coughing on the exhaust. He becomes a distant speck and then is gone.

"I called him a little boy," she grins crookedly.

A little giggle rises out of my throat. "Nice." I giggle a little more and Milagros joins me.

"Well," I say after our giggle fit subsides, "at least he wasn't a hired assassin."

Just then Milagros' cell phone rings. She grabs it out of her bag and answers. She listens for a minute and then says the information is very helpful, thanks the person on the other end, reminds them to call if anything else comes to mind and hangs up.

"Wait'll you hear this one, querida. That was Daniel. He remembered something."

"Oh yeah?"

"Yeah, he said that he was putting on a pair of shoes that Julio gave him and it reminded him of our questions. He said that Julio gave him the shoes because he said couldn't fit into them any more."

"Swollen feet," I say.

"Swollen feet," Milagros agrees.

According to our research on heart failure, as the heart becomes less efficient in its pumping, blood backs up into the peripheral circulation. The lower extremities begin to swell with extra fluid as the veins in the legs swell with the increased blood accumulation. Swollen feet certainly fit into the heart failure picture.

"Huh," I say pondering this new piece of information.

"We got to get back and go see Tyler Brooks again," Milagros states.

"Why?"

"Because I want to know if there are any more unexplained deaths."

"Then we go to the police."

"Then we go to the police," she agrees.

I sit back, satisfied that we are finally going to end this odyssey.

Chapter 13:

It's getting harder and harder to breathe

(*Harder to Breathe,* Maroon 5)

Milagros drops me off at home right around nine thirty Sunday night. I am exhausted from the long day and have visions of a nice, hot shower and then crawling between my sheets.

As she pulls away I see the lighted end of Mr. Ziegler's cigar brighten as he takes a draw on it. Judging by the position I figure he is sitting on his stoop.

"Hey Mr. Z," I call out to him.

"Amanda, I was wondering when you were coming home."

"I was wondering the same thing myself." I see the tip of his cigar moving. He's coming over to talk with me. "Anything interesting going on in the neighborhood?"

"I think the Feds are going to finally make a move on the Russians." He arrives at the fence dividing our properties.

"Oh really? What makes you say that?" I move over to the fence as well so I can make out his silhouette.

"They have their house under surveillance. They've been sitting in that car over there," he gestures with his cigar, "ever since this morning."

A cold chill of dread passes through me. "Are they still there?"

"As far as I know, yes." He takes a drag on his cigar. His face illuminates as extra oxygen meets the fiery tobacco.

"How do you know they are Feds?" I choke out, fear constricting my throat.

"Well, I don't know for certain, dear, but they have to be law enforcement. They're using walkie talkies and I saw a shift change."

"Have they followed any of the Russians?"

"No, I guess whatever they're interested in is at the house."

"Uh huh," I say. Interested in the Russians, my ass. I want to run in the house, bolt the doors and pull all the shades down. After that, have a nervous breakdown.

I am aware of being extremely vulnerable standing out in the night and feel like jumping out of my skin. Exposed. I say, "Well, I gotta go in. Have a nice night Mr. Z."

"You too, Amanda," he rumbles.

I dart into the house and with shaking hands run around doing the door bolting, shade pulling thing. Panic is building in my chest and I swallow a hysterical moan that rises in my throat. I pull back the living room shade and peek out but all I see are a bunch of cars parked on the street. Porch and street lights glint off the hoods and roofs of the cars. There could be people sitting in any number of cars and I wouldn't be able to see them from my vantage point.

"Amanda?" I jump out of my skin.

"Linda! You scared me." I think my heart rate just tripled. It feels like it is going to pound right out of my chest.

"What are you doing?"

"Mr. Ziegler told me there's some guys watching the Russians. I was trying to see them." I move to the other side of the window and pull back the shade again.

"I didn't notice anything."

"Don't!" I yell as she goes to turn a light on.

"Why not?"

"Because then they'll see me looking out at them."

"So don't look out at them."

Linda has not been apprised of the recent goings on. I wasn't trying to hide anything from her. It was more like I was in denial. I decide it's time to confess.

"Look, I gotta tell you something," I say and then I tell her the whole story. She stands there in silence in our darkened living room as I blurt everything out: from the autopsy on the hockey player to the bar where Milagros gets threatened all way to our Miami trip.

"And that's why I'm a little freaked out about the men sitting in a car. Most likely they've been waiting for me to return home," I conclude.

She still hasn't said a word. As a matter of fact, she hasn't moved. She's still holding a glass of water and is in her plaid pajamas and fuzzy slippers. I can't read her expression in the oblique lighting that slants in from the nightlight in the kitchen. I hear the quiet hum of the refrigerator running and then the whir of the furnace as it kicks on. Other than that, dead silence.

"Well?" I finally say, taking a deep breath to try to calm the panic. My hands are freezing cold. I fold my arms across my chest and stick my hands in my arm pits to warm them. I literally feel my knees knocking. Speaking the story aloud has brought it home to me: I have put myself, my friends and family in harm's way.

She clears her throat and says, "Either you two are jumping to conclusions and getting yourselves all worked up over potentially explainable coincidences..." she pauses

"Or?" I prompt.

"Or, you have got yourself in some serious shit."

"What do *you* think?"

"Well, I've never known you to get hysterical or paranoid. But I have to say, the evil people conspiracy is a bit much to swallow. I mean, this isn't a Robin Cook novel for God's sake. This is real life."

"I know, I know," I say. I shift my weight from one foot to the other. The panic is starting to ebb and something else is beginning to take its place; I am starting to feel a little niggling of doubt.

Linda continues, "I mean I don't know as much medically as you do, but maybe the swollen feet thing that your Miami guy had was due to something completely different. It's a very nonspecific symptom and, I would think, hardly definitive for heart failure. If you thought about it, you could probably come up with ten other disease states that could cause swollen feet."

"True," I concede.

"And Milagros getting warned outside that bar? Maybe she didn't hear correctly. It's been shown that people's ability to correctly recall incidents can be shaky, especially when they are scared or in shock. She was all alone; a couple of men approach her. Hell, I'd be scared too."

"Being pursued in the alley," she continues, "well, you never saw the guy, right? You just saw movement and what you think was the bill of his baseball cap. Could you have been mistaken? There's all kinds of debris in alleys that could look like that. Not to mention rats or cats that could have been the source of movement."

"At the time I was pretty certain..." I say starting to waiver in the face of reason.

"Look, obviously this has you concerned. I think the best thing to do is go ask them what they're up to."

"The guys in the car?? What, like go knock on their window and politely ask them why they are lurking in our neighborhood?"

"Something like that."

"Okay, just imagine, for argument's sake, that scenario number two is correct; that there *is* something going on. Should we really just stroll up to their car? What if they have guns? Or grab us?"

"Good point. So here's the solution: call the police."

"And tell them what?"

"That there's a suspicious car that's been parked on our street all day with two men sitting in it. We'll let the police oust them."

"That's not a bad idea," I admit. Why didn't *I* think of that?

"Look, I'll make the call," she volunteers and walks over to the house phone. "What's the make of the car?"

"I don't know."

"I can call Mr. Ziegler. I'm sure he knows."

"No! I don't want to involve him."

"Well, we need to give a description. We can't just call the police without something for them to go on"

"Hold that thought! I have an idea." I run into Brendan's room and dig through his bottom drawer. I pull out the night vision binoculars that Bobby gave him last Christmas. He and Brendan were going to do a night hike and watch animals.

I climb up to the attic and peer out the window overlooking the street. Using the binoculars I look for the car. The world is in varying shades of weird green and black. There it is. Two houses down, near the witch's house. I smirk as I think about her getting pissed if she knew they were there. Maybe she'd put a hex on them and a skunk would come and spray their car. They'd have to sit there enduring the awful smell.

Unfortunately I can't tell the make, model or color of the car. Grunting in dissatisfaction I run down the stairs, call to Linda that I'll be back in a minute, and go out the back door. I grab onto the top of the chain link fence and hop it into Mr. Ziegler's backyard. I stand still for a couple seconds quietly panting but don't hear anything unusual. I cut across his yard and then scale the fence to get into his neighbors', the O'Brien's, yard.

I visualize where the car is in relation to the houses. If I go over one more house and come up the far side I should be able to see the back of the car. Hopefully I'll be able to make out the license plate number and the model.

The problem is I don't know the people next to the O'Briens. But I figure the risk of discovery is minimal.

The night is cold and crisp and as I run across the O'Brien's yard. I make little plumes of fog with my breath. I circle the patio furniture taking extra care to not run into anything else that might be lying on the ground that is undetectable in the gloom. Towards the back of the yard the moon illuminates a statue of the Virgin Mary who regards me with her benevolent gaze. Even though I'm not Catholic I send a little prayer toward her for grace and protection – cover all bases, I figure. If Buddha was back here I'd be rubbing his belly as well.

The fence abutting the next property is made of pressure treated wood and there is nowhere on the O'Brien's side to put my toe to help me over. I take a running leap and vault it in one fluid motion. Amazed and grinning in satisfaction I run over to the gate, ease up the latch and let myself out. Hunched over I creep along the side of the house and then drop to all fours as I get to the bushes at the front. I crawl in between the bushes and the front of the darkened porch to get positioned properly. Kneeling on the ground I pull a branch aside and bring the binoculars up to my eyes. I find the car again and see the heads of two people. I reel back to look at the rear end of the car. It's a Ford Taurus, too dark to tell the color but it looks light, like maybe gray. I can't see the license plate number from my location so I sling the binoculars over my neck and crawl on my hands and knees toward the front steps. Cold, damp bark mulch stabs into my palms. I get to the steps and hold up the binoculars again.

189XKJ. Perfect. I congratulate myself and start creeping backwards to the side of the house. When I get around the corner I stand up and run over to the gate. I unlatch it once again and make my way toward the O'Brien's property. Suddenly I hear a snuffling and then a low growl. I freeze in my tracks. What the heck was that? A little woof followed by another growl tells me it's a dog. Why can nothing be easy, I ask myself?

"Nice doggy. Good boy!" I say in my most pleasant dog-convincing voice as I inch my way toward the fence. Opening my eyes really wide I try to get a fix on where the dog is and his size. The moon has gone behind a cloud so I can't make out very much in the yard. I keep up a patter of good doggies as I slowly back into the fence.

"Who's a good boy? You're a good boy!" I say in a sing song voice to him. I hook my toe onto the bottom rail of the fence and ease myself up. One leg goes over just as he lunges.

"Ahg! Let go!" I shake my leg but he's clamped on to my jeans for all he's worth. I shake my leg back and forth trying to dislodge him. He growls even louder and yanks really hard. I feel myself slipping back into the yard. I grab on to the top of the fence as he yanks my pant leg and then yanks again.

Suddenly a light turns on in the back yard and I am completely exposed.

"Hello?" I hear a voice call.

Great, so much for going undetected. I am like a magnet for disaster. Sighing I turn back to face the consequences of my latest misadventure. I shield my eyes to look toward the back door and say, "Um, hi! I'm your neighbor from a couple doors down? Can you please get your dog to release my pants?" I look down and see it's a little wire-haired terrier. Oh yeah, really ferocious. How could a little thing like that have almost pulled me off the fence? I am not only unlucky; I am a wimp, and a fool. An unlucky wimpy fool.

"Peppi! Come here," a woman about my age steps out clapping her hands.

Peppi, the disobedient little shit, is not listening to his mistress's command. Wrinkling his nose he growls once again and shakes my pant leg. Obviously he wants a piece of me and he's not about to let go.

She walks over and picks him up. Using her hands she pries open his vicious little jaws to finally release my pant leg. Still holding him in her arms she straightens up and looks at me.

"Are you the lesbian from three doors down?"

"Uh, yes. I mean, no. I mean yes, I *am* from three doors down but no, I am *not* a lesbian." I jump off the fence, back into her yard.

"Really? Mr. Ziegler said you are." She says this like it was preached at church this morning and God himself spoke it. [Do you people *seriously* see what I am up against??]

"Well I'm not. Amanda Buscemi," I say holding out my hand to shake hers.

She takes it with her free hand and says, "Donna Dinatelli." Peppi bares his teeth and growls a little to remind me of my place on the food chain.

"I'm sorry I was in your yard," I say trying to think fast of a reasonable explanation. I grab a hold of the binoculars and an idea hits me. "It's just that I thought I saw a fox and was trying to get a better look with my son's binoculars."

"Oh really? That must have been why Peppi was so antsy to get outside."

Yeah right. He heard me creeping around and wanted to get a piece of me, the nasty little wolverine. I peer a little closer at him and he looks pretty satisfied with himself. I'd like to wipe that doggy smirk off his yellow-toothed face.

"Well, anyway, sorry to cause a disturbance." I turn back to the fence

"Did you ever find it?"

"Find what?"

"The fox!"

That's right, keep your lies straight, nimrod, I think to myself. "Only a glimpse. I gave up and was on my way back home." I hook my foot back onto the fence.

"You can go out the front way if you'd like."

Yeah and run into black jacket guy, et al. "Oh that's okay. I left the back door unlocked and would have to walk around to my back yard anyway. Have a good night, Donna. It was nice meeting you!" I say in my best friendly-neighbor voice.

"'Bye, same here," she says as I hoist myself over the fence and make my way back home.

The moon eases out from behind the cloud and I can see my way across the O'Brien's yard. Mother Mary still regards me serenely from her spot. Mentally I turn back to my current problem. When the bad guys didn't see Milagros or me they must have staked out our residences. It must have driven them crazy to not know where we were for a whole day. If they only knew about our trip, I think with a little thrill of satisfaction. Oh wait, if they only knew about our trip we might be in even bigger trouble than we are already. I shudder at this thought.

When I get back home I give Linda the car info and she calls the police. This will at least temporarily get rid of the bad guys watching my home. I sincerely doubt that this will act as a strong deterrent. As much as I hate to admit it, I think I have to see this thing through to the end.

Chapter 14:

Th- th- that don't kill me
Can only make me stronger

(Stronger, Kanye West)

I awake the next morning with clear resolve.
And bleary eyes.
And aching back.

Last night Linda placed the call to the police while I dragged an aluminum lawn chair up into the attic and watched through my binoculars for the police to arrive. When they showed up I saw a brief conversation in which the police shone their big-ass police flashlight into the faces of the bad guys. I took in as many details of their features as I could during this time. One was blonde and scruffy-looking. He was sitting in the driver's seat of the Taurus. The other had darker hair and just looked like a regular guy but I couldn't see him all that well. It looked like they turned over their drivers' licenses at one point. Finally I saw them start up the car and drive off. This pretty much convinced me that they weren't Feds. Wouldn't they have just flashed their Fed badges and told the police to go fry eggs? I think, yes.

Once they were gone, Linda came up the stairs and asked me if I was happy now. For the moment, I replied, binoculars glued to my eyes while I continued to scan the neighborhood street. Are you coming down? She wanted to know. Nope, staying here and keeping an eye out. Shaking her head she departed for bed. I wrapped myself in an old, musty comforter I found stuffed in one of the boxes and watched the neighborhood for the return of bad guys.

Sitting by the window reminded me of a neighbor from my childhood, Mrs. Fletcher. When I was a kid she used to watch my friends and me from behind the curtains in her living room whenever we played out on my front lawn. We could see the occasional glint of her eyeglasses from behind her sheer curtains. We never saw her come out of her house so for us, with our overactive imaginations, she seemed to take on this chillingly creepy persona; a silent, malignant force. Mrs. Fletcher was second on our list of things that scared us, right after the abandoned house five blocks over that was rumored to be haunted. Items three and four on the list: werewolves and dentists. We avoided her property like the plague, taking care to not even touch her lawn as we rode down my driveway and onto the sidewalk. One time we were playing catch and my friend Natalie missed the ball. It rolled onto Mrs. Fletcher's lawn. Natalie, not thinking, ran on to her lawn to retrieve it and a shoe came sailing out and almost clocked her. Nat scooped up the ball with a squeal and made it back on my property before the second shoe could be launched. I guess that was Mrs. Fletcher's way of saying stay off my lawn. She couldn't have made a bigger impression if she had thrown a meat cleaver.

So doing my Mrs. Fletcher impression I kept vigil for the return of bad guys. At some point during the night I must have fallen asleep.

When I wake up filtered sunlight is streaming in through the dusty attic window. A spider is busily working its web in the upper corner of the window. I check out the street for bad guys. It looks all clear. I hope.

Joints creaking, I stand up and try to stretch. My back protests as I turn this way and that and my knees are aching from being bent all night.

Gingerly I descend the creaky attic stairs to find the coffee made and the shower running. I fix a cup and go stand at the living room window sipping the hot brew and scanning the street. All is peaceful.

I ponder our next move. Milagros wants to go see Tyler Brooks again. I wonder if there is a way to bypass Tyler and read the blogs ourselves. Suppose we discover there are more deaths in this group? Do we need to find out if they had heart failure too? How many instances do we need to go to the police? How much will push it from coincidence to evidence? I want this done today. I can't take it anymore.

A lot of what we have is circumstantial. Mike Donowski's death went down as sudden cardiac arrest. No record of heart failure, enlarged heart, whatever. We have Julio Rodriguez who was murdered. Perhaps the autopsy showed signs of the onset of heart failure. Getting our hands on the autopsy report? Not happening.

Actually, now that I take a second look, even though I am convinced that something is going on I don't think we have nearly enough to go to the police.

I sigh, stumped. I am sure Milagros is stewing on this as well and I'll hear from her later on today.

Right now? It's shower time.

I pull the front door closed and step out into the brisk morning air. We haven't had a frost yet and so our garden still looks pretty good I note with satisfaction.

I have checked about twenty times for anything suspicious on the street before heading out. I can't imagine that these guys are so easily thwarted. I'm sure that they are monitoring my movements somehow. I feel creeped out as I envision eyes on my back as I walk down the street. I try for brisk nonchalance as I make my way to the T.

On the T nothing unusual happens; no perv tries to grab my ass; no escapee from Mass Mental Hospital babbles to himself; no potential gang banger slumps in a corner offering challenging stares to the populace at large.

The one ride that will always stick in my mind is one early summer morning this average looking man boarded the T. Once the train got under way the man began to pace back and forth, muttering to himself. He became increasingly agitated and started slamming his one fist into the other hand and calling himself 'stupid' and a 'wimp'. Surreptitious glances told me that the other passengers were just as alarmed as I was. All of a sudden he unbuttoned his shirt, laid it on the seat in front of him and started doing pull ups on the overhead bar. For several minutes all that could be heard was the clacking of the subway train over the tracks and this guy grunting out his chin ups. Then, just as abruptly, he stopped, flexed in the darkened glass at his reflected physique which now seemed to meet his approval. He retrieved his shirt, buttoned it, tucked it in and departed the train at the next stop taking his inner demons with him. Probably the strangest thing about the incident is that everyone just went back to reading their newspapers, tapping away on Blackberries, or listening to their iPods. Boston. You gotta love it.

I arrive in the lab without incident and throw my bag on my desk. Finally feeling safe from watchful eyes I begin to relax. Deke isn't in yet so I stop in Paul's office to see what he needs me to do today. I head back in and start setting up.

"Hey, Deke," I say as I see him enter.

"Hey," he says back.

Whoa, no 'dude'?? What the heck! I look at him a little more sharply but he is going about his business of gathering up some items and then heads out the door. He isn't the most talkative guy on a good day but that was brief, even for him. Maybe he's worried that I'm going to tease him some more about his name. I haven't had much time to think about that so he shouldn't worry so much. The big baby.

❖ ❖ ❖ ❖ ❖ ❖ ❖ ❖ ❖ ❖ ❖ ❖ ❖ ❖

Midmorning my cell phone chirps. It's Milagros.

"Mommy, what time can you get off work?"

"Probably about three. Why?"

"I got something we need to do."

"I haven't seen Brendan since Friday. How about you come over for dinner so I can spend some time with him?" I ask

"That could work. Will you be able to go out in the evening, though? What we got to do is not something we can do at your house."

"Yes I can but here's the story. Black Jacket and his buddies were staking out my house last night."

"No sir!"

"Yes sir. Linda called the cops on them after I snuck out and took down their license plate number."

"No way!"

"Way. So when you come over make sure you aren't followed – I mean it! They could be watching your place too. Park on the street behind my house and come through the neighbor's backyard. They're workaholics and won't be home anyway. When we want to leave we can sneak out the back way so we won't be seen."

"Chica I like the way you think," she says with admiration in her voice.

"Well, I'm desperate; I need to just get this figured out and find enough evidence so we can take it to the police. I can't live like this."

"I agree. Let's make it an early dinner so we can get out at a reasonable time."

"You got it. Be there by five."

We hang up and I go back to completing the next step of my experiment. Deke's been out for most of the morning so I've had no company in the lab. My thoughts keep swirling around our dilemma so it's just as well he isn't around. I wouldn't be good company anyway. The only other call I received was from the City lab to see if I could work tonight; Milagros called in sick. Nice...

Just as I predicted I am done at three. Deke has made himself very scarce today. I'm not sure if he is going to be doing anything else in the lab so I leave a note that the extractions are done and in the scintillator counting. He can remove my tubes when they're done if he needs to use it.

I throw on my coat, grab my bag and head out the door.

I pick up Brendan from his after-school sitter. He's all excited to tell me about his weekend with his father. They did a bunch of guy stuff and even had dinner on Sunday with Philip. Philip stayed over and watched Brendan since Bobby had a shift at the fire station.

"Couldn't Pete watch you?"

"Nah, he wasn't around. He was gone most of the weekend," Brendan says.

"Working at the station?"

"I don't think so. I'm not sure what he was doing."

Probably chasing his little college girl around her dorm bed. But I keep that thought to myself.

We arrive home and start doing the homework and cooking dinner. Along with the drums, cooking is his new interest. He informs me that he wants to play in a band and be a chef when he grows up. That's this week's career choices. Next week it could be a veterinarian. The week after, maybe sports car racer. The best was when he decided that trash removal was cool; wanted to know where he could go to school to learn how to do that. Sweet. Every mother's dream for her child.

Milagros taps on the back door a few minutes after five. I've made a pot of herbal tea that we sip while we wait for dinner to finish cooking and Brendan completes his homework. I have to keep him on task since he loves talking with Milagros and keeps interrupting his work to ask her questions and try his Spanish on her.

While Brendan has stepped out of the kitchen for a few minutes Milagros tells me that she called Tyler

Brooks and he said that no other blogs were posted about anyone else meeting an untimely death.

"If you think about it," I say, "it kind of makes sense. The people posting the blogs are the people in the study. So if one of them dies they just don't post anymore. I would think most of the people enrolled don't know each other well enough to realize if someone else is gone. I don't think the blog site is going to be our best line of investigation."

Milagros is nodding as I'm saying this. "You are probably right. And we won't be able to get the names of all the people enrolled in the study to research it further."

"Right. So are we at a stalemate?" I wonder.

"I've got a next step. That's what we're doing tonight. Will Linda be home so we can go out?"

"Yes, she gets home a little after six."

"Perfect."

"So what are we doing?"

Just then Brendan comes bounding back in so we stop talking. I'm dying to find out what's on the agenda but it'll have to wait. We eat our dinner and are cleaning up when Linda comes in.

I've made a plate for Linda. Milagros visits with her while she eats and I go read with Brendan for a while. He has just discovered Harry Potter and so we delve into the world of wizards, Quidditch games and death eaters. Not too far off from my reality, I decide. I just wish I had a wand or cloak of invisibility to help me.

Finally we sneak out the back door shortly after seven and get into her car without incident. As we drive out of the neighborhood I keep an eye out for any suspicious vehicles. Milagros takes a winding route to make it a little more difficult in case anyone is trying to tail us. Finally satisfied that we're alone we get on the highway, I-93, and head north.

Interstate 93 starts near Rhode Island in southern Massachusetts and runs for a whole whopping 45 miles before hitting the New Hampshire border to the north. As it passes through Boston it is referred to as the "Central Artery". It took me a number of years of living in the Boston area before I realized that. It is the sort of insider information that only the greater-area Bostonians know.

By the way, there are a number of speaking quirks endemic to this area. When a Bostonian talks about their mother or father's sister, they call her Aunt, as in "awnt". Everyone else in the country pronounces it "ant". I got into a big argument one time with a co-worker about the Wizard of Oz. He insisted that Dorothy was calling "Awnty Em, Uncle Henry" during the tornado scene. He rented the movie and paid up the twenty bucks he owed me when he heard the Midwestern pronunciation. Other Boston oddities: rubber bands are called elastics, a purse is a pocketbook, and pizza is pronounced "peet-zer" by the diehards.

Continuing north on 93 I wonder where we are going. If we keep following this road we will be in New Hampshire shortly. There are numerous awesome places such as the Lakes Region, then further north the White Mountains (great hiking), and then finally 93 peters down to the only two-lane highway in the country and takes the traveler into the Great North Woods Region. We aren't going that far, I hope.

"So tell me what's going on." I turn to Milagros.

"Okay, after I spoke with Tyler Brooks and realized I wasn't going to get anymore information from the blogs, I started surfing the internet. I found a website that lists all the clinical trials going on. You can do a search right at the website using key words like diabetes. Based on the information that Tyler gave me, I put in the type of drug that's being tested along with the major sites for the trial. I found the study that I'm pretty sure they're enrolled in."

"What's the type of drug?"

"It's a drug used to treat diabetes. It stimulates insulin secretion. The generic drug name is meglitinides."

"Never heard of it before in my life," I say.

"Me neither. But I guess this is a new, beefed up third generation variety and is being used in an inhaler. Now there are a number of studies going on with that particular drug but only one that states it's studying the effectiveness of the drug using an inhaled form. And this particular study has seven recruiting centers from which they distribute the drug and monitor the people enrolled in the study."

"Lemme guess, two of them are Boston and Miami."

"You got it. The other cities are Baltimore, Houston, Chicago, Seattle and San Jose."

"And you're sure that this is the correct study?"

"Yes, when I found it I called Tyler again and he said that he's certain that I found the right study. He's seen several postings from people in both Chicago and Seattle."

She exits the highway we're on and gets onto another highway, 495 south. To the uninitiated it might seem like we're backtracking since we were heading north earlier but 495 does a huge loop around Boston so we are actually bearing west at this point, not south.

"Huhn. Tell me, I'm curious, what have you said to Tyler that he's so willing to give you information?"

"I tol' him I was interested in participating in a study and wanted to know what it was like. That's why I can ask him so many questions. Like I found out that they go in weekly, do a physical exam – weight, blood pressure, temperature, things like that – also take their blood and have them fill out a questionnaire."

"Sounds pretty thorough."

"Yeah, and get this: some of the items on the questionnaire have to do with heart failure symptoms."

"Really?"

"Yes, they ask about shortness of breath..."

"That makes sense, they're inhaling something. Whatever the drug is suspended in could irritate the lungs or air passages."

"Also flu-like symptoms."

"Ok."

"Dizziness or weakness."

I am silent, taking in what she's saying.

"And," she pauses, "swelling in the extremities."

"Wow," I say. My mind is processing this new information, "So that's probably how they became aware of Julio Rodriguez' possible heart failure."

"Yes!" She slaps the steering wheel for emphasis and glances at me, "I think they are using the data collected in the study to target people who are having a negative outcome. Maybe when they start exhibiting symptoms the study participant is eliminated."

I get a sick feeling in my stomach. "Do you realize how friggin' evil that is? What kind of human beings search for a cure for diabetes on one hand and kill on the other? I find it hard to believe that this is really happening. Like I should wake up and find out that this has all been a nightmare."

"You and me both, mommy. You think I like this? I have been thinking of nothin' else but this and trying to see how we could be misinterpreting or jumping to wild conclusions."

"And?"

"And I just don't see how else the puzzle fits."

"Do you think it's some renegade researcher?"

"That's one possibility. But usually researchers at different sites don't communicate until they are assembling the data. This has taken place at two separate sites."

"So what's the other possibility?" I ask, really disliking the direction of this conversation.

"That it's someone from the corporate side, protecting their investment."

"Ugh," I shudder at how cold and calculating that would be.

I turn to look out the window at the passing darkened scenery. This does not happen in my safe little world. This happens in some parallel universe. Like Linda said, in a Robin Cook novel.

I like to keep my conspiracy theories to government shenanigans and out of the world of medicine and science. *We* are supposed to be the good guys, committed to helping people, finding cures for diseases. I regard myself as part of this group and feel betrayed on some level. Some shift happens inside of me as I realize I have probably been a little too 'Pollyanna' in my attitude. Things aren't all sunshine and roses. Corporate bottom lines and profits can count for more than a few measly human lives.

I hug my arms to my sides and shiver a little at this new perspective.

Milagros is exiting from the highway. We make a right off the exit ramp and are now on some rural road. It occurs to me that I haven't even found out where she is taking me.

I turn back from my reflections to ask her, "So where are we going?"

She shifts a little in her seat and then cautiously glances towards me. "Somewhere, hopefully, that we can get some answers," she replies.

"That's a little vague," I say crossing my arms in front of me. "Care to elaborate?"

"If I tell you, you are going to say no."

I cannot even imagine what she means by this. Aggravated I say, "Just tell me already!"

"You'll find out soon enough," she says as she pulls into a partially lit parking area.

There is a barn with a sign on it that says 'Still River Ranch'. I see a lighted corral with a couple of kids riding horses. One is doing jumps on a shiny black horse jauntily trotting around the inside fence perimeter.

My mind goes blank. I am completely stumped as to why we are here. I look questioningly at Milagros as she pulls up on her door handle.

"You do know how to ride a horse, querida." She makes this a statement. As if everyone in the universe rides horses on their days off from work.

Ravagni

I nod, unable to speak. I can't really ride but I *have* been on a horse once and so I figure that qualifies for whatever she has in mind.

"Good, 'cuz we gonna go for a ride. Just follow my lead." She pushes her door open, looks at me and nods.

I open my door, get out and shut it. For the moment I am on autopilot. I cannot even fathom what she has in mind. She has shocked the words right out of my mouth. No small feat for a smart ass like me.

"Can I help you ladies?" a pleasant low-pitched voice says from behind us.

We turn around to face one of the best looking cowboys I've ever laid eyes on. Okay, I haven't seen a lot of cowboys up close and personal but I'm willing to bet that he's the cream of the crop.

"Whoa," I say under my breath as he smiles and the corners of his eyes crinkle in this sexy, Marlboro Man kind of way.

Chapter 15:

Save a horse (ride a cowboy)

(*Save a Horse,* Big and Rich)

Milagros tells Marlboro Man that we have reservations for an evening ride. He asks us to follow him.

Willingly I go. Watching his backside as he leads us to the side of one of the buildings I thank God some guys do not cave in to the baggy pants fashion. His jeans hug his thighs and butt like a second skin and I almost sigh out loud but catch myself in time.

We go into the ranch office to fill out the necessary forms for the horse rental or whatever they call it. The plan is we have the horses for a couple hours and Marlboro Man goes to great lengths to show us the map of the trail we are to follow.

He leads us to the barn, again giving me an opportunity to admire the muscles of his thighs moving nicely under his jeans as he walks. We stop at the entrance.

"Wait here, ladies," he says and disappears inside.

Once he's out of hearing range I say, "Alright, what's going on? You say we have to go somewhere tonight and this is it? Horse riding? "

"Horse riding is just a means to an end. You'll see. By the way, when I made the reservations I tol' them we were expert riders. That way we can go out by ourselves. So act like you know what you're doing."

"Ah, perfect! I've been on a horse once," I hiss at her. She is unbelievable.

Marlboro Man comes back leading a beautiful chestnut horse, "This here's Applejack." He brings it to Milagros and helps her up.

She scales it like a pro and sits attentively while he adjusts the stirrups to the appropriate length. He tightens some straps and then hands her the reins.

A stable hand is now bringing another horse towards us. The horse is all black except for a white marking on his face.

"And this," he turns to me, "this is Beelzebub."

"What?" I say. This doesn't sound so good. "How'd he get that name?"

Marlboro Man smiles, "Oh, he was a little wild in his youth. He earned his name back then."

Great I get a horse named after a demon from hell. This just keeps getting better and better. I look at the horse. He is standing still, no twitching or quivering, no chomping on his bit or anything else that I imagine would show an unpleasant nature. But what do I know?

"So he's fine now?" I ask, still hesitating I look over at Milagros. She's giving me this intense bug eye stare that says, 'just shut up and get on the f'ing horse'.

I sigh and stick my foot in the stirrup the way I saw Milagros do it. Marlboro Man has me by the waist and helps me all the way up. I settle into the saddle and look back at Milagros with a look that says, 'see, I'm going along but this better be worth it'. At least I hope that's what my look says. Probably I don't fool her for a second.

Finally the adjustments are made and he hands Milagros a walkie talkie explaining it's in case we run into trouble, get lost, something like that. He asks if we're all set. Once we give the affirmative we are led around the perimeter of the corral and pointed to the path we are to take.

We head off at a rolling pace. It quickly becomes dark as we leave the lights of the corral behind us. There are no clouds so the three quarter moon is nicely illuminating the path. Also they have these well-placed solar path lights that we are following. Milagros has taken the lead and my horse docilely follows hers.

"I still don't understand why we're riding horses," I say to her once we are well out of earshot of the stables.

"We need a way to get to a certain location."

"Well, what's the location? Enough with the mystery. Tell me now or I'm turning back."

I hear her sigh and then she says, "I'll tell you but first you have to promise not to yell at me."

"Fine, fine, I promise I won't yell."

"The main branch of the pharmaceutical company whose drug is being used in the diabetes study is close to this ranch. I want to go there and poke around, see what we can find."

"Are you out of your mind?" I yell immediately breaking my promise. "Milagros, first of all you don't just saunter into a place like that. I'm sure it's all locked up."

"I think I got a way to get in."

"Ha! Okay, even if you do, then where exactly do we look? I'm sure there's no big neon sign pointing out the way."

"I found the name of the person who is heading up the investigation. They are based out of this facility. My plan is to find that person's office."

I pause, running out of arguments for the moment. She *is* resourceful, I'll give her that, I think grudgingly.

We amble along for a few moments as I try to sort out the logistics. "Okay, so we find this person's office. What do we do, ransack it?"

"Of course not, we just take a careful look."

"That's the plan; just take a look? You realize what you are proposing is illegal. It's this little felony called breaking and entering." Add this to my indictment list. Helga, get the shower ready.

"First, we are not going to get caught. Second, even if we did they wouldn't call the police. That could lead to us talking about our suspicions. They would risk getting investigated."

"Okay, so instead they bump us off. Even better!" I throw up my hands in exasperation. "You do realize that if these people are capable of what we think they are, they won't hesitate to get rid of a few more people."

"That's why we aren't getting caught, mommy." She says as she sharply pulls her horse's reins to the left. He bucks a little but then goes left off the trail and crashes through the underbrush.

"Hey where are you going?" I call out.

"This way," she calls back over her shoulder. "We have to go off the trail."

I pull on Beelzebub's reins. He does a little horsey protest and continues on the trail.

"Hey, Bub," I say, "this way." Once again I pull the reins only a little harder. He pulls back on the reins and stops dead on the trail.

"Come on. Pretty please?" He snorts and shakes his head. Great. Now what?

"You need some help?" Milagros calls back to me. She has stopped and is watching me trying to convince demon horse to follow her.

"I guess so." This is humiliating; first a dog rats me out, now this horse refuses to listen to me. It's like the entire animal kingdom is conspiring against me.

She slides down off her horse, loops the reins around a small nearby tree and walks back to me.

"Give me the reins, chica," she says holding out her hand.

I give them to her and she makes a little clucking noise as she starts to walk toward Applejack. Beelzebub goes willingly with her.

"Oh, here we go; he listens to you but not me. Why did *I* end up with a horse named after Satan's minion? I should have a horse named Buttercup or Honey Pie," I complain. "But no, I get this charmer."

"Shhhh! Don't talk like that in front of him. Horses are very sensitive."

"Oh, what? Like I'm gonna hurt his *feelings*??" I reply sarcastically, "You'd think he'd get over it what with being named after a demon and all."

She ignores me; which is probably the wisest thing to do. I'm getting myself all worked up over this latest escapade and complaining about the horse is my way of venting. Immature? Yes. Do I care? No.

She gives the reins back to me and climbs back onto her horse. We start up again.

"By the way, how do you know we are going in the right direction?" I want to know.

"I have a GPS with me. I plugged in the address before we came out here."

I should have known. Her talents are wasted in the lab, I contemplate. She could be a detective, a private eye for God's sake. I picture her as one of Charlie's Angels aiming a gun and yelling, 'freeze' like Drew Barrymore. Hmmm, which one would I be? I could be Lucy Lu, I think as we jostle along. Yeah, I could kick major butt, just like Lucy. And who was that hottie that was her boyfriend in the movie? Oh, Matt LeBlanc. Yeah, he could be my boyfriend. That would be good. As I imagine peeling off his shirt, I smile happy in my little fantasy.

All of a sudden Beelzebub whinnies as he slides a little and scrambles to find his footing.

"Ahg!" I say as I grab the reins tightly breaking from my daydream. We are descending a hill. I decide I better pay closer attention to what is going on.

"You okay?" Milagros calls back to me.

"Yes, but how much longer?"

"About six hundred yards. So maybe over that next hill."

Great. A little closer to incarceration. Or meeting my Maker.

We are at the edge of the woods abutting the back of one of the buildings. We've tied the horses to trees and are scoping out our best approach.

"Here, mommy, put this on," she tosses me a knitted ski mask and some latex gloves.

"Great," I mutter as pull on the gear. If I'm going to be a criminal, I might as well look the part. "Is this because you anticipate security cameras?"

"It's a logical precaution," she says and then points to the back door. "Stay here. I'm going to try opening the back door."

She starts creeping toward the building. I am holding my breath. They could have motion sensitive lights out here. Every muscle is tense and on alert. If the lights go on I am going to immediately untie the horses so she and I can make our escape as quickly as possible.

One of the horses gently neighs behind me, "Shh!" I hiss turning to give a warning glare. It's probably demon horse.

I turn back around and see that Milagros has made it to the building.

Now I see her pull something out of her pocket but it's too dark to make out what she's doing. She's probably picking the lock. Apparently her talents know no bounds.

I stamp my feet to get the circulation going as well as to have something to do. I make a lousy criminal; I have absolutely no patience.

Oh my God, it looks like she just pulled the door open. I open my eyes wider trying to see better and it looks like she's motioning me to come forward. I sprint up to the door.

"Do you think there might be an alarm going off somewhere?" I say in a low voice, glancing nervously around.

"Maybe, but I doubt it," she whispers back and points up in the dimness to a slowly blinking small red light. "I think it blinks faster if it's armed and then tripped."

"How do you know these things?"

"You don't want to know but I got that piece of information from the same place as I got the lock picking kit."

"You're right, I don't want to know. Let's get a move on. This is making me really nervous. What are we looking for?"

"The office of Steven Morris. I'm hoping they have nameplates on the doors. Let's go up to the second floor. Most offices aren't usually on the first floor."

We are in the stairwell having this discussion so we start to creep up the stairs. My ears are straining for any noise. All I hear is my pulse hammering away and my jagged breathing.

We reach the second floor door and Milagros slowly and quietly pulls it open. After making sure the hallway is empty we start tiptoeing forward. Milagros pulls out a penlight and flashes it on the nameplate of the first door. Doris Naughton. Nope.

Next is Mike Smith and then Caleb Mwazawi. We continue down the hallway and find a number of other offices along with the restrooms and a break room.

We come to the end of the hall with no luck. Milagros points to the ceiling and I nod my agreement that we go up to the next floor.

We've been in the building for maybe two minutes but it feels like two hours. I am sweating profusely under the ski mask and the sweat is stinging my eyes.

On the third floor we continue searching for Steven Morris' office. The pen light shines on the fifth door down and we read 'Steven Morris'. Milagros looks at me with wide, excited eyes. I give her a thumbs up and she turns the knob.

Morris' office looks like a regular office with a desk and chair, computer, phone, some stacks of papers. Off to one side is a small table with several chairs around it. There's a wall of bookcases containing binders and journals behind the desk.

"You go through the papers, I'll see if I can get onto his computer," she whispers to me.

I nod my understanding and dive into the first stack

by the light of the computer screen. I hear Milagros clicking away.

The first folder looks like financial estimates for some project. The second appears to be a proposal for a different project. The third, a rough draft on another project. It looks like he's the clearinghouse for all the projects.

I reach the bottom of the first stack with no luck and turn to tackle the second stack. Again, there's nothing that looks like it has to do with the meglitinides study.

I straighten the two stacks and look to see what Milagros is doing. She hasn't had any luck with getting into his computer and has taken to opening drawers. One has files in it so she looks through each of them before closing up the drawer.

Taking my cue from her, I open the drawer nearest to me. There's an employee handbook, directory, and other personnel-related items.

I close that drawer and try the middle one. It's locked. I look to Milagros who is already whipping out her lock picking kit. She goes to work on the lock and after the longest minute of my life, gets it open.

She slides it open and there are pens, a box of staples, paper clips, rubber bands. She pulls it back a little further and we see the bottom of a manila folder. I grab the exposed edge, slide it out and open it. It contains a number of sheets. The heading on the top says 'MEM-PHIS'. It is a spreadsheet with a bunch of numbers. I focus on the headings of each column. The first column says 'ID' and has numbers like 07-10275 under it. Next column heading is ΔG'. Then 'INS'. I start to slide the paper back in the folder when Milagros grips my wrist. She points to a column a few spots to the right that says 'BNP'. My pulse quickens. I scan down the BNP column. Most of the numbers are very low; less than values of twenty. I flip to the next page and one number in the BNP column springs out at me: one hundred twenty two. It is bolded. There is a scribbled notation on the side that says, 'watch'. I flip to the next page. All BNP's are low again. Page four, the highest value is a thirty seven. It isn't bolded, though. I flip through the sheets. One has a value of seven hundred forty. The notation on that line says "done". The last page has two bolded BNP values fifty-one and sixty-one. No notes are written there.

I turn back to the first page. The other columns have incomprehensible headings: LPA, VAMP8, HNRPUL1. Those columns have pluses and minuses in them. Very strange.

Suddenly we hear a low but distinct throbbing noise. Milagros and I look at each other and simultaneously whisper, "Elevator!"

I cram the folder back in the drawer while Milagros flicks off the computer screen. We dash out the door, turn left and sprint for the stairwell door at the end of the hall.

I want to look back but am afraid this'll slow me down. We crash through the door and push it closed. Taking the stairs at breakneck speed we reach the bottom and lunge through the same door we entered.

We burst into the cold night air and do an all out dash for the woods. Milagros reaches the horses first and unties them at lightening speed. She tosses Beelzebub's reins to me and I make a flying leap onto his back.

"Heeyah!" I say, and I flick the reins. Beelzebub just stands there.

"Come on go," I say as I push my body forward a couple times trying to get him started. He shakes his head and neighs his answer to me.

Nervously I glance over my shoulder. I don't see anyone coming out, no alarms ringing or lights flashing but I am desperate to get this beast moving.

"Beelzebub, go. Come on! Giddy up!" I plead, rocking back and forth in an attempt to jump start him. I drag the ski mask off and lean down, "Please, please, pretty please."

"Kick him," Milagros has stopped her horse and calls back to me.

Of course, like in the westerns. You are supposed to use the spurs that are attached to the stirrups. I raise my legs up and hit his sides. He gives a snort and looks back at me.

"Do it harder!" She calls to me.

I raise my legs up even higher and kick his sides with all my might. Beelzebub gives an angry whinny, rolls his eyes back until I can see the whites shining in the moonlight and he takes off at a mad gallop.

I am holding on for dear life as he plunges through some thickets. "Whoa!" I yell. This seems to have the opposite effect as he digs in and races up a hill and down the other side. I peer over his head and ahead see a rapidly approaching group of trees. Giving a yelp of terror I pull on the reigns but Beelzebub ignores me. We enter the woods and branches lash at me. It's all I can do to hold on to the horse and protect my face. I bend low over his neck and try pulling hard on the reins at the same time. This is having no effect on him at all. If anything he runs harder in full-out demented hysteria.

He darts right and then left around trees. I clench his sides with my thighs to keep from being flung off his back. I try looking around his head to see where we are headed. We're going up a hill with small trees and some loose rocks that he is scrambling over. This doesn't slow him down, though. If anything, it seems to make him even more frantic. I can feel his powerful legs working beneath me. We reach the top of the hill at full throttle and hurtle down the other side at a terrifying pace.

I yank with all my might at the reins while jouncing clear out of the saddle and then slamming back onto it again and again. This sends jolts of pain up from my crotch and stars sparkle in my vision. I struggle to sit up a little higher to get better leverage on the reins when wham! I see a supernova of stars and the last thing I remember is hitting the ground hard.

Chapter 16:

Slowly, gently night unfurls its splendor ...

(Music of the Night, Andrew Lloyd Weber as sung by Michael Crawford)

Slowly I become aware of a soft undulating light filtering through my eyelids and the strains of Phantom of the Opera quietly playing. Halfway between sleep and wakefulness I try to remember what I was dreaming: I was going fast and trying to get through these trees. No, wait, that wasn't a dream. I pull myself to full consciousness. I open my eyes and am looking into the craggy face of an elderly American Indian man who is sitting on a footstool near me. A fire is burning in the fireplace; its flickering orange flames cast irregular shadows on the walls and scattering shadows on his features.

"Easy, easy," he says as I try to sit up and instantly get dizzy and collapse backward onto the couch's soft cushions. He shifts an ice pack back onto my forehead.

"Where am I?" I manage to croak out.

"You're in my home," he hands me a glass of water and some Tylenol. "Here take this."

"How did I get here?" I ask after swallowing the tablets.

"I was outside and heard you crashing through the woods and found you knocked out on the ground. I carried you back here."

It all comes rushing back to me: breaking in to the Allagaro building, the wild escape. I groan. My head kills. I wonder where Milagros might be. She must be worried about me.

"My horse?"

"Gone. He will probably return to the stable on his own."

"I have a friend who'll be looking for me," I try sitting up again.

"We will go find her once you feel a little better," he says placing a gentle hand on my shoulder.

I slump back. My stomach feels queasy. I raise my hand to my head and feel a lump the size of an ostrich egg on my forehead under the ice pack. I wince at how tender it is to my touch.

Remembering my manners I say, "I'm Amanda Buscemi, by the way."

"Sam Ward."

"Thank you for taking care of me, Sam."

"It's my pleasure, Amanda."

"I lost control of the horse I was riding. He was doing a full out gallop. I must have hit a branch."

"You are fortunate to have only a bump."

"I'm sure you're right. I should have known better than to go riding at night. Again, thank you."

He raises a hand as though to stop me from saying more "You are welcome. Perhaps our paths have crossed for a reason."

"A reason?"

"Yes," he says. The wood in the fireplace suddenly gives a loud pop as water buried deep in the wood is released. The heat permeates me like a warm hug. Sam continues, "Often seemingly chance meetings have a purpose. I might have something to learn from you or you from me."

"Well, I'm not sure I buy into that whole thing. My friend Linda says stuff like that to me too."

"Why do you think it might not be true?"

"It's too wooooooo for me," I say for lack of a better word. I flutter my fingers to help translate my made up word and then wince as even this small movement causes a bolt of pain in my head.

"Ah, you are a woman of reason."

"That's right, Sam, a woman of reason," I answer him slowly. "You hit the nail on the head. I'm a scientist. I don't go in for all that mystical, spiritual stuff." Finally, someone who understands me!

"I see. Well let me challenge you with a new way of thinking."

"Okay, shoot."

"Since you are a scientist you might recall that most new scientific ideas are met with derision and resistance until the weight of evidence proves the idea to be true. For instance the concept that the world is round instead of flat."

"I'm tracking with you. Like evolution explaining how we got here."

"Exactly. So one of the newer scientific theories is quantum physics. Most specifically particles not physically connected can have an impact on each other."

Quantum physics is used to describe how subatomic particles act. Newtonian physics (apple falls from tree, hits Sir Isaac Newton on head, he discovers this is gravity) does not apply at the ultra-small level. Everything is actually energy waves, not the little particles circling a nucleus the way we were taught in basic chemistry 101. The really bizarre part of this is researchers have found that these "particles"/energy clouds/energy waves are influenced by the observer. This has lead to the current thought of energy fields that extend out from our consciousness and has connections into matter that goes beyond our basic understanding of how matter interacts. At least this is my feeble understanding of it.

"Yeah, I've heard a little about it. Frankly, it's pretty freaky and difficult to wrap my mind around."

"Fair enough. And I'm not trying to get into a heavy scientific debate. I just want to orient you to what I am going to propose."

I must admit that despite my pounding headache, I am intrigued so I say, "Okay, Sam, give it to me. You have my full attention."

"Excellent. So what I'd like you to consider is that we are not as separate as it appears on the surface. That all of humanity is part of the same fabric. Just like sub-atomic particles affect each other though they are not directly connected, on a more macroscopic level each of us influences the other. Your pain is my pain. My joy is yours. We are all interwoven and, therefore, no meeting is chance. Random." He pauses looking me steadily in the eye. His deeply lined face radiates a kindness, a gentleness that is almost tangible.

As Michael Crawford sings about opening up the mind to the music of the night Sam, in perfect sync continues speaking slowly and deliberately, "We may choose to *not* find out the reason for our paths crossing. But that doesn't mean there isn't a purpose. That I won't impact you and you won't impact me in some way."

"Huhn. That's pretty mystical, Sam." Mystical, heck, I feel like I'm in a Star Wars movie. I half expect to see Yoda come tottering out with his walking stick saying in his high-pitched growly voice, "Of the same fabric we are. Interwoven you will see."

Sam answers, "It may sound mystical but that is only because this is a fairly new concept; it is asking for a paradigm shift, a change in how a person will view and reference the world. Perhaps in the future this will be a widely accepted concept."

"Maybe," I allow. "But I prefer to stick to the ideas that are currently accepted. They work pretty well for me."

His face creases into a gentle smile, "I would think that people made similar statements when they first heard the theory that the world was round instead of flat."

I shrug non-committally and shift the ice pack to redistribute the cold. I have never been challenged to consider that perhaps my ideas are antiquated. This is something new and slightly disturbing.

"You say you have a friend that says similar things?" Sam asks.

"Well, Linda doesn't talk about quantum physics but, yeah, she claims we are all interconnected."

"So my challenge to you is to think about this, as a scientist. Look for proof of this interconnectedness. I'll bet you will be surprised once you raise your awareness, how often something happens that confirms this concept."

"Like you think of a friend that you haven't talked to in years, the phone rings, and it's her."

He chuckles and his eyes crinkle, "Something like that, Amanda. Just be open. And return to see me in the beginning of November. I invite you and your friend to be my guests at my tribe's medicine fire ceremony. After that we can have dinner at my home and you can tell me of your journey since this meeting. My dearest hope is that you will overcome the sadness that has invaded your life for so long."

Just then we hear a truck engine and bright headlights shine through his cabin's front window.

"I believe your friend is here." Sam stands up and holds out his hand to help me up from the couch. I grab hold of his hand and let him pull me up.

I say, "Wait a minute. What makes you think I am sad?"

"I see it here," he touches my cheek, "and I feel it here." He places his hand over his heart. "But it is time to let you go on your way." He presses a business card into my hand.

"And how do you know that whoever has pulled up to your house right now is my friend?" With a lurch I suddenly realize it could be the bad guys. They might have tracked me down and are going to finish the job that the tree branch started.

Sam puts his hand on my shoulder to guide me to his front door, "After I brought you back here I called the Still River Ranch to tell them I had one of their riders. They got in touch with your friend and said they'd bring her over as soon as she returned to the ranch."

"How did you know that I was riding from Still River? Did you use your mystical powers?" Once a wise ass, always a wise ass.

Again, the smile, "No, Still River is the only place around here with stables. I saw the horse run off and figured that's where you must have come from."

There's a rap on the door. Sam pulls it open and Milagros is standing there with Marlboro Man.

"Chica!" she cries. She grabs me and hugs me tightly. "Are you alright?" She pushes me to arms length to look at me better. "Oh my God, look at your head! What happened?"

"Hey Milagros. I had a disagreement with a tree branch. The branch won," I say trying to make light of my injury. The Tylenol has helped a little.

"I am just so glad to see you!" She turns to Sam, "Thank you so much for taking care of my friend."

"Ms. Buscemi, I am so sorry," Marlboro Man steps up, "I had no idea Beelzebub would bolt like that."

I look over at Milagros. She won't meet my eyes. I'm sure I'll hear about the tall tale she told later.

"Don't worry about it, um," I pause because I don't recall ever getting his name.

"Mike," he supplies.

"Right, Mike, I'm just glad all I got was a bump."

"Sam," he leans in and shakes Sam's hand, "thanks for rescuing our rider. Ladies, we should get going?" he looks to us.

We both nod our heads and make for the door. At the threshold I turn back and say, "Sam, I enjoyed talking with you and I'll see you in November."

"I enjoyed it as well. And please bring both Linda and Milagros to the ceremony," he says with a twinkle in his eyes.

"So who was that guy," Milagros wants to know. We are walking back to Mike's truck.

"Obi Wan Kenobi," I say.

"Huh?" She looks at me questioningly.

"Nothing," I say.

Mike has opened the passenger front door and assists me with climbing in. As I lift my leg to hoist myself into the truck pain shoots up from my crotch. I flash back to banging up and down in the saddle as Beelzebub slalomed through the Worcester County countryside. I wonder if my va-jay-jay will ever be the same.

"Sam Ward?" Mike says bringing me back to the current conversation, "That man single-handedly saved the conservation area around Still River. He's a professor at UMASS Lowell."

"Really," I say.

"Yes, he's also on the leadership counsel for the Nipmuc tribe. You really should consider going to the fire ceremony. It's an honor to be invited; rarely do outsiders get to go. My ranch hands and I are invited due to our good relationship with the tribe over the years."

"I might just do that," I say.

We are finally heading back home. Milagros hounded me until I called Ron Lee. He was working tonight in the emergency room at BI so she brought me in to get checked out.

Once I receive a clean bill of health she brings me home. We pull up to the same spot that we departed from hours earlier, in front of my neighbors' house that live behind me.

"Let me help you get in," she says.

"No, no," I grab the car door handle, "I can make it back okay."

It's past midnight and I just want to get to bed. We say good night and I get out of her car.

All is quiet in the neighborhood. My neighbors' cars are in their driveway and I see the glow of their television from what I assume is their bedroom window.

I skirt the cars and creep to their back yard. Quietly I lift the latch on their gate. I step through and carefully ease the gate closed so as not to make any noise. Two steps in and the backyard is flooded with light.

Crap! I make a run for the fence dividing our yards and hurdle it like an Olympic athlete. Okay, like an *aging* Olympic athlete. I land sideways on my right foot and feel a bolt of pain.

"Amanda, is that you?" I hear Joe's voice.

Why can I never catch a break? I wonder.

"Hey, Joe," I call back.

"What are you doing out here?"

"I thought I saw a fox," it worked once so let's try it again.

"Oh yeah," he steps into the light on his porch, "I heard about that. The guy next door thought he saw it too."

"Really?"

"Then the guy next to him said it wasn't a fox, it was a fisher cat."

"What the heck is a fisher cat?" Good God I have started an epidemic of animal sightings. Imagine what it would be like if I said I saw a UFO.

"I think it's in the weasel family but bigger and more ferocious," Joe explains.

Swell. "I doubt something like that would show up here," I say trying to break the momentum of my lie.

"That's what I thought too but we used to get 'possums in our garage in the middle of Detroit when I was a kid. So you never know."

"Well, whatever it was, I think it's gone now."

"Okay, talk to you later."

"Good night." I turn and hobble to my back door.

I let myself in and drag myself wearily to the bathroom to wash up. I get a look at myself in the mirror and shudder. The swelling has gone down considerably but I am going to have a doozy of a bruise. Between that, my aching hinter region, and the twisted ankle I feel like I've been through a war.

All I can manage to do is brush my teeth and extract a pricker from out of my tangled hair. I can't even imagine what horrors tomorrow holds. Tonight I am just thankful to be alive.

Chapter 17:

Gravity is working against me

(*Gravity*, John Mayer)

The next morning I can barely move. John Mayer's song Gravity plays in my head as I get out of bed. Yup, gravity is definitely working against me. Never mind the quantum stuff Sam was talking about, regular old physics has played havoc with my body.

Last night I had wrapped my ankle up in an ace bandage before going to bed in an effort to subdue the swelling. That seems to have helped with the swelling but I can't put much weight on that foot. I gimp down the hall to the bathroom

With trepidation I look in the mirror. My forehead has gone from the angry red it was last night to the beginnings of black and purple. I remove a piece of straw and wonder what else is living in my hair.

I do a shuffle-hop-skip to the kitchen. Linda glances up at me and then does a double take.

"What in the world happened to you?"

"Don't ask. All I can say is you wouldn't approve." Shuffle-hop-skip, shuffle-hop-skip I reach the coffee maker. I pour myself some of the brew and suck it down while standing, balancing on my one good foot since I can't figure out how to get my coffee mug over to the table without spilling it.

"Is Brendan up?" I ask before she can grill me anymore about my physical state.

"He snagged a granola bar and went up to the attic to practice his drums."

Brendan has taken to the drums like a fish to water. He set up shop in the attic so he won't disturb us. I tried to dissuade him since it's pretty cold up there but he doesn't seem to mind.

Linda goes to take her shower and I ponder my present condition. I cannot fathom trying to work today and decide I should call in sick. I can't remember the last time I took a sick day so I refuse to feel guilty for doing it now.

I get Brendan off to school, call in sick to Paul, and then log on to the internet to do a little research.

In the car last night I found an old Target receipt in my purse and used the back of it to write down as many column headings as I could remember from the document we saw in Morris' office. Now I pull that out, flatten it as best I can and put it next to the keyboard.

The first heading I wrote down is CD4. I think I know what that is. It's a marker on a certain type of immune cell called a helper cell. Why they would be testing for this I have no idea. The test is used to assess the immune status of people infected with HIV. I go to the search engine dogpile.com. I plug in CD4 and get exactly what I expect; a bunch of websites concerning HIV. I go back and plug in CD4 and diabetes. There's a study regarding HCV infection (hepatitis C virus) and diabetes. Is that why they did the counts for CD4? I put in CD4 plus heart disease. Slim pickings again.

Next I do LPA. I get about a million things: from Little People of America to an engineering group to lipoprotein A. The last one sounds the most promising. Lipoprotein A is associated with heart disease. I read about that for a while. Nothing pops out regarding LPA associated with diabetes.

Moving on to VAMP8 the very first hit on the search engine gives me not only a discussion on VAMP8, which I learn is a gene associated with early onset heart attacks but also discusses another item I was going to look up: HNRPUL1. I do a bunch of reading which almost puts me into a mental coma.

By late morning my brain is about as saturated as it can get. I dial Milagros. She picks up on the second ring.

"How are you, honey? I didn't want to disturb you in case you took the day off and were resting."

"Well you guessed right. I *did* take the day off. But I haven't been resting. I've been studying up on all those cryptic headings we saw in Morris' office."

"And what have you found out?" she asks.

"LPA, VAMP8, and HNRPUL1 all have to do with predicting heart disease. VAMP8 and HNRPUL are gene variants that are associated with 'early-onset of myocardial infarction', which I think means having a heart attack in your fifties or younger. The LPA gene shows a three-fold risk of severe coronary artery disease," I read from my notes to her. "I think what they are trying to figure out is if one or more of these genes is causing a subgroup in their study to experience negative outcomes. Maybe an increased susceptibility to heart disease is skewing the study and if they can eliminate the subgroup, they can have better outcomes. They are using BNP to measure the outcome.

"The CD4 is kind of stumping me," I continue. "Usually you think of CD4 having to do with HIV infection but I guess it can gauge immune status in general. Maybe there's some sort of immunocompromised condition that might weaken the heart."

"Or maybe," Milagros interjects, "the drug itself compromises the immune system or attacks the heart and you can measure it with the CD4 count."

"Hmm. That's a good point." We are both silent as we ponder this. "Well, anyway, that's what I've been doing. I'm not sure how helpful it is to solving this whole thing or adding to our case that they are covering something up."

"But maybe once an official investigation is started this can be evidence that they were aware of the problem but didn't stop the study. Remember the cigarette companies with their internal memos? The memos showed they were aware of the association of cigarette smoking with lung cancer decades before it became public knowledge. Maybe this is what we can get them on; that they know that their drug is causing heart failure and that they are covering it up."

"That's one angle," I say. I recall, however, that despite the public pillorying of the cigarette companies not much was really done to them legally for all their maneuverings and cover ups.

"Well let me tell you my news," Milagros says. "I got to see the autopsy report on Julio Rodriguez."

"How did you do that?"

"I went to ask Benny if he could get it for me. But he wasn't in. So I called the Dade County coroner from his office. Said I was from the coroner's office up in Boston and asked them to fax it to me."

By now this sort of outrageous behavior doesn't surprise me. Impersonating someone from the coroner's office? Sure, why not! Instead I say, "And they just did it?"

"It was easy. I said we needed it for some records up here to fill out an insurance form. No one even questioned it. They faxed it right away. No one down in pathology even saw me do it."

She is so lucky. If I had done that I would have been caught red-handed.

"Okay, so what did it say?"

"He died from his stab wounds. We already knew that. His heart was three hundred ninety five grams."

"So within normal limits," I say.

"Within normal limits," she agrees. "But he only weighed a hundred forty pounds."

"So he was a lot smaller than Mike Donowski."

"Exactly. His heart might have been enlarged for his size."

"But we have no way of proving it," I point out.

"Which is why I asked them to run a BNP test."

"And they agreed?"

"Yes."

Okay, now I am just annoyed. How can she get anything she wants? I used to think that people fell under her spell because she is so pretty. But that doesn't explain her success this time since this was done on the phone. She just has some special magic mojo. Our maybe a set of balls I was unaware of.

"So what's the result?" I ask, burying my resentment.

"I haven't heard back from them yet."

"Ok. You *do* realize that some of the stuff we have has been obtained illegally. We can't go to the police and tell them everything without incriminating ourselves."

"I know. That is a problem."

"Heck yeah!"

"So I think we need to keep going. I just don't know what our next step is."

"Well I know what my next step is," I say suddenly realizing I'm exhausted, "I am going to crash for a while. Maybe I'll come up with something after I've rested."

"Okay, querida. You get some rest. I have to get ready to go to work."

We hang up and it is all I can do to keep my eyes open. I crawl into bed for a little cat nap.

I wake up to a darkening bedroom. I look at my alarm clock. Four ten. That was more than a cat nap. But I feel about twenty times better so I know I needed the rest.

I jump into the shower, get dressed and go out to collect Brendan from the sitter. My ankle is still tender. I limp down the street to the sitter's house. I don't see Mr. Zeigler on my journey. I consider this a small miracle or perhaps a change in fortune: imagine the story that would be circulating if he got a load of my battered condition.

At home we eat dinner and get the homework done. Philip has another local hockey game so as soon as Linda comes home I leave.

Pulling a baseball cap on to hide my forehead I check to see if there are any suspicious cars. I don't see any but that doesn't mean I'm not being watched. I choose to leave by the front door. I figure if the bad guys want to waste their time following me to a hockey arena, they can. I'll save my fence hopping for another day.

Mr. Ziegler is out on his stoop.

"Hey Mr. Z," I call.

He gets up and walks over to me, "Amanda, how are you?"

"Just fine and yourself?"

"Fine, fine."

Now's my chance to use his snoopiness to my advantage and I say, "Did the Feds raid the Russians yet?"

"No, they haven't been back all day. Maybe they collected all the evidence they can by observing them and are getting warrants ready to search their house."

"Hmm, maybe." I'm relieved to confirm that I don't have those guys hanging around watching me but wonder how they are keeping tabs on me.

"You need to be careful out here alone at night, darlin'"

"Why's that?" Now what? My stomach does a little flip flop.

"There's some wild animal roaming the neighborhood."

Oooooh, *that!* Relieved I say, "A wild animal?"

"Yes, Donnelly over here," he gestures with his cigar to the Donnelly house over my shoulder, "he says it was a bobcat." Harold Donnelly is fifty-four and lives with his mother across the street from us. He seems pretty shy and quiet but, of course, Mr. Ziegler can draw him out.

"A bobcat?"

"But Bucceli says he thinks it was a wolf."

Good God has this story got legs. I feel a twinge of guilt that I started this whole thing but there's nothing I can do about it now. Bob Bucceli lives across from Mr. Z and is an exaggerating big mouth. He is always bragging about his sons. "Bobby junior this, Stevie that..." I have had to listen to this windbag boast for years. Ugh. He got real quiet, though, when Phil got his hockey scholarship to Boston College. His loser sons barely made it into community college.

"I'll keep an eye out. Thanks for the heads up."

We wish each other a good evening. I head for the T trying hard not to limp within eyeshot of Mr. Z.

Bobby and I arrive at the rink at the same time but have come from different directions. We meet under the now-lit street lamp.

"So let me see the new hair," he says. I had called and thanked him for his generosity but he hasn't seen me since the transformation.

I do a little twirl.

"Take the cap off," he says, "I can't see it that well."

"Uh, I didn't have time to style it today," I say. The last thing I need is for him to see my forehead. I don't have a good explanation worked out for the bruise.

"That's okay, come on!"

"No!" I say a little more shrilly than I intended. I reel it back in and say as calmly as I can, "It looks really good when it's styled and I wouldn't want you to see it when it's not at its best."

"That's okay," he repeats. "Come on, let me see."

"No, now stop!"

His mouth has compressed to a thin line as he looks at me a little more closely. "What are you trying to hide?"

"Nothing!"

"Oh really." He makes it a statement, which means he doesn't believe me. "Is that a scratch I see on the side of your face?"

I rub the side of my face. I didn't think it was noticeable.

"Yeah, just a little one."

"Amanda, take off your cap."

This is only going to get worse if I refuse. Reluctantly I remove the cap. And his eyes narrow as he brushes my bangs back.

"Who did this to you?" He says in a tightly controlled voice.

"What? No one did this to me! I had an accident."

"An accident," he says flatly.

I might as well come clean, or at least partially clean. I can't admit that I had the accident while committing a felony. I say the only part of the story that I can, "Milagros and I were riding horses and mine went nuts and bolted. I hit a tree branch and got knocked off."

"Why were you riding horses?"

"We just decided to do it. On a lark."

"When did you do this?"

"Last night."

"On a work week night you and Milagros just decide, 'on a lark', to go horseback riding."

Dang, I should have said Sunday. That sounds a little more realistic. Now I have to stick to my story and it doesn't sound too believable.

"Yes," I say as convincingly as possible.

"Are you seeing some new guy?"

"No!" Great, now he thinks I'm being abused by a new boyfriend. "Look let's drop it. No one beat me up. Even though you don't believe me, it's the truth." I cram the cap back onto my head.

Just then Philip arrives.

After we wish him luck we go to Dobsky's. Bobby's nephew, Anthony – Anna's son, is there. He's going to go to the game with us. Bobby doesn't have an opportunity to quiz me anymore about my condition. For that I am relieved.

BC loses the game but Phil gets two assists so we're happy for him.

I dart out as soon as the game finishes, declining the invitation to a late night burger with the boys once Phil gets out of the locker room.

Getting off the T I start my three block walk to the house. The streets are dark and lonely. I suddenly feel a little more vulnerable without anyone else out on the street.

My heightened anxiety causes me to keep glancing over my shoulder. I feel like someone is there but I don't see anyone. The hairs on the back of my neck are standing on end. I hunch my shoulders and cram my hands deeper into my jacket pockets.

I turn the corner to my street. Just a half a block to go, I encourage myself.

My breath comes out in little bursts of frosty condensation. My ears strain for any noise. With all the houses buttoned up tight against the cold there is dead silence. As I pass a tall fir tree someone steps out in my path.

"Ah!" I yelp.

"Whoa!" the other person says.

I focus in the light from a distant street lamp and see it is a teenager with a filled trash bag in his hand. "Oh my God, I'm sorry! I didn't expect to run into anyone out here," I say.

"No prob. Just be careful. Someone saw a bear out here."

"A bear?"

"Yeah," he says lifting the lid on the trash can sitting at the curb and placing the bag inside. "My mom said we have to make certain to keep all the trash covered. That's what might be attracting the bears."

"Uh, probably a good plan," I say.

"Yeah, but I don't really think that there's any bears around here."

"No?"

"Nah, my friend says it might be a mountain lion."

Oh crap. Next thing you know it's going to be a saber tooth tiger. "Really, why is that?"

"They have bigger territories and are more likely to come into densely populated areas," he says this with all the certainty of teenage wisdom and experience.

"Swell. Well we better both be getting in then, eh?"

"Yeah, take care."

I head home shaking my head. This is like the telephone game. Each time the story gets repeated, it gets more and more distorted until the final version is nothing like the original. A bear, I think to myself. A mountain lion! Pah! Any of you folks notice some bad guys with machine guns, maybe??

Chapter 18:

You live, you learn

(*You learn,* Alanis Morrisette)

The next morning I arrive in the lab ready to immerse myself in the next leg of the experiment that Paul has planned for me to do.

Deke comes in but we don't talk that much. Once again he seems to be preoccupied. I wonder if he had a setback in his study. He's studying the effects of a new cholesterol medication on the coronary arteries in rats. Testing on an animal model is usually the first step on the way to getting it ready for human trials. It is also part of his doctoral thesis about how fatty streaks in the arteries lead to inflammation. This inflammation is the first step in the process of plaque building up in the arteries surrounding the heart; the beginning of the vicious cycle of coronary artery disease; a condition that has kept cardiologists and researchers in business for decades.

He's been asked to be a guest lecturer for an undergraduate class and leaves mid-morning to go do that.

While my stuff incubates I go over to the scintillator to retrieve the data from Monday's experiment. I now have the tedious job of entering about eighty values into the database. I open my desk drawer to get the jump drive – which is an improbably small device that can store a bunch of information. Each study has its own database that we store on a jump drive as well as our hard drive. We do that so Paul can take the data home and look at it if he wants.

The jump drive is not in my desk. I pick up some stacks of papers lying around. Not there either. Maybe Paul took it. I go ask him. He says he did take it and then gave it to Deke. He wanted him to look at some of the numbers.

I go over to Deke's desk and open his drawer. There it is. I grab it out, go over to my computer and insert the end of it into the USB port so I can access the necessary file.

I click on the proper drive to open up the jump drive. We list each study in folders so we can keep everything straight. There are five different studies that Paul has going in various stages. But instead of the five folders I expect to see, there's two. The first is the name of Deke's study and the second one says 'MEMPHIS'.

My heart skips a beat. I open up the folder and there are a number of folders inside the initial one. I look at the labels: AWE RRED, MEMPHIS 1 and MEMPHIS 2. Barely breathing I click on MEMPHIS 2. There are all these documents inside the folder: Control, Field Study, Proposal, Test, etc.

Deke! Why does he have these files? Could it be an odd coincidence that he has something labeled with the same name as the clinical trial Milagros and I are investigating? I glance up at the door. I don't want to get caught. I open the document labeled 'Test'. It looks identical to the document I saw in Morris' office. My hands shake and become super-clumsy in my panic. I copy all of the documents onto my computer and yank out the jump drive.

I run over to Deke's desk, slide open the drawer and place the jump drive back in and then run back to my desk. I sit there shaking and trying to digest the ramifications of what I just saw. This doesn't make any sense. My mind is a jumbled confusion. Deke! For God's sake what would he be doing with this stuff?

I think about the jump drive in the drawer. Now I'm not certain if I put it back in the right spot. I run over to Deke's desk again, open the drawer, move the jump drive from the right hand side to the left and run back to my desk.

I lean back in my chair trying to look casual. My mind is completely numb. I can't even fathom why Deke is involved in this. I think of his dedication to his work over the several years I've known him. This doesn't gel with the mental picture I have of greedy corporate executives; smoking their cigars and drinking scotch, sitting on expensive leather chairs at their exclusive country club deciding to dispatch hit men to rid their world of the likes of Julio Rodriguez. Once again I picture his drawer as I open it. Maybe the jump drive was in the middle. Yeah, I think that's where it was.

I dash back over, open the drawer, move the drive to the middle, and close it. Running back to my seat I bump my hip on the counter as I turn the corner of the bench. Swearing under my breath I flop into my chair and massage my hip bone. That'll leave a bruise. At least Bobby won't see that one. I pick up a paper and make like I'm studying it.

Deke is one of the good guys, isn't he? I rub my hands on my jeans, they've turned all sweaty. My mind is whirling around this puzzle. I try to remember if he overheard any part of conversations I had with Milagros. Is that how they became aware of our investigation? Wait a minute! The jump drive was right next to the paper clips. I distinctly remember now.

I run over to Deke's desk one more time, move the jump drive next to the paperclips, close the drawer and scramble back to my desk sliding on the floor as I round one of the benches.

I am still breathing hard from the back and forth marathon when Deke walks in.

"Hey," he says.

"Hey," I say back.

He walks over to his desk and places some papers on it. My heart is hammering in rapid staccato. I pretend to be sorting some papers while I watch him. I hold my breath as he opens his drawer. He drops something in it and closes it.

He goes over to the coat rack, hangs his jacket up, and puts his lab coat on.

Oh snap, I forgot to look for the real jump – the one that I am supposed to be using to store all my data. Maybe I can wait until he leaves and go over to look for it. No, on second thought I don't want him thinking I was anywhere near his desk.

"Um, Deke?" I say trying to keep my voice even, "I don't have the jump drive for the CURFEW study. Do you have it?"

"Oh, uh, sure," he says. He walks back to his desk and removes it from the USB port on the side of his computer. So that's where it was. He walks over and hands it to me.

"Thanks," I say.

"Sure," he answers.

His casual California attitude is distinctly missing. He hasn't called me 'dude' in days. I have interpreted this as being preoccupied with something. I guess I was right; he was preoccupied with something: how to cover up murder and keep an eye on me. I just don't understand how he got involved in this mess.

He is placing a bunch of tubes in a rack, writing on them as he goes along. I peel my eyes away from him and put the jump drive in. I click open CURFEW folder, click on the appropriate document and start entering the data from the scintillation counter. I glance up now and then checking to make sure I know where Deke is and what he's doing.

My alarm goes off signaling the end of the incubation. I go over and do the next step of the experiment. It's almost lunch time. I don't want to leave the lab with all those downloaded documents on my computer. What if Deke discovers them?

Keeping watch out of the corner of my eye, I go back to my desk. I click on the document folder where I stored all of the files. I save all of them onto my jump drive and double check to make sure that I didn't forget any of the files. I then remove it from my computer tucking it into my jeans. I drag and drop all the pilfered files on my computer into the Recycle Bin and then empty the Recycle Bin. If he really wants to, I suppose he can still find them. But he'd only do that if he was really suspicious. I think I've done a good job of acting normal.

I stand up and say, "I'm going to lunch. I'll be back in a while."

"Mhmm," he says. He's writing some stuff in a notebook and does not glance at me as I walk past him.

I throw my jacket on and leave.

As I run to the T I place a call to Milagros. When she answers I say, "Are you free right now?"

"Yes, why?"

"I need you to get to my house, ASAP."

"Ok, why?" She repeats the question.

"Look, I don't have time to explain right now. I'm hopping on the T. Just come through the back way."

I start to hang up and say, "And make sure you aren't followed."

The doors slide closed on the subway car.

I come through my neighbor's yard arriving a few minutes before Milagros does. I'm not sure our secret entrance is secret anymore but I'm hoping it is. I haven't seen any signs of the bad guys.

When she comes through the door she says, "What's going on mommy?"

"You aren't going to believe what happened," I blurt out, "I used the wrong jump drive that I took off Deke's desk this morning. He has all the MEMPHIS files."

"Are you kidding?" Her eyes are enormous.

"I wish I were. I've been freaking out all morning."

"I don't understand. How is Deke connected to all this?"

"I have no idea but obviously he is."

We are both silent as we mull over this latest twist. Finally I say, "Well, that was the bad news. Now you want hear the good news?"

"There's good news?"

"Yup. I have all the files." I whip out the jump drive, brandishing it in the air with a flourish and then plug it into my home computer.

"You rock," she says and holds out her fist. I bump my fist to hers.

"So here's your job. Copy all the files onto my computer and then start looking at them."

"You got it." She sits down and starts the process. When she's done I direct her to delete the files off the jump drive so all that remains are the original files on Paul's research projects. While she does this I run to the bathroom.

She is just completing the task when I come back into the family room. I take the jump drive and slide it back in my pocket.

"I gotta get back. Don't call me. I'm not sure how much Deke will be around. I'll call you when I get a chance."

"'Bye," she says already engrossed in examining the documents.

Back in the lab I don't see Deke around. I do the next step of the experiment. I now have half an hour before I will have to go back to the bench. I sit down at my desk and click on the internet connection. I am determined to find the link between Deke and the files.

I go to a search engine and type in memphis clinical trial. The first and second choices don't look promising but the third one does. I click on it and it describes the MEMPHIS study.

I learn that MEMPHIS stands for meglitithiazole mediated physiologic increase in insulin secretion and sensitivity in type 1 diabetics. It's a study that tests a new drug combination. Not only does the drug have a new super form of meglitinides which stimulates insulin secretion. It also has a thiazolidinedione in it which improves the sensitivity of cells to insulin and allows for increased uptake of glucose where needed.

The beauty of this new meglitinidic drug is, in theory, that the few functioning insulin-producing pancreatic cells diabetics might still have are turned into super-factories. It's even been shown in an animal model to stimulate the cells to divide and grow. This coupled with a drug that increases glucose uptake into cells is a formidable double-whammy. I recall the second-hand report from Mike Donowski's roommate that he was able to decrease the amount of insulin he had needed to inject; a definite sign of disease improvement. It would be exciting if it weren't for all the appalling things that have been happening to the participants in the study.

I keep reading and discover the name of the pharmaceutical company that is backing the study. It's called Allagaro. I never asked Milagros the name of the company whose building we broke into. I go back to my search engine and type in Allagaro. I find the company website link and click on it. Sure enough it's located in Boxborough MA, right off 495. I navigate around on their website. I don't see very much that helps me. I am about to log off when I notice under the company logo it says "a subsidiary of Meade, Albright, Mutaki Industries".

My heart sinks. This is the connection. Deke is doing this for the almighty dollar. He *is* the cigar-smoking, scotch-drinking cruel executive. He is not my friend after all, he is my enemy. I have been a fool.

I can barely get my work done as my mind is filled with this latest revelation. Every little noise makes me jump. I keep expecting Deke to walk through the door.

Milagros texts me to say she has to leave for work and we haven't had an opportunity to discuss what she's found from studying the files. Both of us are working at the City lab tonight so we'll go on break together to update then.

Bobby has Brendan every Wednesday so I don't have to stop and collect him on my way home. I get off at my T stop and start my trek toward home.

Coming out of one of the shops is the handsome Tris McEvoy. We see each other at the same time.

Hi face breaks out into a genuine smile and he says, "Well hello Amanda Buscemi. Fancy meeting you out here on the street."

"Hi Tris. What a pleasant surprise. Do you live around here?"

"Just a few blocks over," he indicates the opposite direction of where I live.

"I'm sorry I haven't called you. I've been kind of busy."

"That's okay. I was worried about you after the restaurant fire. I looked for you outside but didn't see you."

Ah, yes, I all but forgot about the fire. I've been busy committing so many more felonies since then that the fire has dimmed by comparison. But how could I have forgotten to call a hunk like this?

"Oh, we were there. I guess we just got lost in the crowd," I hedge.

"Well I'm just glad you made it out safe," he gives me the thousand watt smile again. "Hey, can I buy you dinner tonight?"

"Oh, I'm sorry! I'm working tonight," I say. Actually, I realize that I am very, very sorry. Here is this guy who is not only good-looking but appears to have some style and class. Opportunities like this don't come around all the time so I say, "How about tomorrow?"

"That would be great. And how about you give me your number so we can make plans?"

He takes out a Blackberry and types in my cell phone number as I recite it to him.

"Perfect. I look forward to tomorrow."

"Me too," I say.

We make our goodbyes and I continue on my way toward home.

I only have a few minutes before I have to leave. I grab an apple out of the frig and throw a load of laundry in the washer. I am way behind on chores.

I arrive at City lab right at five. I check to see what bench I am working and then head over to it. I see Milagros. Our eyes connect. I see worry and fear radiating from her, even from this distance.

We take the late dinner break at seven thirty. In the cafeteria we buy our meals and sit down across from each other and away from everyone else.

Milagros starts first, "I didn't have as much time as I would like to figure everything out but it looks like the MEMPHIS 1 study started first, a couple years ago. It was a much smaller study. It looked successful, if I'm reading the results correctly. That must have been why they made it a national, multi-site study recruiting thousands. They named it MEMPHIS 2. But it looks like they started tracking BNP's right away. So maybe there was a fatality or two in MEMPHIS 1, but it wasn't documented. Then they started doing lots of blood collections. I think they were trying to figure out why there were negative outcomes."

She takes a bite of food and continues after she's swallowed it, "One of the things they are looking at is if there's genetic predisposition."

"The ones I looked up yesterday," I say, "VAMP8, et cetera."

She nods. "They also looked at a viral component. I saw they tested for actual viral infections such as adenovirus,"

"Doesn't that cause the common cold?"

"Yes. I wasn't sure about that one. It's a respiratory virus. The medicine is inhaled but I didn't see any association with heart disease. Also they looked at the coxsakie virus. That can cause an inflammation of the heart called myocarditis so at least that one makes sense. And they looked at cytomegalovirus, also linked to heart disease I found out. That might be why they were looking at CD4 counts – to check the immune status in the presence of viral infection."

"So I'm trying to make sense of this," I say. "If they know some people are susceptible to heart failure as a direct or indirect consequence of using this drug, why would they continue with the study? I mean take this to its logical conclusion: even if you clean the data up a little bit and get it past the FDA, people are going to start dying once this hits the market. We have at least two instances we know that had adverse outcomes. Two out of what, two or three thousand people in this study? That's 0.1% occurrence rate. How many diabetics are there in the U.S. alone? Probably tens of millions. We are now talking about potentially hundreds, if not thousands of people dying as a result of taking this drug. Even if you don't care about people, you care about the money. A law suit would put these jokers right out of business."

"That's if a link can be *proven* between taking the drug and going into heart failure."

"I guess that's what they call risk management," I say. "How cold and calculating do you have to be to do that?"

"Apparently very, chica, 'cuz there's more to this story."

I've put down the sandwich I am eating. My appetite is completely gone. I adjust my baseball cap that is starting to feel like a tight band around my head and say, "What else?"

"There is one more study."

I look at her. "Is that the one in the folder labeled AWE RRED?"

"Yes, it stands for Accelerated Weight Reduction with Replacement Energy Drink."

"A weight loss study?"

"Not just any weight loss study. The protocol states that it is looking to see if participants who ingest an energy drink half an hour prior to each meal have greater weight loss than those that drink water."

"Ok..."

"But that isn't what the study is really doing."

"What's it doing?"

"They've divided the participants into four groups: group one drinks the energy drink, group two drinks the energy drink with meglitinides supplement added, group three has the thiazolidinediones added, and group four has the drug combo added."

"They're trying to isolate which drug is causing the problem."

"Yes. And they are eliminating the diabetic component to get a clearer picture of what's going on."

"What have the results been?"

"They are monitoring with BNP and it looks to be about the same number of people having increased levels of BNP in this study as those participating in the MEMPHIS study."

Before I can say anything more my cell phone rings. I look and see that it's Linda. I answer it and hear Linda on the other end of the phone yelling over a bunch of background noise that I have to come home right away.

I listen in stunned silence and say, "I'll be right there." I close up the phone. I am now in complete shock as I stand up, looking blankly in front of me.

"Mommy, what's going on?" I vaguely hear Milagros' voice through the fog that threatens to engulf me.

I lower my eyes to meet hers and choke out, "My house is on fire!"

Chapter 19:

Burnin' ring of fire

(*Ring of Fire,* June Carter as sung by Johnny Cash)

Milagros drives me from the hospital to my house. When we get there the street is blocked off with fire engines, police cars and an ambulance.

She pulls over and I jump out of her car and start running down the sidewalk. I dart around groupings of people that are standing outside watching. I get close and see Bobby and Brendan standing out in the street near one of the fire trucks. I call to them but they can't hear me over the commotion. I keep moving toward them, pushing my way through the onlookers.

Finally Brendan sees me, breaks away from Bobby and comes running toward me. His face is dirty from the smoke and tears have streaked rivers down his cheeks.

"Mom!" he yells as he runs, crashing into my arms. I pick him up and bury my face into his neck.

"Oh baby I'm so glad you're okay," I sob.

"Mom, my drums were in there!" He cries.

I set him down and get on my knees so we're eye level, "I know, I know, we'll get you another set. Don't worry!" I am so grateful that he is safe I would promise him the world.

Bobby has come over now. I look up at him, "What happened? Were you in the house?"

"No, I was just bringing him back when we saw the fire trucks pulling in."

"What started the fire?"

"I have no idea. No one was home. Linda and I arrived around the same time, right as the fire trucks were pulling up."

We turn and look at the fire fighting efforts. My breath catches in my throat as I try to bite back a sob. Firemen are working at the walls with hatchets. Hoses are pumping plumes of water into the house.

I see Linda making her way toward us. Her face is covered in soot as well and as our eyes meet I see the pain and despair in them. When she gets to me we hug each other and cry. It looks like everything is gone. So much for our home. It is even more Linda's loss than mine. She owned the house, I just paid her rent.

I feel a hand on my back and turn to see Milagros standing there.

"I'm so sorry! What an awful thing," she says with a look of compassion in her eyes.

"Thanks," I sniff, "it looks like all our things are gone."

"But at least everyone is fine, yes? And that's what you have insurance for. You do have insurance?" she looks at Linda.

Linda nods and wipes her eyes, "I just can't imagine what could have caused the fire."

"The fire marshal will figure that out," Bobby says.

We silently watch while the firemen chop into the house to vent it and then flood it with streams of water. The smoke grows thicker as they get more and more of the fire extinguished.

Some of our neighbors come up to us offering condolences. The house on either side of ours is virtually untouched. A testament, I suppose, to the speed at which the town's fire department responded.

At some point someone puts a blanket around my shoulders. I stand there shivering more from the shock than being cold.

Finally the fire is out and the firemen are packing up their hoses. The fire chief comes over and speaks to us. He reminds us that we can't go back to look for anything as it is too hot. We can come over the following day once the marshal has inspected it.

We stand alone on the street as the last emergency vehicle pulls away.

"Come and stay at my house tonight," Bobby says.

Linda declines as she's already called her daughter who is coming to pick her up. I accept his offer with a grateful smile.

"You can stay with me if you'd like," Milagros says.

"Thanks but I think I'll take Bobby up on his offer," I say, "Brendan will probably want to be with both of us."

Reluctantly she gives me, Brendan and Linda hugs and then walks back up the street to her car.

Linda's daughter pulls up and eventually she leaves with her. Bobby goes to get his truck which is a little ways down the street. Brendan and I take one final look at the remains of the house. Smoke oozes from windows and the gashes in the walls.

The fire is out and the cold night air is sinking into our bones. We are shivering when Bobby pulls up. We get into his truck and he turns the heater on full blast. Brendan and I huddle together to try to warm up.

Now that the shock is wearing off questions start whispering in the back of my mind: what if the fire was intentional? What if it was the Allagaro bad guys that set it? And what if this is their warning shot across the bow and next time it'll be a direct hit?

Chapter 20:

When all you got to keep is strong
Move along

(*Move Along,* All American Rejects)

I wake up at the crack of dawn the next day. Brendan is curled up against me like a kitten. Bobby insisted Brendan and I take his bed and he slept in Brendan's bedroom.

Quietly I extricate myself from the covers and creep out of the bedroom. I head down the stairs to the kitchen. Bobby is already there with a fresh pot of coffee made. A little television sits on the counter and the news is on.

I walk in and say good morning. He returns the greeting and tells me to help myself to the coffee. I fix myself a cup and take a seat at the table where I can see the screen.

"Did we make the news?" I ask.

"No, I guess it wasn't exciting enough."

"Mpmf. It was exciting enough for me," I say sipping my coffee. How weird is this, having coffee with Bobby in the morning after sleeping in his bed last night.

We watch the sports, weather and traffic reports in a relatively comfortable silence.

"Are you going to send Bren to school today?" He asks.

"No I don't think so. I want him to get as much sleep as he can."

We are silent a little longer as the newscasters recap the latest awfulness that's happened: a murder in Dorchester, a pedophile arrested sixteen years after he's done his deeds, and a business man is exposed for hiring illegal aliens.

Bobby clears his throat and says, "I know it's kind of early for you to be figuring everything out, where to live and all that, but have you given it any thought?"

My stomach sinks. Besides losing all our stuff, we've lost one of the most important things: a place to live.

"No, not really." I give a heavy sigh and rub my face. "I guess that's the first thing I have to figure out."

"Well, I 'm bringing it up because you guys can stay here as long as you want."

"Where would you put us? You only have three bedrooms."

"I was thinking maybe Brendan could share my room and you could have Brendan's. I don't mind. It'd be nice to have the little guy around more."

"What about Pete?"

"I called him at the station. He's fine with it."

"Jeez, this is awfully generous of you, Bobby."

He makes a shrugging motion, "Just think about it. If nothing else stay until you can find a decent place to live."

"Okay, thanks."

"Later I'll call the fire chief and find out when we can get over there to see what can be salvaged. In the meantime let's have some breakfast."

He extends his hand across the table to me. I slide my hand in his and he gives it a reassuring squeeze.

Late morning Bobby, Brendan and I head over to the wreckage that once upon a time was our home.

I called Paul to let him know what happened and that I needed to take the day off. He told me to take as many days off as I needed.

We pull up to the ruins. Linda is already there speaking with the fire marshal. After we introduce ourselves he tells us that we can look for anything that survived. That he'll know in a day or two what happened.

I walk up the driveway and look at my car. The tires on the right side, the side that was facing the house, are flat and the paint is bubbled and scorched. I sigh and turn away

I join Linda in the wreckage. I look back to see that Bobby is still talking to the fire marshal. Brendan is standing with him. I told him to stay back since I don't want him getting hurt.

"Linda, I'm afraid this is all my fault," I say as we turn over a charred piece of wood that was our kitchen table.

"Why do you say that?"

"Milagros and I have been doing some more digging and there really is something going on."

She is crouched down and pulling on something. She stops what she's doing looks up at me.

I shift my feet and self-consciously fold my arms, "We kind of broke into this pharmaceutical company named Allagaro a couple nights ago." Slowly Linda stands to face me and I spill my story: the files in Steven Morris' office, the escape, my discovery that Deke had the files also, my copying them onto our home computer. "So I think they've been watching me and they torched the house to either warn me off or to divert my attention away from any more investigating." I conclude my confession.

By this time tears are swimming in my eyes. "I am so sorry. This is all my fault," I say gesturing to the carnage. "You have every right to be really mad at me."

While I've been speaking Linda has remained quiet, regarding me steadily. Finally she says, "Well I don't know if that is the reason our house burned down. I think we should leave that up to the fire marshal to investigate and decide the cause. I don't think you should jump to conclusions."

I let out the breath I have been holding. I thought she was going to be really angry with me. I mean, she should; I indirectly caused her to lose everything.

"However," she continues, "if there really is something going on I think you should go to the police. You shouldn't be taking matters into your own hands. If these guys are dangerous, and I'm not saying I am buying this story completely, but if they are, your first responsibility is to your family. What if Brendan was home? What if they do something to you? You want Brendan to grow up without his mother? You seriously need to reconsider." She pauses and looks around at the cold sodden debris that was once our home. "Let's not worry about what caused the fire right now. Let's just work on salvaging what we can."

I nod my head. We both turn back to the task at hand. We lift and move charred wooden beams and sections of dry wall, calling to each other as we find an item that is relatively unscathed. We begin creating a little pile on the sidewalk out front.

I find an album that I'd put together of Philip's school days; the best papers and art work from each grade. A little tear leaks out the corner of my eye and slides down my cheek. I sniff back more tears as I place it in the growing pile even though it's charred and dripping wet.

Linda calls to me. I look over and she holds up a warped cymbal from Brendan's drum set. I nod and she drops it before Brendan can see.

We finally finish and go back out to the sidewalk. Bobby has put everything in a couple boxes and Mr. Ziegler has come out and is talking with Bobby.

"Girls," he rumbles in his gravelly voice, "the missus and I feel awfully bad for you. We're sorry that this happened."

"Thanks Mr. Z," I say.

He hands me a thick envelope and says, "I went around this morning before people left for work and this is what I collected from all your neighbors."

I take a peak inside. It is stuffed with money.

"Oh Mr. Z," I say starting to hand it back to him, "this is too generous. We can't accept this."

"Nonsense," he replies pushing it back toward me. "There's all kinds of stuff you'll need right away before your insurance claim kicks in. People wouldn't have given if they didn't want to."

Right. I picture Mr. Z marching to each neighbor's house, cigar clamped in his teeth telling people how much they were going to give. Probably made them open their wallets in front of him so he could pluck out their 'donations', leaving only enough for coffee and a bagel and telling them they can stop at the bank during lunch.

"Well, thank you."

He gruffly squeezes my shoulder, pats Linda's arm and ruffles Brendan's hair before leaving us.

Brendan helps Linda get her box over to her daughter's car.

Bobby turns to me with an odd little smile on his lips. "Mr. Ziegler is under the impression that you two are lesbians. Is there anything you'd like to tell me?"

I roll my eyes, "The man is incorrigible. I can't convince him otherwise. He has all the neighbors convinced that we're lovers."

He smirks, "Well, while you stay with me I can't have any of those wild lesbian parties. I live in a quiet Catholic neighborhood."

I narrow my eyes to let him know I don't find this amusing. "I'll try to keep it under control," I say, sarcasm dripping from my voice.

We get the boxes back to Bobby and Pete's house and unload them into the kitchen so Brendan and I can go through our salvaged stuff more thoroughly.

Bobby runs out for some groceries and I go take a shower. I peel off my smoky clothes and put my bra and panties in some soapy water in the bathroom sink.

I'm glad I was wearing my new Victoria Secret things yesterday so that they survived. My boobs have never looked better. It's amazing what a decent bra can do. My sophomore year in high school was the epic boob growing year for me. As freshmen my friends and I jokingly formed the Itty Bitty Titty Club. When we returned in September to start tenth grade I was a 34A. By November I was a B cup and March, a C. As the remnants of the snow disappeared my friends informed me I was no longer a member of the club. I argued I was still an IBT member in spirit but they were having none of that. Ever since then I have been in denial. I always squeeze the girls into a C cup bra. The expert bar fitter at Vickie's got me to try on a D. The transformation was startling.

I wash my hair with the shampoo Javier made me buy and scrub until I'm sure all the smoke is washed away. As I get out of the shower my cell phone rings.

Without looking at the number I answer, "Hey, sweetie," assuming it's Milagros. She called me while I was picking through the debris at my house. I had told her I would call back and then forgot to do it.

"Hello," I hear Tris's rich voice come through, "that's a nice greeting!"

"Oh! I thought you were my girlfriend," I say and actually blush.

He chuckles and then says, "I guess that explains it. I was calling about dinner tonight."

That's right; I was supposed to have a date tonight. I let out a little sigh and say, "I'm sorry, Tris, I'm going to have to take a rain check on that dinner."

"How come?" he asks with, I believe, a twinge of disappointment.

"My house burned down last night."

"What?"

I repeat myself even though I know he heard me the first time. He was only expressing disbelief. I feel as though I should be pinched to see if I'm dreaming; like I am living outside of reality.

"How terrible! How did it happen?"

"We won't know for a while yet." Although I have my suspicions, I say to myself.

"Was anyone hurt?"

"No, thankfully. But you can understand how I might not be in the mood to go out tonight."

"Sure, sure. But maybe that would be the best medicine..." he trails off with the suggestion left on the table. I smile a little. I'll give him an A for effort.

"That's really sweet. But, honestly, no. I can't."

"Maybe another time?"

"Of course and thank you for understanding."

We make our goodbyes and I hang up. This is the story of my life; wrong place or wrong time. I wonder if I'll ever hear from Tris McEvoy again. He'll probably lose interest and move on to some less disaster-prone woman.

I towel off the rest of the way and slide into a pair of Bobby's boxers and tee shirt so I can wash my one set of clothing.

I gather up my stuff and open the door. I run into Pete in the hallway.

"Hey," he says.

"Hey back. Thanks for letting Brendan and me stay with you guys for a while."

"Sure, no problem," he says not really looking me in the eye. "Sorry about the fire, that's a tough break."

He moves past me and climbs the stairs to the bedrooms.

I go into the family room where Brendan is playing a video game. I get him to turn it off and go take a shower, instructing him to toss his clothes out into the hall so I can wash them.

He bounces down the hallway, seemingly unaffected by the events of the last twenty four hours. Wishing I could recover that quickly I schlump into the kitchen and put the kettle on for some tea. I hear Brendan toss the clothes into the hallway making airplane bombing noises. I go collect his clothes as he turns the shower on. I hear him break into song, "I'm bringin' sexy back, yeah! Them other boys don't know how to act, yeah!"

A pretty good Justin Timberlake impression, I have to say.

I put our clothes into the washer and get that going. The tea kettle starts to whistle as I walk back into the kitchen and Bobby comes in laden with groceries. I help him unpack while our tea steeps.

"Pete's home," I say.

"Yeah, I saw his truck."

I lower my voice, "I don't think he's very happy that we're here."

"What makes you say that?"

"I just didn't get a very welcoming vibe from him."

"He'll get over it."

"I don't want to cause friction between you. I can go stay with Milagros if this is a problem."

"Amanda, don't worry about it. Pete isn't upset with me because you're staying here."

"Well he wouldn't even look me in the eye," I say, holding out my piece of evidence.

"That's because he's in love with you."

"Huh?"

"He probably can't look you in the eye," he explains patiently, "because he's been drooling over you for years. Now that you're staying here, it probably makes him uncomfortable that you're in such close proximity. But it's more than just an attraction; he's been mooning over you lately."

"Ha! That's a good one," I reply sarcastically. "Has he ever said anything to you?"

"No, he wouldn't. But lately he's been asking about you more. Wanting to know if I know where you are, if you're seeing anyone, stuff like that."

"That's silly. You're wrong. He's always done that flirty thing with me but that's just goofing around. You should know better than that."

"Think what you want, but I'm telling you: he's fallen for you."

I make a shooing motion with my hand. What a ridiculous notion. Pete chases tail. He flirts with me for the following reason: flirting is reflex for him. Some men whistle to pass the time; others jingle the coins in their pocket. Pete flirts. It's what he does. End of story.

Ignoring Bobby I fix my tea and head to the bathroom. Now that Mr. Sexy Back has vacated it I can get in there to put on some makeup. Oddly, most of the bathroom stuff survived; maybe all the tile and porcelain protected it. Or maybe even God decided I deserved some mercy.

I take extra care applying my makeup. I try to do it the same way that the makeup counter lady showed me. I apply an extra coating of foundation to my forehead. It is still purple but the edges of the bruise are turning yellowish. Just lovely. When I am done I survey my handiwork. I think I did alright. I don't look like a circus clown or a prostitute – that's my grading scale – so I zip my makeup bag and move onto my hair.

Done in the bathroom I move our stuff from the washer to the dryer. I get a pot roast with potatoes and carrots ready to put in the oven. We have agreed to go out clothes shopping and I figure the pot roast can cook while we are out. We can have an early dinner when we get back. Bobby has to be at the station by seven that evening.

Oh goody, an evening with Pete. Just what the doctor ordered...

Chapter 21:

Hello, hello
I'm at a place called Vertigo
(*Vertigo*, U2)

I wake up the next morning disoriented. I sit up and look around realizing where I am. Flopping onto my back I let out a big sigh and rub my eyes. Oh God, it isn't a dream. Here I am living with my ex-husband and the biggest skirt chaser that ever lived. And then Bobby decides to tell me his crazy idea: that Pete's in love with me! How ridiculous, I think derisively.

Last night's dinner, as well as the whole evening, was uneventful. Bobby left for work but Philip had come for dinner and stayed afterward so he and Brendan were good buffers for the uncomfortable feeling I was getting from Pete. I still don't buy Bobby's theory but I'm not sure why Pete is acting kind of jiggy around me.

I get out of bed and tenderly tread down the hall to the bathroom. My ankle feels much better so I peal off the ace bandage. I examine the suspect limb and decide that I'll put the bandage back on after my shower just for the extra support.

Today, I decide, Brendan needs to get back to school. I make a pot of coffee and call Bobby on his cell phone while it's brewing. We agree that as soon as he returns from his overnight shift he'll drive Brendan to school and then drop me off at Milagros'. She and I finally spoke the previous evening and she wanted me to come over to her place in the morning.

When I get to her condo she buzzes me in. Greeting me at the door Milagros has her hair caught up in a clip with a few loose strands curled around her face. Navy blue sweats complete her look of casual gorgeousness. Even dressed down she looks terrific. She offers me a cup of coffee and I accept.

I walk the few paces it takes to get to her living room area. And once again take in her décor. The L-shaped couch is eggplant purple, ultra-suede and super stylish. Milagros can go out on a fashion limb and will wind up making a bold statement instead of a faux pas. Once she brings my mug into the living room we sit down kitty corner to each other. I take a sip and wait expectantly for her to tell me why she wanted me to come over. It doesn't take her long, only seconds, before she says, "I've been going through the notes I took while reading the files at your place."

The fire has destroyed my computer and with it, all the Allagaro files. This is a major set back. If we go to the police with nothing to back up our claims they are going to file it right in the trash and laugh us out onto the street. And even if they decide to follow up, they would have to do things the legal way; you know, crazy shit like getting a search warrant. I doubt there's enough probable cause, or whatever they call it, to get a search warrant. I envision the DA going before a judge to ask for a search warrant: "Well you see, your honor, these two crackpots claim that there's this evil corporation. And that people are dying because this here evil corporation doesn't want to give up on a drug study they got going on..." "What's that? Uh, no your Honor, there is no evidence. They claim it's all been altered or destroyed. We have only their word."

Yup, that'll work.

"What do you mean, following up?" I ask bringing myself back to the current conversation, "What was there to follow up on?"

She never mentioned that she took notes. I peer at her over the brim of my coffee mug as I go to take another sip of her Kona coffee that she grinds just prior to brewing. It is close to ambrosia and I make a point of never refusing a cup when she offers.

Milagros replies, "When I was looking at the files for the test results, I wrote down anyone that had positive results in any category."

Tucking a long piece of escaped hair behind her ear she pulls out a piece of notebook paper from a folder she's been holding on her lap and lays it on the cocktail table so we can both look at it.

"See, this one," she points to the first handwritten line on the paper. "This one had an elevated BNP."

"Uh huh," I say looking at it. There's a number, 07-00278, then more numbers, B = 91 CMV +.

"If there was any other test that was positive I wrote that down as well." She gives me a moment to digest this. Then she points to another line in the middle of the page.

12-00151 has a positive HNRPLU1. The BNP is low, though, at 2.8.

I flip the paper over. The back is three quarters filled as well as the front. We have, by my estimate, about fifty to sixty participants that she has singled out for one reason or another.

"I have no idea what this means," I say. I lay the sheet down.

"I know, that's what I thought at first too, querida. It was all just a jumbled mess. I've been looking at this data for the last twenty four hours and it's been driving me crazy. So what I did was I created a spreadsheet and put each person in with any results I recorded to see if there's something that stands out."

She removes another sheet from her folder. It's a spreadsheet that has all the data on it and some of the numbers are highlighted. It appears similar to the original document that we hijacked from Morris' office, just with a lot less information on it.

"So I decided the first thing I should do is prioritize by the test that indicates heart failure, BNP. I figured that was what got me interested in this in the first place so I should stick with that."

"I agree. That's what I would have done."

"Then I started looking at the two people we know had heart failure and see what other test results were positive for them."

"Wait a minute. How could you tell which of these were Mike Donowski and Julio Rodriquez?"

She draws another notebook sheet out of the folder and says, "Because, chica, I found the key as well."

She has the key. Why didn't she tell me before?

I push aside my irritation and grab the sheet out of her hand. I scan down the list. I find Mike Donowski's name first. The corresponding number that is used to identify him in the study is 07-01113. I go back to the spreadsheet with all the test results and find his number. His BNP is 330. The other test result that is positive is VAMP8 var. Possibly var stands for variant. I've seen that designation before.

"What's with this triangle shape?" I ask. After VAMP8 var she had written $\Delta = 55\%$.

"It was next to the BNP result so I wrote it down."

"Maybe it means a change in BNP levels?" A triangle shape, called delta after the Greek letter for which it represents, is used in the sciences to indicate change. If you said the delta temperature today was 20 degrees, that would mean the temperature changed by 20 degrees.

Milagros agrees that it is a reasonable guess which is why she wrote it down.

I scan further and find Julio Rodriguez, ID number 09-00882. I go to the other sheet and find his test results again: $BNP = 117$, Δ 48%, HNRPUL1 +.

"So both Mike and Julio had positive BNP's," I state. "They both had a genetic marker that predisposed them to coronary disease. *And* they both had a fairly large change in their BNP result. I would think that is significant since a person's BNP shouldn't change in such a short period of time. According to this, Mike's delta BNP was 55% so that means," I do a quick mental calculation, "that the previous BNP result was approximately 170."

"Yes, that's exactly what I was thinking too," Milagros agrees.

"Okay," I do a mental knuckle-cracking and pencil in 'previous BNP = 170' on the line next to VAMP8, "his result at the time of death was just under 1,000? So what would be the percent change?"

Milagros jumps up, runs to her desk and comes back with a calculator. She punches in some numbers and says, "If he goes from 330 to 980 that is almost a 300% increase."

"Wow, that's huge. He went from 170 to 330 to 980. So there must be some sort of multiplying effect; once the heart failure kicks in, it gets worse. And it gets worse quickly."

"If the drug causes the first injury to the heart, maybe continuing to take the drug speeds up the disease progression," she adds.

I look down and find Julio's ID results again. "He was 117 and had a 48% increase over the previous result. What would the previous result be?"

"79," comes the reply after she plugged the numbers into the calculator. I write that on his line of results.

"Hmm. If he experienced the same situation as Mike his next BNP would have been about 350."

"Actually it was 322."

"You got the results from the Florida coroner's office?"

"Yes, I forgot to tell you with everything else that happened."

"Damn. That's actually pretty scary that we could predict his BNP number."

She nods. We both sit for a few moments lost in our thoughts. I am troubled by how we haven't seen anything that pin-pointed the exact pathway that's causing the escalating BNP numbers. But maybe that is what's also troubling the study investigators. Based on the data we've seen, maybe they are thinking that if only they could find out what is causing the heart failure they can correct it somehow – like excluding a certain population of people – and have a successful study. They'd be one step closer to releasing a new super drug that can help possibly millions of people. And, more importantly to them, I'm sure, make an enormous stack of money.

I have to admit, this is interesting as an intellectual exercise. That's if you can forget people are dying due to this.

"Maybe," I say thinking out loud, "maybe the drug or what the drug is suspended in has a cardio-toxicity for certain people."

"You'd think they would have looked at that."

"Yeah, I know."

"Well what about the AWE RRED study? Did you get a chance to look at that?"

"Not as much. But like I said, they were looking at BNP numbers on these people too."

"Did anyone have increased BNP or a large delta BNP?"

"Yes, these last three entries." She points to the bottom of the spread sheet.

One had a BNP of 88. The ΔBNP was 5%. No significant change. The second one was 104 with ΔBNP of -17%. That would signify an improvement. The last entry was 56 and the delta was 68%.

"It looks like we might have something with this last person."

"That's what I'm thinking too."

"So we have one person out of how many in the AWE RRED study?"

"Fifteen hundred."

"Ok, one person out of fifteen hundred that is showing the same outcome as in the MEMPHIS study. That's actually less than our estimated 0.1% occurrence rate."

"*But*," Milagros says. "if you think about it, you wouldn't use the whole fifteen hundred as the calculation."

"Why?"

"There's four groups in the study. Right? Well, this person is part of the group that received the drug combo. So you would only want to calculate using one quarter of the fifteen hundred. That would be three hundred seventy five. One in three hundred seventy five is," she pushes the calculator buttons, "0.3%."

"That makes sense. But we have to realize that this is only one person so it could be just a coincidence."

"True," she agrees. "But remember that when I was writing all this down I was using BNP as my criterion. I only recorded anyone that had a BNP over fifty. There might have been more that were under fifty but had a big delta."

Hmm. She has a point. I wish we still had the files so we could look at them.

She flips the spreadsheet back over to the front and using her finger scans down the column with the heading Δ. We find five additional participants that have delta BNP's of greater than 30% on the front and a whopping seven on the back.

"We didn't initially look at these people because we were focused on the BNP result. But if the delta BNP is signaling an approaching case of heart failure, then all these people are at risk."

"And should immediately stop taking the drug," I add. I grab up the calculator, "How many participants are in the MEMPHIS study?"

"Almost four thousand."

"Okay. So if we use a change in BNP of 30% or greater as another determinant of negative outcome, then we have twelve additional people." I plug in those numbers, "That's a 0.35% rate."

"Is 30% a reasonable cutoff?" She asks.

"I don't know."

We go back to top and discover that most participants' Δ is close to zero; ranging from -17% up to 9%. There is nothing in the teens and then a 22%, two 25%'s, and a 26% that we had overlooked before.

I recalculate the rate and come up with 0.45%. I show Milagros the result.

"Wow, and we have to realize that I wasn't focusing on the delta BNP when I went through all four thousand participant results. I was using other criteria. So there might be more victims that we haven't identified yet."

We're both solemn as we ponder this. It could be doubled, tripled, hell even ten times what we have on this paper. I was starting to feel hungry for lunch but the thought of all these people unwittingly taking a drug, thinking it is helping them when in fact it's attacking their heart makes me feel queasy.

I look over to Milagros. "Boy what I wouldn't give to see those files again."

"You and me both, mommy," Milagros says. "That's why I went over to your lab to see if I could retrieve the files off your computer."

My mouth drops open in astonishment. "Wait a minute. You know that I stole the files off of Deke, therefore *Deke is one of the bad guys!* So do ya *think*, for one little, eensy teensy weensy moment that going back to the lab might be just a little bit dangerous?" I look at her with bug eyes.

"Don't worry; I had a good cover story."

I lean forward, "Really. I'd love to hear but first let me ask you, did you ever wonder why Deke was in possession of those files?" I give a bit of a dramatic pause here to get her full attention. "Well here's a news flash: Allagaro is a subsidiary of Mead Albright Mutaki. And Deke? His name is Decatur Albright; as in the Albright part of Mead Albright Mutaki. His father is one of the founders of that company."

She looks at me dumbfounded and, for once, is speechless. I sit back on the couch, grimly satisfied that I have finally brought her up short. My gratification is short-lived, though, as I realize that if I had told her about Deke's relationship with Allagaro that evening in the cafeteria she might not have acted so impetuously. But then the fire happened and it slipped my mind since then. Would knowing this have stopped her from going to the lab? That I don't know.

I rub my temples, where the most significant pounding is occurring. I wonder just how much higher my blood pressure has to go before I'll have a stroke.

"Alright well you can't take it back. And you made it out in one piece so tell me your story, Nancy Drew."

Milagros recovers and says, "I went in and Deke wasn't there. So I looked in and around his desk for the jump drive but couldn't find it."

"Did you look in the USB port on the side of the computer?" I ask, remembering my oversight.

"Of course, mommy, that's the first place I looked. So I went over to your computer, logged on and started looking for the files you deleted."

"Wait a minute. How did you log on? You don't know my password."

"I figured you had it written somewhere. And you did, it was under your mouse pad. Otherwise I would have called you and asked for it."

Great. Outwitted in two seconds. Am I really that lame?

"So I was just kind of cruising around in your computer. I didn't really know what I was doing but figured it was worth a shot. That's when Deke came in."

I draw in my breath like I'm a kid being told a scary story around the camp fire. "What happened?"

"He asked who I was and what I was doing. So I introduced myself and said you sent me over to get a personal document off the computer for you. He told me that they had a computer virus that wiped out a bunch of stuff and that your computer was one of the affected ones. They had to put in a new hard drive and so you wouldn't be able to recover any files that were on the old hard drive."

"This is bad."

"I know."

"No, I mean this is really, really, *really* bad. I didn't realize that they knew we had the files. I thought that *if* they burned my house down, and I don't know if that's true, but if they did it, that it was a warning or maybe they were trying to distract me. But they also got rid of my work computer. I think we can be pretty certain they know we have or had the files."

"Well, they did their job because now we have very little to work with."

"And even less we can take to the police."

We sit there in depressed silence.

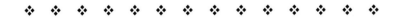

We decide we need some comfort food so head out to a café down the street. We start with some soup and then share a plate of fries. We try to counterbalance that with salads. I am sure that this is fine for Milagros but I will gain ten pounds and it'll take six months to lose.

We don't talk much during lunch. We are both a bit overwhelmed with a feeling of impotence and need a mental break.

We've just arrived back at her apartment when I have a sudden thought, "What if we have a way of contacting at least some of the study participants?"

"What do you mean?"

"Well, we still have Tyler Brooks. Maybe if we give him the list of affected participants we can get him to go on that blog and track down as many of them as possible."

"That's a good idea! We could warn everyone and shut the study down."

I get a little adrenaline rush from having a plan.

"But do you think that would really work querida?"

"I think that might be the best plan and the *only* plan we have," I assert.

"Think about this: these guys are computer savvy. They put a virus in the university computer system and corrupted your computer to the point it had to be replaced. So we have to assume that they are probably monitoring the blog site. If we have Tyler put out a blog they will probably shut it down really fast."

"And we get Tyler involved," I say. "I don't like putting anyone else at risk like we are."

We sit back on her couch dispiritedly. Hell, it wasn't such a good plan after all.

Milagros says, "All we have are names. We have no idea what part of the country these people live. If we did we might be able to track them down individually."

We are silent for a while as we contemplate this impossible hurdle.

"Wait a minute," I say. I grab up the spreadsheet again, my mind clicking away.

"What is it?" Milagros asks.

Holding up my finger to indicate I need a minute, I scan down the list and see the pattern. "This might work!" I exclaim.

"Tell me!" Milagros cries.

"Okay, okay. So you see Mike Donowski's ID? 07-01113?"

"Yes?"

"Now look at Julio's: 09-00882."

"Okay."

"What are the study sites again?"

"Boston, Miami, St. Chicago, Seattle, Baltimore, um, Houston and San Jose."

My heart is pounding. "So what if the first part of the ID is a site identifier? The numbers go north to south and east to west."

"How so?"

"Well, Boston is site zero seven. Moving down, Baltimore would be zero eight."

"And Miami zero nine!" She catches my excitement.

"And it keeps going that way with Chicago being ten and Houston eleven."

"So these two people that start with zero eight, we know their names. We at least have narrowed it down to a region of the country – Baltimore!.."

"And we can try looking for them on the internet phone directories. I bet some of the names are unique enough that we would be able to find them relatively easily."

"Chica, you are a genius!"

Just then my cell phone rings. I look at the number. It looks familiar but I can't place it.

"Hello?" I answer it.

"Amanda!"

"Oh, hi Tris," I say as I glance over at Milagros who cocks an eyebrow at me. I hold up my finger, telling her to wait a minute.

"How have you been?"

"Okay, considering," I say.

"Were you able to salvage anything from the fire?"

"Not much, just a few things. I'm just glad that no one was home and the fire hadn't spread to any of my neighbors' houses." I say. Milagros gets up and goes into her bathroom. I hear the faucet run and a cabinet door close.

"Yes," he says, "I'm sure it could have been much worse."

We talk for a few more minutes about the fire. I haven't heard from the fire marshal so I still don't know the cause. Yes, I have a place to stay.

Milagros wanders back into the room. She now has different clothes on.

Then he says, "I've been thinking of you all day. I know how awful I would feel if this happened to me. And I thought, I should just call and see if you'd like to go out for dinner tonight. I know your schedule might be all thrown out of whack but you still have to eat."

He pauses. I don't know what to say. It seems a little strange to be considering anything as normal as a dinner date when my whole life just literally went up in flames.

"Maybe," he continues as though sensing my reluctance, "maybe we can have some laughs and I can help you forget about your troubles for a few hours. What do you say?"

"Dinner tonight?" I say, finally finding my voice, "Well...I'm not sure." Milagros is gesturing wildly. I say, "Can you hold on a minute?"

I cover the mouthpiece and say, "What!" in a hoarse whisper.

"Is that the guy from the restaurant?"

"Yes."

"Well you should go out with him!"

"But we're working on all this stuff," I motion to the papers laying scattered on her cocktail table.

"I have to go to work. You should go out and have a nice dinner. Forget about all this terrible stuff for a few hours," she says.

"But I could be looking up all the names tonight so we can make the phone calls tomorrow."

"We can do that first thing in the morning. Go have a nice time! You deserve it."

She says this with such emphasis that I actually believe her. I *do* deserve a nice dinner out; especially with a handsome, charming, sophisticated man such as Tris McEvoy.

Still I hesitate. I mean, lives are hanging in the balance. Shouldn't I be working tirelessly to find each person I can and warn them?

"Go," Milagros mouths the word to me.

Caving in I get back on the cell phone, "Tris? Sorry about that. Yes, I can go to dinner tonight."

"Excellent! Any ideas where we should go?"

"Well, I don't have a lot of clothes right now so I'll be in jeans. Let's not make it anywhere too fancy. Oh, and I'm living in Cambridge right now so let's do something that's within walking distance or I can take the T."

"I can pick you up..."

"No, that's okay." This is my standard rule on a first date. I meet them at the restaurant. They only get to know my residence if we get past the first couple dates.

"Alright, well how about The Billiard Club? That's definitely casual enough for jeans, it's in Kenmore Square, and they have a nice variety of food choices."

"It's perfect. I know exactly where it is."

"How about seven?"

I agree to the time. We say our good byes and hang up.

Milagros is all smiles and happiness for me. She goes on and on about how I should go have a great time. That I look so good now.

She sits me down on the toilet seat top in her bathroom and does my make up, clucking over the bruise on my forehead. She uses this stuff she claims will cover the bruise.

Next she drags me to her closet and makes me pick out a top to wear with my jeans. This takes a while since, not all her cute little tops looks so cute or little on me. Some I put on and peal off immediately. Others we consider might work. Finally I fit into this nice cashmere sweater in pale pink that wraps across the front and ties at the side with a silk ribbon; very classy yet a little on the sexy side.

Just perfect for a first date!

We decide to leave all the papers at her place. Milagros drives me to Bobby's before going to work. Once again she makes me promise to have a good time and leave the whole Allagaro drug investigation behind for the evening.

She peals off as I stand on the sidewalk watching her brake lights as she gets to the intersection and turns. For some reason I feel a little melancholic and I don't know why. I shake it off and go in the house.

Bobby is gone to pick up Brendan from school. Pete is no where to be seen. I wander around straightening and putting things away as best I can.

Finally they come home. Brendan gives me a very enthusiastic greeting. We settle into getting the homework done. While he is toiling away I go find Bobby. He is watching the early news on TV.

"Hey Bobby?"

"Yeah?" he says still looking at the TV.

"I've got something going on tonight. Are you going to be around to watch Brendan?"

He pulls his eyes from the screen and considers me in the pretty pink top. I flush as I know he's figured out that I am going on a date.

"I've got the evening shift again. Do you need me to change it?" he says with just a little bit of an edge. He shouldn't have to change his schedule so his ex can go out on a date, is the underlying message.

"No, don't worry about it. I'll ask Linda to watch him. Her car survived so she can come over to pick him up."

"Is this going to be disruptive for his schedule? I mean how late are you going to be?"

"I should be home by nine thirty at the latest. That should be okay for him."

I call Linda. I tell her about my date tonight with Tris and ask her if she can watch Brendan. She assures me that she can do it and would be delighted, "I've missed my little firefly."

With that done I have a couple hours to kill before my date. I go shower and do my hair and make up again. By six thirty I have Brendan ready at the door. Linda pulls up and I bring him out.

He seems thrilled to see her and they drive off together. Brendan rolls down his window and waves to me until they disappear from sight.

Chapter 22:

You got soul, you got class

(*Ain't No Other Man,* Christina Aguilera)

I arrive a little before seven at the restaurant. I scan the entryway and then the bar for Tris. When I don't see him I go into the bar and order a glass of wine.

A group of business men are checking me out. I smile to myself: I think I can get used to this. I take a sip of wine and glance at the entrance.

A few more sips of liquid courage and I am feeling much more relaxed; not as keyed up as I was when I came in. Tris is the first decent prospect in a long time. I mentally tick off his attributes once again: good-looking, considerate, good sense of humor, probably a good job (alright, I don't know that one for sure but he *looks* like he has a good job).

I have run the gamut of bad dates. One man took me to a really nice restaurant, ordered a bunch of expensive items to impress me and then at the end of the meal 'realized' that he forgot his wallet. I paid and he apologized over and over and said he would make it up to me. I never heard from him again.

Another time the date had gone really well but turned sour when he wanted me to put on a black leather bustier and six inch stacked heel boots that he brought with him. I think he might have had a whip and ball gag also. I didn't stick around to find out.

The stories go on and on. But I'll stop there. After all, this is not a story about my dating mishaps.

When Tris finally comes in my heart does a little flutter and I get that funny feeling in the bottom of my stomach that is a combination of happy and excited and scared all at once. He looks around and catches my eye. I raise my glass to him across the room. He smiles and makes his way over to me.

"Hi, am I late?" He comes up and takes my hand in both of his. An exciting Tris hand sandwich.

"No, I just happened to catch the bus at the right time and got here a little early."

"Oh good. Wow, you look great!" he holds my hand out appreciatively and I do a little twirl for his benefit.

"Thank you," I say, basking in the glow of his male admiration.

"Do you want to get a table right away or have a drink at the bar?" he asks.

I examine my glass of wine and say, "Why don't you get a drink? We can get a table a little later."

He sidles over to the bar and gets a glass of wine also. When he comes back we clink glasses and settle in to getting to know each other.

He is an only child, recently divorced, is a CPA at large firm in the financial district in Boston but would like to open his own practice and do consulting. For fun he likes to ski and play guitar. He also runs.

When the conversation turns to me it is hard to think of things to say. I mean where do I start? My shotgun wedding? My unfulfilled dreams of becoming a doctor? I stay with the stuff that doesn't make me sound like a loser. I talk about being a mom, working at the university. I tell him a few funny stories about my neighborhood just to keep it interesting. Boy, if he only knew the half of it.

We move into the dining area. Once we've ordered our meal and a second round of drinks my cell phone rings.

"I'm so sorry," I say glancing at the number. It's a local number that I don't recognize but I get so few calls I figure it must be important.

"Hello?"

"Hi, may I speak with Amanda Buscemi?" I hear an official-sounding male voice on the other end.

"Speaking."

"Ah, Ms. Buscemi, this is Officer Collins, I'm calling on behalf of Chief Stone, the inspector for the fire department."

"Yes?" My pulse quickens. This must be in regards to the house fire. I stand up and make a gesture to Tris indicating I'll be back in a moment. I go out on the sidewalk.

"We have a preliminary report and would like to go over it with you and your housemate at your earliest convenience."

"Can I hear the results over the phone?"

"We prefer to do this in person."

"Well I prefer to hear this as soon as possible." Bureaucratic nonsense, I fume. Just give me the news, buddy.

"I suppose I can do that as long as I set up an appointment for you with the inspector also."

"Sure, sure. I'll come in first thing in the morning. Now what have you got?"

He clears his throat, "The preliminary findings are that the fire originated in the living room and rapidly spread to other areas of the residence. An accelerant might have been used but so far has not been detected. The burn patterns indicate a downward pattern which is typical in accelerant-related fires but show no pooling or other unusual burn patterns."

"I'm sorry; I have no idea what you are telling me. Are you saying this is arson?"

"This is what we suspect, ma'am, but usually a trail of accelerant can be traced to an exit point so the arsonist can safely leave the premises and then ignite it. We did not see this."

"So this isn't arson?"

"No, ma'am, this means we aren't dealing with your average, run-of-the-mill arsonist. This person knows what they are doing."

I steal myself to ask the next question, "Who would know how to do this?"

"Someone with specialized military training or a fireman."

The last statement is still reverberating in my mind after I have hung up: someone with specialized military training. *Or a fireman.*

Suddenly a bunch of things click into place. Pete is a fireman. Pete was at that bar when I got drugged. Pete was near the restaurant when we were being watched by Black Jacket and escaped through the alley.

Where was he on the night the house burned down? Brendan said he wasn't around on Sunday when he was with Bobby. So who knows where he was? But he was in an ideal position to know that no one was home.

Pete. I've known him forever. Could he really be part of this?

I lean against the front window of the restaurant. My mind is whirling at all this information.

I remember bits of conversations: Bobby telling me that Pete's been asking about me lately; Brendan saying Pete was not at home on Sunday night which is when my house was being staked out. He's been acting funny around me too. Maybe feeling guilty?

First Deke, now Pete. Is there no man I can trust?

Lost in thought I don't realize that Tris has come out of the restaurant until he says my name. I give a little start as I come out of my ruminations.

"Are you okay?" he asks.

"Huh? Oh, Tris, I'm sorry. I didn't mean to leave you back there. I just had to take a few minutes to think after I hung up."

"Can you tell me what it was about?"

"It was the preliminary report from the inspector regarding the fire. They think it might be arson."

"Arson?!"

"Yes, so I needed to stay out here for a minute and sort out some stuff in my head."

"Well, if you want, I make a really good sounding board," he says and gives me a smile.

I smile back, trying to recover. "That's okay, let's go have our dinner."

We head back in to the now noisy dining room.

Despite my misgivings about involving one more person in any part of the drama, I tell Tris about the report. He listens attentively, even asking some thoughtful questions.

Eventually we move on to other subjects. I am starting to relax again. I sip some of the wine, a very good cabernet by the way, and eat my salad. He tells me a funny story from his youth that has me laughing by the end.

Every table is filled and the conversation level has gotten progressively louder and louder. It's also quite warm. I tug a little at the neckline of Milagros' sweater. Even though it is beautiful, I should have chosen something different, maybe with short sleeves.

"It's warm in here, isn't it?" Tris says to me. He is looking at me closely.

"Whoo, boy, is it," I exclaim.

He throws some money on the table and stands up. "Come on. Let's get out of here."

He grabs my coat and helps me into it. Winding our way through the packed dining room we finally make it to the entrance. I trip on the door's threshold and he grabs a hold of me to keep me from falling onto the sidewalk. I look up at him and he bends down and kisses me gently on the mouth. My breath snags a little in my throat as he pulls away. I slit my eyes open and regard him in the

oblique lighting from the street lamp. He looks rugged
and handsome. I find I want him to kiss me again. As if
I said my thoughts aloud he leans in and kisses me one
more time. My lips part and I feel his tongue slowly glide
over my bottom lip; my toes curl. I move my tongue forward slightly and tentatively brush his tongue. He
thrusts deeper into my mouth and I let out a little groan.
This is the best, most sensuous kiss I've had in long time.
My legs feel like jelly and there're some stirrings in the
places that have been dormant for a while.

When we finally come up for air I stumble against
him a little. Tris puts his arm around my waist and says
softly, "Come with me."

My feet seem to move of their own volition. I think to
myself, what am I doing? He doesn't think I'm going to
sleep with him, does he? I'm not going to sleep with him!
Am I?

We round the corner and I giggle as I trip again.
Clumsy! What's my middle name, Grace? Have a nice
trip, see ya next fall! This strikes me as hilarious and I
start to laugh. Tris laughs with me. Maybe I said it out
loud.

We are at his car, a shiny dark expensive-looking
thing of beauty. He opens the door and helps me in.

"Oh, no," I say, "I, I can't. I need to go home."

"I'll drive you home, Amanda. Don't worry."

"No," I put my hand out to stop him from closing the
door, "I can get the bus-sh-sh-sh. I mean bus."

He takes my hand off the door and places it on my
lap. "I insist," he says and closes the door firmly.

I lay my head back on the headrest. It feels all
wooden and filled with cotton. I'm vaguely aware of Tris
walking around to the driver's side, climbing in and starting the engine. I swing my head a little to look at him. It
lolls over more than I intend. I move my hand to the con-
sole between us and try to push up. My muscles aren't
responding well and it takes a herculean effort to right
myself.

I look at him. He goes double as my vision gets blurry. Alarm is rising in me. Something is terribly wrong. Dread fills me as I say, "You aren't going to take me home, are you?" But it comes out more like 'hue arn gon' tay me ho-o-ommmme are hue'.

He puts the car in gear, looks at me steadily and says, "No, Amanda, I am not."

"Oh fffffuck," I say as my head lolls to the right and I feel myself slumping against the door.

Chapter 23:

I will remember you

(*I will remember you*, Sarah McLachlan)

"...least detectable."

These are the first words I hear as I regain consciousness. I try to move my limbs but they feel leaden and weighted down. I only succeed in wriggling my hands and feet a tiny bit.

I slowly become aware of my surroundings. I am achingly cold from lying on a bare cement floor. Panic rises as I realize that my hands are tightly bound behind me.

My face is pressed against the gritty floor but I don't move. I keep my eyes closed and try to get a sense of where I am. But even more important, I listen to the nearby conversation.

I recognize Tris as one of the speakers. He is talking with another man.

"If it's potassium chloride we run the risk of elevated blood potassium levels."

"That's what I thought too. A lot of them are like that – showing up in the blood in some way. I eliminated curare because if poisoning is suspected it will definitely be detected."

Curare! Poisoning! My heart rate instantly accelerates. These guys are discussing ways of doing me in. Oh crap! I try to twist hands free of the restraints without moving my arms and drawing attention to the fact that I'm awake. Instinct tells me that I should pretend to still be out cold so I can hear more of what they're saying.

"Digitoxin was one I considered," Tris continues, "but it's too chancy. It might show up in the liver."

I feel sick. I allowed this man to put his tongue in my mouth! Now he's busy plotting my demise as coldly as if I were a lab rat. I feel the acid rise in the back of my throat. I swallow it down and continue to listen.

"Still that might work. A car accident might not warrant a toxicological study of the liver."

"True but if it *is* done we are looking at a murder investigation. We can't chance it. We have to make it look accidental. No questions. No loose ends."

They are silent for a few moments.

"Ricin? I'm not sure we have it but that won't be detected."

"Hmmm," I hear some clicking like keystrokes on a computer, "you get internal bleeding."

"So? You get internal bleeding when you slam into a tree going sixty miles an hour."

"It says here you also can get kidney and liver failure."

"We're using a lethal dose. There won't be any opportunity for organ failure."

"Okay, let's keep that one on the list. Did you say we have it?"

"I'm not sure. Do you want me to go check?"

"Not right now," Tris directs, "Let's see what else we have."

Tap, tap, tap.

"Glutamate can cause a stroke."

"Glutamate? As in NutraSweet? Jesus Christ!" I hear what sounds like a nearly full can thrown into an empty trash can.

"You'd have to drink tons of the stuff to stroke out, you moron."

"Still, why risk it."

There's a pause and then, "Strychnine. That might work. Even though it's detectable it could be explained because it's been found laced into cocaine and heroin. We can inject a cocktail of strychnine and cocaine."

Nice, I can die being known as a drug addict. Now I'm pissed. I might be more mad than scared right now. How dare they besmirch my memory! I want to kill these assholes.

"I'm not sure we have either one of those substances in house, do we?"

"I doubt it. Besides, I don't know about the others but I don't think Amanda does any drugs," Tris says.

That's right; I say to myself, I don't do any drugs. Thank you very much. Wait a minute...did he say others?

"Well, let's keep it on the list right now. If I have to check about the ricin I can look for cocaine too," the other guy who's not Tris says.

"Here's another one: selenium. It causes cardiovascular collapse."

"Cardiovascular collapse? I bet a coroner would be suspicious. Besides if they look for trace minerals like arsenic, selenium could come up."

I hear a sigh and then more tapping on the keyboard.

"Wait, look at this! Why didn't I think of it before? Succinylcholine! It breaks down into compounds found naturally in the body. It's undetectable. It's perfect!"

They are quiet for a few moments then the guy-not-Tris says, "Uhho, the lungs can get edematous. That's a problem."

That's right, fuckers, I think. Kind of hard to explain water on the lungs when I'm wrapped around a tree. I feel of thrill of victory; they haven't figured out a way to do me in yet without making it suspicious.

"Here's a thought: instead of crashing into a tree how about the car plummets into a river? That would account for the edema."

"That could work," Tris agrees.

"We'll need a river that's isolated enough so no one sees the car go in and tries to rescue them but off a main road so it doesn't look odd that they're in the area."

There it is again: he just said it, *they, them*! This could only mean...

Milagros! Oh no!

❖ ❖ ❖ ❖ ❖ ❖ ❖ ❖ ❖ ❖ ❖ ❖ ❖ ❖

In my panic I must have moved because I hear Tris say, "Looks like Sleeping Beauty is walking up"

Slowly I open my eyes. Tris has crouched down near me. I see him peering at me dispassionately as my eyes refocus.

"How long have you been awake?" he asks.

"Long enough to realize that you're an evil bastard," I spit out.

He sighs, "Amanda, Amanda, I honestly wish it didn't have to come to this. Every step of the way I kept hoping you'd give up."

"If I can figure it out, someone else will be able to as well," I respond.

He knits his eyebrows a little. This thought must have occurred to him too.

"If you stop the clinical trial right now, all you're looking at is one person who's died of heart failure. If you continue, more people are going to get sick and eventually it'll come out," I reason, pressing my advantage.

"But we're working on a solution right now," he says as he stands up. "We'll have a different formulation shortly and switch it out at all the sites."

He begins to walk away from me.

"And what about all those people enrolled in the study that are going to start getting sick?" I call after him, "What are you going to do? Are you going to make sure each of them meets an untimely death just like Julio did?"

He stops and then slowly comes back toward me, eyes flashing. "Do you have any idea what's at stake here? This is a twelve *billion* dollar industry! This drug could corner the market. Hell, I could win the Nobel Prize for a drug that restores pancreatic insulin production!"

He is agitated. He has started pacing and runs his fingers through his hair. "We've isolated what caused the situation and are fixing it."

"Steve, come here and take a look," the other guy calls.

Steve! So his name isn't Tris, it's Steve. *As in Steven Morris.*

He walks over to the table where they have a lap top set up and bends down to look at whatever the other guy has on the screen.

Other Guy says, "This river's pretty isolated. The nearest residence is several hundred yards away."

"Won't they still hear a car crashing through a guardrail?"

"I'm not sure."

They bend over the laptop again looking for a place to dump our bodies.

While they're distracted I furiously wriggle my hands back and forth trying to loosen my bonds.

"Let me go out to my car. I have some maps out there," Other Guy says.

When we are alone Steve turns away from the computer screen and looks at me. I struggle to sit up and topple over. He sigh's, grabs a folding chair and places it next to me. Then he helps me up and gets me seated in the chair.

"What I don't understand," I say once I'm seated, "is how we met. It isn't like you had any idea I was going to be at that restaurant. So if you planned this whole dating-kidnapping scenario, how did you make it look like a chance meeting?"

He grunts out a mirthless chuckle, "Sheer dumb luck. I couldn't believe when you walked right past my table that night we met. It seemed like a very lucky break for me. I made my mind up at the spur of the moment to go hit on you."

"You mean you didn't plan it?"

"No, not at all. I was surprised as hell to see you

there. But then I got to thinking that if you needed to be taken out at some point it would be much easier if you knew me and went with me willingly. As it turns out, that's the very thing that happened."

"Wow, well you're quite the planner now, aren't you, *Steven Morris*?" I reply sarcastically.

"So you figured out who I really am, huh?"

"Yeah, I'm brilliant; a day late and dollar short. So who's Tris McEvoy?"

"I don't know. I lifted a business card out of the jar at the front of the restaurant where people throw them in to win a free dinner. If you had looked at the card you would have seen that I scribbled out the business number and put my cell phone on there instead."

"Ha! You see, Steve, Mr. Big Planner, if my death is investigated and they look at my cell phone records, they'll see you called me. They'll trace it back to you." I say, spotting the loophole and triumphantly pointing it out to him.

"Sure," he says, "except for the fact that it was a pre-paid cell phone which in now sitting at the bottom of the Charles."

Well, damn. I should have known. My spirits sink as I see my one glimmer of hope fading.

"So why did you decide tonight was the night? I mean, heck, you just burned my house down. Wasn't that enough?"

"I thought it would be. But then there you two were, back to snooping the very next day."

"You don't know that. You got rid of all the files in the fire!"

"Unfortunately for you, your little friend, there, took all those notes."

"She didn't take any notes," I go with the bald-faced lie.

"Nice try but we know all about the notes she took while reading the files. Even though you had an older, incomplete file you were still able to piece together most of what we were doing."

"How do you know this?" I ask.

"We bugged your friend's apartment. We heard your whole conversation. I have to say, I was impressed that you got as far as you did. And figuring out the ID codes associated with each city, that was a nice piece of work."

"Gee, thanks. I'm flattered," I say. My mind is whirling around this whole business. If they bugged Milagros' apartment, did they bug my house? If they did they would have heard me telling Linda the whole story. Then they are going to have to eliminate her as well. I feel wretchedly sick to my stomach at the thought.

"How about my house? Did you bug that as well?"

"Never got the chance. There was this nosy old fart that was always hanging around."

Thank God for Mr. Z, I think. At least he saved Linda from my fate.

"Then how did you set it on fire?"

"He was out snooping around the neighborhood with his flashlight. Someone came up to him and said they thought they had spotted a bear, if you can believe that, the next block over so he took off with them. Otherwise we might not have had the chance."

A bear. My supposed fox sighting had escalated to a bear. Under other circumstances I would be busting a gut. I mean, talk about the power of suggestion! But I'm a little focused on my survival right now.

I think about the night he approached me at the restaurant. He was sitting with two other men.

"So your friends are going to remember that you came over and talked to me. What are you going to do, pay them off to forget they ever saw me?" I ask.

"Don't get too smug, Amanda, those were guys I hired to watch you. They had just come off their shift and were updating me when you came strolling through."

My heart sinks. I have got to be the unluckiest person in the world. We just *had* to go to that particular place. And that's how I met this scumbag.

I look at him sitting there with his arms folded; being all superior. All that nice stuff he said: lies. The kiss? What I thought was the romantically glorious kiss? Another lie.

With anger and resentment boiling away in me I say, "I'm just curious what kind of man can kiss a woman one moment and plot to kill her the next."

He gives me a small cruel smile and says, "The kind of man that *wins*. I wasn't planning on kissing you but then you tripped in the doorway. That draws people's attention and later they might remember you, or worse, me. So I kissed you. People tend to turn away and give a couple their privacy. And then not get a good look at us. Look, this is business, Amanda. We made the business decision to keep the study going. We *believe* in our product. We *owe* the world this product. You and your friends are just blips on the radar screen. I know that's hard for you to hear, but it's the truth. The history of science is riddled with these kinds of sacrifices."

"Easy for you to say, you're not the one getting murdered."

"Probably but there's no other way."

"There's always another way. Look, I won't say anything. I'll tell Milagros that our lives are at stake. That we can't say anything."

"Nice try, but no. We couldn't trust you."

"Somewhere inside there has to be a decent human being. How can you look me in the eye and do this?"

"I don't *have* to look you in the eye. I have people to do this for me."

He's resting one of his butt cheeks on the table and now stands up and says, "As fun as this is, debating with you, I have to go get some stuff." He takes a roll of duct tape off the table and wraps it around my chest and the chair to secure me to it.

"Be a good girl while I'm gone," he pats my head and moves toward the door.

As soon as it clangs shut I try to stand upright as much as I can. My legs are straight and I am bent over from the waist. I look like an L turned on its side. To make matters worse, my feet are duct taped together so I can't walk. I take a hop forward, become unbalanced and crash to the floor. To save my face I'm able to turn just enough to the side so that my shoulder hits the cement first with a terrible jarring motion. I literally see stars.

Just then I hear the door open and Other Guy comes back in, "What're you doing?"

He rushes over to me and rights the chair. After he does that he asks, "Where'd Steve go?"

"He said he couldn't take it any more and is going to turn himself in to the police," I say.

"Very funny," he pulls out his cell phone and makes a call.

"Where are you?" he says when, I assume, Steve picks up. He listens for a moment and says, "Don't forget the hypodermics." And then he hangs up.

He glances at me to make sure I haven't moved and then opens up a map on the table.

"So what do ya say there, guy? Care to let me go free?" I ask gamely.

He ignores me, studying the map intently.

"I mean right now all you are is an accomplice to kidnapping. But murder? Come on, you don't really have the stomach to murder me, do you?"

He doesn't respond.

"I'm the mother of two boys. You'd be taking their mom away from them." I pause for effect, "I'm sure you have a mom. You wouldn't want someone killing her now, would you? You know us moms! Always meddling!" I try for a chuckle; like this is just some inside family joke. Oh, that ol' mom, she's always getting herself into a pickle!

Nothing.

"This would be like killing your own mother. You'll never be able to look at your mother again without thinking of me!"

Still he ignores me.

Trying another tack I say, "People saw Steve and me having dinner. When I go missing they will trace my steps and it'll lead to him."

Silence.

"He'll turn on you in a heartbeat. That's the kind of guy he is, a two-faced piece of shit. He'll say you killed me, that he had nothing to do with it. Then it'll be your ass in prison for the rest of your life. Do think a guy like Steve would clam up and *not* point the finger at you?"

He turns the map over, looks at something and then flips it back to the original side.

I sigh. "He'll be out in two and you'll be an old, old, *old* man before you even have a chance of getting out. You'll be so old your penis will be like a shriveled up kidney bean. Even the most desperate old lady won't have you."

Still nothing.

"She'll be like, 'back in the Truman Era, when I actually had sex I don't recall ever seeing such a pitiful piece of manhood.'" I say in my best little old lady voice, "'Why is that really what a penis looks like? It looks more like a shriveled up kidney bean. Or the stub of a cigarillo. Is that what happens from all those years of spanking the monkey in prison?"

I wait for a reaction. Then I say, "Waxing the dolphin?" Pause. "Chokin' the chicken?" I search for another phrase, "Slapping the salami," He doesn't even twitch! "Bop the bologna," I say desperately. "Wanking the wookie!"

Other Guy straightens up from his map studying and sighs. Ah ha! I think to myself; I finally got to him. He stands, grabs the duct tape and pulls off a section, walks over to me and slaps it on my mouth. Then he goes back to the table and starts doing something on the laptop.

Damn, now what? How am I going to be able to plead for my life? I was going to offer my body as a last resort like Mata Hari.

I try pushing the duct tape off with my tongue. It holds fast. I push again as hard as I can. It still sits tight on my mouth but I think I sprained my tongue if that's possible.

Now that I can't speak I take to examining Other Guy's profile. I fantasize about biting his nose or head-butting him.

I let out a sigh through my nose. My thoughts turn grim. These might be the last hours of my life. I'll never get to see Brendan grow up. When Philip finds the girl he wants to marry I won't be around to meet her. I'll never see grandchildren. I try to swallow the huge lump that's formed in my throat.

I'll never get to do the cool volcano hike in Hawaii that I read about. Or ride a gondola in Venice. Or take that camera safari in Kenya.

And Milagros. She's just starting off her life. Her list must be even longer.

I go back to that firelight conversation I had with Sam Ward. It seems like ages ago but it has only been four days. I have a great sadness; that was what he said. I ponder the statement. Could he, in his tribal wisdom, have been able to so keenly see into my soul that way? Or do I wear my heart on my sleeve and he was just the first person to call me on it? Either way he hit the nail on the head.

I go back to that awful night almost twenty years ago.

I lost my two best friends when I was eighteen years old. Natalie and I grew up together. We lived down the street from one another and walked to school every day from first grade on up. Jennifer moved into the neighborhood just before we started fifth grade. She was a natural fit into our twosome. Rarely were we apart. We were so close we started calling each others' parents Mom and Dad.

We were on the girl's softball league together: Jen was short stop, Natalie pitched and I was an outfielder.

We tried out for the pom pom squad together – they made it, I did not, even though they worked for weeks with me on the routines (seriously, are you surprised by that one?)

If one of us liked a boy, the other two had to approve him. The approval process was a complicated and ever changing formula: determine his astrological sign (an Aries or Capricorn were out for Natalie), his favorite song (had to be kind of macho but with a sensitive side, like Poison's Every Rose Has Its Thorn or Billie Jean by Michael Jackson but Wake Me Up Before You Go Go by George Michael was lame and instantly disqualified him), and extracurricular activities (sports were good but chess, debate club or being a gear head earned a negative rating).

Our families attended the same church and we all had the same crush on our youth pastor. And during long sermons we would leaf through the hymnal and irreverently put 'under the sheets' after each song title (How Great Thou Art *under the sheets*; The King is Coming *under the sheets*) until we had tears rolling down our cheeks and stomach aches from suppressing our giggles.

And we spent one summer hanging out next to Jen's pool. In a show of solidarity we never went in it because she broke her leg and couldn't go in herself. Instead we'd play Monopoly, Uno and spit. The top 40 radio station would blare all the recent hits in non-ending fashion. And we'd practice make up and hair do's on each other.

In the spring of our senior year Nancy Nelson had a party at her house. I wanted to go but was scheduled to work that night. I couldn't get anyone to switch with me and I was really mad. This was going to be the party of the year. Nancy's parents were gone and so there'd be drinking and dancing and all the other stuff that goes on when parents aren't around.

I went to work that night steaming with resentment. Every purchase I rung up irritated me. I would look at the clock and wonder what my friends were doing right then. I had been hoping to see Tommy Cartwright at the party. He'd been making a special effort to say hi to me at school and I was hoping he was building himself up to ask me out. He was supposed to be at that party.

Right about the time I was locking up the store for the night Natalie and Jennifer had decided to go joyriding with a couple guys they liked. As I was turning onto my street they were flying down Route 107. And by the time I had safely pulled into my driveway, they had crashed head on into a tree. The impact was so hard that it literally split the car in two. Police estimated that they were going close to eighty at the time of the accident. No one survived. I found out about it at two o'clock in the morning when the police pulled up to Natalie's house to tell her parents.

Their deaths devastated me. We were closer than sisters and had our whole lives planned. We had all been accepted to the same college, we were all going to live on the same street and have our babies at the same time so they could grow up together and be best friends just like we were. Our husbands were all going to go golfing together every Sunday and watch the kids on Saturdays so we could go get our nails done and treat ourselves to lunch out.

None of that was ever going to happen. My whole world imploded in those few awful seconds. I should have died with them, I thought. Maybe in a way I did.

Maybe I've just been waiting for that my whole life.

With the proverbial life flashing before my eyes right now I look at my current relationships with a new perspective. I realize that I have been holding people off at arm's length. In my moment of new found clarity I see that it is because I didn't want to ever suffer such a devastating loss again.

I think of Linda; such a sweet and loving soul. We've been friends for more than a decade and yet I've never told her that I love her. I never even thought about whether I loved her or not. It was too risky to think in those terms. So I blocked it out.

And Milagros; with her warm smile and expressive face. I *do* care about her. I always lecture her about being safe and feel panicked when she is out at night on her own. Again, I never said, hey Milagros you are special to me. I love you. I never did it because I was keeping her at a distance. I didn't *want* to care. Because when you love, you can get hurt. So instead I would be all gruff and grumpy. I had to protect myself from life. Sarcasm was my sword, defensiveness my shield. And she put up with me! *Linda* put up with me.

Tears are pooling in my eyes now. So many years wasted, I think with disgust. So many years I could have filled my heart with love and accepted the love of others; made my life fuller, richer, so much more wonderful. Instead I hid behind my fear of loving and was in such denial I wasn't even consciously aware I was doing it.

So much for all those stupid psych courses I had to take in college. They didn't help me in the least to recognize my own pathology.

I have this overwhelmingly heavy sensation in my chest that expands and presses on me till I feel as though I can't draw any air into my lungs. It grows and grows until I feel completely engulfed.

I realize that this is what regret feels like.

The tears finally spill from my eyes and run down my cheeks. Big drops splash onto my jeans. My nose gets runny and I snort up a bunch of snot that threatens to come out.

I do love Linda! I say to myself. I *do* love Milagros! I love! I love! I scream inside my head.

I lean my head back and the tears stream into my hair. They are hot and stinging. I feel the rivulets as they course through the roots of my hair and into my ears.

My last few minutes on this planet are *not* going to be moments of regret or fear I promise myself. They are going to be moments of love. I may not be able to ever tell them of my feelings but I am going to love them with all my heart.

And suddenly the weight on my chest lifts. I literally feel like my heart is growing bigger; like in the movie *How the Grinch Stole Christmas,* at end when the Grinch's heart grows ten sizes. That's exactly what it feels like; my heart is expanding with love. It aches, but in a good way.

I raise my head and look at Other Guy. He is studiously ignoring me. I wonder if he loves. I think maybe, if he does, he can find it in his heart to not kill me, to not kill Milagros.

Just then the door bangs open. I look over but it isn't Morris. It's Milagros, I see with a sinking heart. I was hoping so desperately that she was going to escape.

She is being pushed into the room by Black Jacket from the restaurant. Her eyes are as big as saucers and when she sees me she cries out and runs over to me.

"I'm so sorry, I'm so sorry," she sobs into my neck as she hugs me.

I shake my head back and forth trying to let her know that it's okay; not her fault. She notices the tape on my mouth and peals it off.

"Are you okay?" she asks.

"So far. And you?"

"I'm okay too."

"How'd they get you?"

"He came up to me just before I got in my car after my shift at City," she nods with her head at Black Jacket. "He held a gun on me and made me drive out here."

"Where's here?"

"You don't know? We are at the Allagaro buildings."

"I wasn't certain. I was knocked out while I was being brought here."

She's kneeling on the floor in front of me. She sneaks a look at our captors. They are over by the table that's holding the computer and maps. They are talking among themselves. She starts working on pealing the duct tape off my ankles.

"Do you know what they intend to do with us?" she whispers.

"They're going to kill us." I whisper back.

Her eyes become shiny with tears. She puts her hand on my leg and rests her forehead on my knee.

"This is all my fault, querida. You wanted to stop but I just kept going. You don't deserve this."

"*Neither* of us deserves this," I say.

The door opens again. We look over in grim expectation. But once again it isn't Morris with the dreaded drug to kill us.

It's Deke.

Chapter 24:

You can't always get what you want

(You Can't Always Get What You Want,
The Rolling Stones)

"You!" I hoarsely shout as Deke comes in.

I see two guys behind him. One I recognize from the night they were staking out my street. His was one of the faces illuminated by the policeman's flashlight, the blond, scruffy one.

He roughly pushes Deke into the room. Now I notice that Deke's hands are bound and he has a cut on his temple and his jaw looks swollen.

"Dude!" he says, "What are you doing here?"

"Me? What are *you* doing here?"

By now he has staggered over to us and is crouching down next to Milagros who has continued to feverishly work on my bound ankles.

"I found out these squids who work for my dad were trippin' a study."

Milagros flashes me a look that says what is he talking about?

"He means he discovered these guys at Allagaro were doing something sketchy concerning the same clinical trial we've been investigating," I explain.

"You knew about that too?" Deke asks.

"Yeah, but how did you know?"

"My dad asked me to go check out the facility with him while he was here a few days ago. They were showing us all these solid projects they had going on. I ended up reviewing a study they had and happened onto the MEMPHIS study."

"How'd you 'happen' on to the MEMPHIS study? I'm sure they didn't just have it sitting out," I say.

"No but these boners didn't know I got my undergraduate in computer science. I hacked into the files just to see what else was going on that they weren't telling us. At first I didn't know what the file was but it looked suspicious so I copied it onto the jump drive that I had in my pocket to look at later."

"Did you get a chance to look at the files?" I ask.

"A little. It was kind of outside my area of expertise but it looked like they're tracking adverse outcomes on a diabetes study. I kept the jump drive locked in my desk drawer and was going to look at it more the next day. But when I came in to the lab on Wednesday we couldn't log onto the computers. IS department said we were rippin' a major virus and it tonked our systems. I went to get my jump drive out of my desk. That's when I discovered someone had snaked it."

"So the Allagaro guys got rid of all the existing outside files," I say.

"Looks that way," he agrees. "So what did you femmes do to get yourself in this mess?"

"You know that BC hockey player that died?"

"Yeah..."

"Well, he was in the MEMPHIS study. Milagros discovered it when they brought him in to City Hospital. It's a long story but we've been looking into it for over a week. I accidently found the files on your jump drive, copied them and took them home to read. I didn't know why you had them. I thought you were part of the cover up."

"No way, man. That would be bogus."

"Why didn't you ever say anything to me?"

"Dude, I was being ace on this. I didn't even know you were looking at this too. You kept it on the down low pretty well."

"Well not down low enough," I say. A surge of guilt overcomes me: I know how these guys found out that

Deke had the files. Milagros and I talked about it at her place. His death will be my fault. Wait a minute!

"Deke," I say, "isn't your dad, like, the president or something of the parent company?"

"Affirmative, he's the chief scientific officer," he says.

"Well, what are you doing here? I mean, they can't kill the CSO's son, can they?"

"Evidently they can," he responds. He notices Milagros working furiously to free my legs and says, "Milagros, I have a set of keys in my pocket. Get them out and you can saw through the tape with them."

She dives her hand into the front pocket of his cargo pants and comes up with the keys. Now she starts hacking at the duct tape with them..

Deke continues in a low voice, "I hadn't talked to my dad about this yet. And they knew I hadn't. I tried to tell them that I had and they blew me off."

We look over at the cadre by the table. They are quietly talking and pointing to the map on the table.

"Do you know how they are going to kill us, mommy?" Milagros finally speaks.

"Succinylcholine," I tell them. "The guy who kidnapped me, I thought his name was Tris? He's actually Steven Morris. He's out right now collecting the stuff."

"Man, that's cold," Deke says.

"Isn't that what they use in surgery? Doesn't that paralyze your muscles and you suffocate unless they put a tube down your throat?" she asks with a quavering voice.

"I think so," I answer, not able to think of a way to make this less frightening for any of us.

"We need a plan," Deke says. "I know this looks bleak but we can't just let them do this. We have to fight."

"Great, any suggestions?" I say.

We look around. We are in a storeroom or small warehouse area. Metal shelves holding various types of boxes divide one side of the room up into aisles. It's diffi-

Ravagni

cult to tell if there is any other exit than the one from
which everyone's been coming and going. The table sits in
between us and the door. I am still tied to the chair
although Milagros has finally sawed through the tape on
my ankles. Deke's hands are tied in front of him. Milagros is the only one not bound in some way. They could
make a run for it but I wouldn't be able to.

"First thing I am going to do is get you out of this
tape," she says and starts to work on the portion wrapped
around my chest.

"No! Get Deke's hands free first. He's the strongest
and can fight if it comes to that." I whisper.

"Alright, that's enough of that," Black Jacket has
walked over with his gun trained on us.

"You," he points the gun at Milagros, "throw me
those keys."

Reluctantly she complies. He bends down and scoops
them up. Then he makes her sit on the floor about three
feet from me. He makes Deke sit three feet away on the
other side of me.

He walks back over to where the others are but
remains turned toward us; his gun out and pointing at us.

"Milagros," I say out of the corner of my mouth.

"Yes?"

"If they go for me or Deke first I want you to make a
run for it."

"Amanda..."

"I'm serious," I say with vehemence, "whoever can
escape, should. This isn't a bravery contest. This is survival."

I've been saying this while looking at Black Jacket
who has once again joined in the conversation at the
table. So even though he keeps glancing over at us he
isn't noticing that we are talking. Milagros hasn't said
anything so I tear my eyes away from our captors and
steal a glance at her. She has her legs drawn up to her
chest and her head is bent down on her knees.

212

"Do you hear me?" I whisper.

She nods but keeps her head down, her long dark curls hiding her face.

"Promise me that you won't try to save me; that you'll try to escape."

She raises her head and looks at me. Tears are streaming down her face. "I can't promise you that," she says.

"Milagros, the odds are stacked against us. There will only be moments for whoever is supposed to go second and third to escape. This is your only hope."

"But – "

"No buts. Listen," I say glancing at Black Jacket to make sure he hasn't yet noticed us talking, "I love you! I know I've never told you this before. And I'm sorry for that! But I do love you so very, very much. And that is why I want you to try to escape. And if you love me, you will do that! If you stay, you'll only end up in the same condition as me."

Just then the door to the room opens and Steve Morris walks back in carrying a bunch of stuff in his hands. My heart sinks. This is it, I think.

Morris deposits the paraphernalia on the table. The group gathers around Morris as he shows them a vial with clear liquid; the deadly succinylcholine I assume. Other Guy peels open the packaging for a syringe and attaches a needle to it.

My heart is racing. It looks like the end is rapidly approaching.

"Dude," Deke whispers, interrupting my thoughts.

"What?" I say out of the corner of my mouth looking straight forward as Black Jacket turns slightly toward us.

"Get ready to run toward the shelving."

"Huh?" both Milagros and I say in unison.

Suddenly the room plunges into total darkness. I hear shouts and a folding chair clangs to the floor.

"Come on!" Deke yells.

I stand up as best I can and run hunched over in the general direction of the shelves. Someone grabs one of the legs of the folding chair that I'm attached too halting my forward motion. I heave to the right. The hold continues. I turn as hard as I can to the left. Whoever is holding on now grabs the back of my chair and pulls. I fall backwards and hear an "umpf!" as we hit the ground.

Hoping one of the legs has hit my assailant in a vital spot, I roll on my side and try to stand. I am on my knees and struggling to get up when I am grabbed again and pulled back down. I topple over and hit the floor with a grunt. Flailing my legs in a wild, lunatic style I kick him a couple times. On the second kick I make contact with something yielding and hear an "ahgh." I don't feel hands grabbing me anymore so I stop kicking and begin twisting and wriggling away like a sidewinder snake.

I hear Milagros yelling for me over the din and I wriggle toward her voice. "I'm coming," I huff, "I'm coming."

Hands grab me. I yell and start to flail but then realize Milagros is shouting in my ear, "Mommy it's me! Stop!"

She grabs me by the front of my sweater and pulls me toward her. I push with my feet against the floor to help her as she continues dragging me away from the center of the room and into the relative safety of the shelves.

I feel a cold draft and realize the door to the outside must have opened. Dim moonlight filters in. I see some shadowy figures running out the door. Now the commotion is outside.

Close by someone starts toward the door. I wonder if it might be Deke. Milagros says, "Hold still. I found box cutters."

I lie still while she slices through the duct tape holding me to the chair on my left side and then my right.

Once done she pulls the tape off just as the door closes and we are again engulfed in complete darkness.

"Oh shit," she cries in frustration. "I'm gonna try to get your hands free. Hold on."

I feel her hands find the slight gap between my wrists. Trying not to envision the sharp razor slicing through my skin instead of the tape I hold my breath. Her hands are icy cold on mine as she takes her first tentative cut on the tape. I pull my hands as far apart as I can and suddenly I am free.

Ripping the tape off we each give a triumphant little cry. I hear the box cutter clatter to the ground as she drops it and then hugs me. We cling to each other. Sounds of commotion are filtering in from outside.

After a few moments Milagros says, "What do you think is going on out there?"

"It sounds like there's fighting," and just then something thumps heavily against the door and we both jump.

"Maybe we can find another way out of here," she suggests.

"Deke went out that way," I say feeling guilty that we aren't out there helping him. I start crawling toward the door. I'm not sure what I'm going to do but I can't abandon him.

"I'm coming with you!" Milagros cries and I hear her coming up behind me.

I crawl forward a couple feet, wave one of my hands in front of me to make sure there aren't any obstacles and then crawl forward again a couple feet repeating the process.

All of a sudden we hear a loud bang. It sounds like a gun.

"Sweet Jesus!" I cry out and turn around and start crawling in the opposite direction. I bump in to Milagros. "Turn around! Go back!" We start crawling back in the same direction we came from. Another gunshot sounds and then another. Now we are scrambling as fast as we can.

All of a sudden I am grabbed around the middle and slammed into the floor. I scream and start flailing at the heavy body on top of me.

"You fucking bitch!" Morris screams at me as he tries to put his hands around my throat. "You've ruined everything."

I twist and grab at his hands to keep them from completely closing on my neck. Extra weight pushes me harder into the floor as Milagros jumps on yelling, "Get off her you bastard!"

Dull thwacks tell me she is pummeling his back. He heaves his body to throw her off. She yelps as she lands a distance away. Morris, then, shifts his body back toward me but this has given me the opportunity draw up my right leg and in a split second I have shot out my foot. I don't make direct contact, but it feels like I might have hit the side of his head. In an astounding fete of survival I contort my body and bring my other foot around. I thrust it out again and again. He crumples on top of me making horrible gagging noises. I must have hit him in throat. Panicked, I wriggle and push until I get him off me and start crawling away.

"Em, are you okay?" I call out. I know I'm giving my position away but hopefully Morris is still incapacitated.

"Yes," she yells back. "Where's Morris?"

"Dying of a collapsed trachea if we're lucky!"

I feel a draft coming from behind. Someone's come in! Someone who probably has a gun! My hands and knees pound the floor in an effort to put as much distance as I can between me and the door.

A flashlight shines into the room. Its beam is circling around. It's only a matter of time before we are discovered.

"Amanda!" I hear someone call.

I stand up and start running blindly, hands out in front of me. I slam into a shelf and boxes start tumbling down on top of me. I put my hands up to protect my head.

Meanwhile I try to keep an eye on the circle of light that's sweeping the warehouse. It swings around and catches me as I become buried in the pile.

"Amanda," again my name is called. Someone is digging through the boxes. I try to move but most of my body is immobilized by the weight of the boxes.

Box after box is lifted off of me. My torso and head are freed first followed by my arms and finally my legs. I lay there battered and stunned. In the wash of the flashlight's beam I blink.

"Are you okay?" Milagros asks me.

I am lying on my back and lift my head a little in the direction of her voice. "Milagros? What happened? Who's here?"

The flashlight swings around and illuminates a face that has become all too familiar: Pete!

I drop my head back onto the floor. I am so confused. What is he doing here? Is he one of the bad guys after all? Black dots start forming in front of my eyes and fill more and more of my vision. An odd buzzing comes from inside my head. I try to speak but my mouth won't work.

Then all is blank.

Chapter 25:

Amen I,
Amen I,
I'm alive

(If Everyone Cared, Nickelback)

The first thing I'm aware of is the light. Brilliant fluorescent light is filtering into my awareness. I slit my eyes open and raise my hand to block out some of it.

"Don't try to move too much. We've stabilized your neck," I see a female's face come into view.

"Am I paralyzed?" I ask. I have this big brace around my neck and don't know what to do with my hand that is raised to my eyes. If I move it will it cause some sort of irreparable damage?

"Do you feel this?" she asks.

"Ow!" I say as I feel a sharp pressure on my foot.

"I'd say chances are pretty good that you aren't paralyzed," she smiles, "but we're gonna keep that neck steady for the ride to the hospital."

She moves out of my line of vision. I lower my hand and lay there looking at the ceiling lights. Where is everyone? I wonder. What happened? I was moments from dying an extremely unpleasant death and now I am laying here very much alive. A surge of joy sweeps through me at this heady thought.

"Okay, we're going to lift you onto the stretcher now," the female EMT tells me. "On three; one, two, three."

I am hefted onto the stretcher which is then elevated to waist height. A wave of pain moves through me as I am jostled. A blanket is tucked around me and they wheel me outside. Pulsating white and blue lights pierce the night. A cacophony of sounds assault me: a police radio squawks, snatches of a nearby conversation, a man's voice calls out, and there's the distant but unmistakable sound of a horse whinnying and then snorting.

The EMT's stop at the ambulance and I say, "Hey, where's my friends? Is everyone ok?"

"We can't really say," says the male EMT, "but there's a bunch of police cars around so maybe they're over there?"

"Where're you taking me?" I ask as I am lifted into the back of the ambulance.

"UMASS Med," comes the answer. They lock my stretcher in place in readiness for the ride to the hospital.

The next morning I awaken to the sounds of a hospital coming to life. I hear people walking by and talking, a cart is rolling past, there's the distinct metallic scraping sound of a bed curtain being pulled back.

I recall that I've been placed in an observation bed in the ER with the promise of being released in the morning if I get a clean bill of health. Once I was x-rayed and examined, they gave me something to help me get some rest.

And now I am awake.

Slowly and painfully I turn my head and relief washes over me as I see Milagros sleeping in the chair beside my bed. She must have come in after I fell asleep. I smile as I look at her; she is slumped onto a pillow that is wedged between the chair and the wall. She has a blanket wrapped around her and a lock of curly dark hair rests against her cheek. She looks just as beautiful asleep as she does awake. On the other hand I am wiping the drool from my mouth and am sure my eyes are all puffy and my hair is standing on end.

Although I'm dying to ask a million questions I let her continue sleeping. What matters most is that we're both still pulling air into our lungs.

I feel a swell of elation move through me and smile to myself; we're alive! I still can't believe that we were minutes away from meeting our doom and were saved in the eleventh hour.

And speaking of being rescued, what happened? Pete was there. Was he our rescuer? If so, how did he find us? For that matter, how did he even know we needed rescuing? And whose gun went off? Was anyone shot?

I turn a little to get more comfortable and horrible pain shoots up my side. Now I understand why I was kept for observation. I suck in my breath to try to contain it

"Are you alright?" Milagros asks.

"Oh, you're awake! I tried to keep quiet so you could sleep."

"That's okay, querida," she stretches her legs out, "so how do you feel?"

"Wicked sore."

"I bet. You should have seen the pile of boxes that you were under. You're lucky to only have some cracked ribs."

"So that's why it feels like someone's sticking a hot poker in my side," I say. I must have conked out before they had a chance to tell me about my ribs.

I want to hear all about what happened but need to get comfortable first.

"Can you raise the back up a little?"

"Sure, sweetie," she says and walks to the end of the bed, finds the control and raises the back up until I indicate that I'm good.

"Okay, so tell me, what happened?" I demand.

Just then the curtain around my bed is pulled back.

"Mom!" Brendan cries out and comes dashing up to me.

"Bren! Am I glad to see you! Come 'ere," I say.

Needing no more encouragement he clambers up on the hospital bed and falls into my arms. I grunt at the sharp pain but am so glad to hold him that I don't say a word.

I bend my head down to his and breathe in the watermelon shampoo smell of his hair. After getting my fill of hugging and kissing him I turn to Linda and Milagros who are standing side by side grinning and say, "So tell me what happened!"

Milagros turns to Linda and says, "You tell her first."

Linda says, "I brought Brendan back at nine thirty last night but you weren't home yet. Pete was there and let me in. I decided to wait until you came home so I could hear about your date. By ten I had Brendan tucked in and then I called your cell phone. It was turned off."

"That was because my date drugged and kidnapped me. His name wasn't really Tris McEvoy but Steven Morris who was heading up the MEMPHIS study. He must have turned my cell phone off so it wouldn't ring."

"Well, I knew you would never turn your cell phone off," Linda continues, "so I became really concerned. I started telling Pete everything you had told me about the hockey player, going to Florida, the guys staking out our neighborhood, you two breaking into the Allagaro building. He got quite upset and called Bobby at the station. They decided you might be in danger."

"And we were right," says Bobby walking up to my bed. He bends down and kisses me on the cheek. "How are you?"

"Okay, a few cracked ribs but it could have been much worse. So go on! What happened after you guys thought I was in danger?"

Bobby looks rough; his face is unshaven and dark shadows are under his eyes. There is a discoloration on his left cheekbone.

Bobby picks up the story, "Linda agreed to stay at the house with Brendan. Pete came over to the station to get me then we drove out to the Still River Ranch. We figured we'd retrace your steps so we could sneak in the back way like you two nut jobs did. The guy at the ranch, Mike, remembered you and volunteered to come with us."

"You rode a horse?" I can't help but smile. Bobby went on a hunting trip in Montana once where he had to ride a horse. The horse took an instant dislike to him and kept trying to bite him the whole time. And when it wasn't biting him it was trying to knock him off by rubbing against boulders. He vowed to never get on the back of another horse as long as he lived.

He looks chagrined, "Yeah, I did."

"It didn't happen to be called Beelzebub, did it?"

"No, why?"

"Never mind, go on." I say.

"Well we got there and started checking out the different buildings. None of them seemed open. We were just standing there like jackasses thinking that we were wrong about where you were when we saw a car pull in to the parking area. It was Milagros and some guy. It looked like he was holding a gun on her."

"He kidnapped me as I left work," Milagros chimes in.

"So we followed them to the building where you were being held. As soon as we saw them go in we called the police."

Just then I notice Deke has joined the group.

"Hey Deke," I say.

"Amanda, I'm so glad you're okay. You are, aren't you?"

"Yes, and you?"

"I'm alright. Just glad my favorite betty is still around."

"Bobby was telling us how he and Pete tracked our movements and found out where we were," I explain.

"Cool," Deke says. He turns to Bobby and they shake hands.

Bobby continues, "After we saw Milagros go in and called the police we found a high window that we could climb up to and look in. We saw you two in the middle of the floor and the kidnappers over at the table. We weren't sure what was going to happen but wanted a contingency plan in case the police didn't arrive in time. Pete and Mike went around to the back and found the circuit box for the building. We decided that if we needed to we would cut the lights. While I was hiding around the corner, waiting for them to return another car pulls in and there's Deke getting manhandled into the same building."

"Yeah, I could've taken the stupid assmunches but they had a gun," Deke interjects.

"Deke!" I exclaim.

"Oh right, sorry little dude," Deke runs a hand through his shaggy blonde hair. "Didn't mean to offend."

"No prob, Deke," Brendan responds. He has comfortably nestled in under my left arm while Bobby's been telling his story.

"So anyway Pete and Mike come back and we decide that if it looks like any of you are in danger that we'll cut the lights. We heard someone else coming and hid again. We see this guy walking up carrying some stuff."

"That would have been my date, Mr. Wonderful." I say.

"Yeah, a real sweetheart," Bobby rejoins. "So we climb back up to look in. The three of you are sitting together and the kidnappers are gathered around this table. Your Mr. Wonderful dumps the stuff he has onto the table while the others are looking at a map or something. I saw that Deke has noticed me so I let him know to that we were there and to keep it quiet." At this point Deke is nodding his head. "When we saw the one guy getting a hypodermic ready we figured this was not a friendly tetanus shot. Pete ran around to the back and threw the breakers on the circuit box."

"And the lights went out and you saved our lives!" I finish for him.

Bobby grins, "Basically, yeah. Mike had found some old tree branches that he broke off into clubs. As those guys came running out of the building we started clobbering them."

"Wow," I say, relishing the image of Morris and his gang getting their asses kicked. But then I remember something. "Wait a minute, we heard gunshots."

"I was getting to that," Bobby replies, "One guy that came out had a gun drawn. I whacked his arm with the tree branch. He lost his grip on his gun and it went sailing. We were fighting each other when Deke came out. He saw the gun and made a mad dash for it while I kept beating on the guy and trying to subdue him."

"Cool, so did you shoot him?" I ask Deke.

"Nah, I couldn't get a clear shot on him," Deke responds. His voice is laced with regret.

"So each of us – me, Pete and Mike – had a guy we were fighting. Then the door to the building banged open and that guy that you were dating –"

"I wasn't dating him!" I interrupt, "I went out with him once and the date ended very badly."

"Whatever," Bobby says. Clearly he's enjoying telling his story and getting in a zing or two at the same time. "So he comes charging out and starts firing at us. He winged both Pete and Mike before Deke nailed him with a shot of his own."

"Damn straight," Deke says, "My own version of karma."

"Pete and Mike got shot?" I ask, very much alarmed.

"Yeah, they were both brought here as well."

"How bad are they?"

"Mike got hit in the leg and Pete took a shot in the shoulder. Mike's wound was in and out so they cleaned it out and he's on IV antibiotics right now." Bobby hikes a thumb over his shoulder in the general direction of the emergency area. "Pete had to have the bullet surgically removed. He's in recovery or maybe on a floor by now."

"Oh my God!" I say. "But they're both going to be okay?"

"Yes, they'll be fine. I can't say the same for your boyfriend."

"Morris?" I say ignoring the boyfriend comment, "He's dead?"

"No but he's in critical condition. Deke shot him in the gut."

"Deke! Was that a lucky shot?"

"No way dude, I was on the shooting team in college. I won the Distinguished Pistol Shooting competition my junior year as an undergrad and was a runner up for the General Custer trophy that same year. So when I shot that poser I meant to bring him down and make him stay down."

I realize Deke is our own Austin Powers, he's a man of mystery. He's like one of those nested Russian dolls: the first layer, the one he shows to the world, is the casual surfer dude. But underneath that exterior he's the son of a wealthy businessman and preparing to take over the reigns for his father's business one day. And under that he's a crack shot with a pistol. Something I never would have envisioned him doing. What's next? I find out he's a Republican?

Just then Mike is brought over in a wheelchair. We all greet him and ask him how he's doing. He tells us he's going to be alright and just finished signing out. One of his ranch hands is coming to pick him up. He asks Bobby if he'd like a ride back to get Pete's truck. Bobby accepts.

Before they leave I say to Mike, "Thanks for helping, Mike, you didn't have to get involved but you did. We really appreciate it."

"My pleasure. I have to say I was wondering how you ended up way over by Sam Ward's place since it was in the opposite direction of where you were supposed to go for your ride the other night. Now it all makes sense."

I feel a little twinge of guilt for deceiving him at the time, "Sorry for not being truthful when we took your horses for a ride. I understand if you're angry with us."

"Nah, your hearts were in the right place." He chuckles then shakes his head, "You gals are quite a handful."

"That's an understatement," Bobby throws in his two cents. He turns to Linda, "Are you going to be able to get everyone home or should I come back?"

"I can take them. What about Pete?"

"He's going to be in for a couple days."

Just as they leave a nurse comes in to check on me. She tells me there are some detectives who want to speak to me.

Milagros bends down and whispers in my ear, "They already interviewed me. I tol' them we got the files from Deke, chica. They don't know anything about us breaking into Allagaro."

I look at her.

"...Or the restaurant fire." She concedes and looks away.

I continue staring at her as I feel the beginnings of a headache forming behind my eyeballs.

"...Or using false identities those couple times."

I raise an eyebrow.

"...Or invading people's privacy."

We lock eyes and hold for a couple heart beats in time. I give her a little wink, my lips curve up slightly and I whisper back, "It'll be our little secret."

 *Epilogue:*

The rest is still unwritten

(*Unwritten,* Natasha Bedingfield)

The day has been clear and mild but as evening sets in it has become increasingly cold. The fire has kept us warm, though, and the ceremony was intense and primal. It's touched some deep part of me. To make this even better I am flanked on either side by two people that mean the world to me: Linda and Milagros. We are sitting cross-legged on blankets the Nipmuc tribal elders supplied and have witnessed the medicine fire ceremony; an honor few outsiders have ever experienced.

Across the flames sits Mike and two of his ranch hands. As the ceremony ends I see Mike smile at me, the golden-orange flames giving his skin this warm, burnished glow. I smile back. At his invitation we returned to the Still River Ranch last week and took a ride on Applejack and Beelzebub. Demon horse had gone through a retraining program – some kind of horse psychotherapy – and Mike wanted me to take him for a ride to see if he was adequately rehabilitated. Frankly I thought a priest and holy water was more in order than rehab. I was hesitant but, as usual, Milagros conned me into it.

Okay, if I'm being honest, I wanted to see Mike again. So Milagros didn't have to do much arm twisting to get me out there. There's something pretty enticing about a cowboy. The phrase about wild horses dragging me away comes to mind – literally. But 'Bee', as I've taken to calling my steed, behaved himself.

As I turn my eyes to the glowing logs one more time I reflect on how truly fortunate I am.

Despite my fear that Milagros and I were going to be found out for our misdemeanors and felonies, the police were more interested in the unfolding criminal case against Steve Morris and James Skogquist, the other Allagaro scientist that conspired to commit murder and fraud. All told there were thirty five study participants that suffered some ill effects of the drug cocktail they were taking. Multiple lawsuits have been filed against Allagaro and Steve, once he recovered from his injury, now sits behind bars awaiting his trial for murder, conspiracy to commit murder, arson, and kidnapping. His lawyer has his work cut out for him.

I have decided that Sam Ward's theory has some merit; that there is a purpose to the things that happen to us. Even though we suffered quite a harrowing experience if I hadn't gone through what I did I wouldn't have had my realization about my fears and how they were affecting me. I feel like I have a new lease on life.

Brendan and I are still living with Bobby and Pete while Linda settles with the insurance company and has her house rebuilt. Pete has pretty much recovered from being shot in the shoulder. He is still going to physical therapy but finally returned to fight fires and is hitting on anything in a skirt. I went to visit him while he was still in the hospital. Halfway down the hall to his room I could hear the tinkle of female laughter. When I got to his room there he was surrounded by a bevy of nurses and was regaling them with stories of his heroics.

Some things never change. It is comforting on some bizarre level.

And speaking of some things never changing: Bobby has taken to teasing me about all the men that had to come out and rescue me, some even taking a bullet for me...once an ass, always an ass.

Oh, and one final note: I got a call from Mr. Z. They finally found and trapped the wild animal that was menacing the neighborhood. It was a raccoon. I guess the little guy went down hard and fought them off till the end. Mr. Z and two other guys kept him trapped under a bush with their rakes and shovels until animal control came and got him. They released him back in the wild. Somewhere I envision him doing the Caddyshack dance.

I hear you pal, I'm alright too!

Coming Spring 2010...

It Keeps Getting Better

Are terrorists about to unleash some new horror? Not if Amanda and Milagros have anything to say about it. Follow our intrepid duo into their new adventure as they work to uncover and thwart a nefarious plot.

Will they figure it out in time?

Stay tuned...

LaVergne, TN USA
22 January 2010
170913LV00001B/86/P